No Plans to Fall

KIRI PATTERSON

Book Cover by Karyssa Adair

ISBN:979-8-9906373-1-3

For Joseph

You are the reason I believe in Happily Ever Afters. Thank you for always believing in me and my ability to write this book, even when I didn't. I'm one lucky girl because you're in my life.

*

---

* For Content Warnings please see my website at www.kiripatterson.com/content warning

Chapter One

MARISSA

Ripped strands of plastic draped over the old wooden doorway of the fair's haunted house, the strobe light flashing shapes in and out of my vision. If I tripped, I would take my friend Faith down with me, and then she really might kill me. I pulled my long brown hair away from Faith's grip and out of my eyes. I wish I hadn't forgotten a hair tie tonight.

Oh well, can't change the past.

"I bet your second graders wouldn't even be scared in here," I said to Faith over my shoulder, trying to lighten the tension.

Rose snorted. "Oh please, you just wait. Your turn is next."

Rose was always a little feisty, but tonight I would pay for my spontaneity.

"I hate both of you right now," Faith growled, pressing her face harder into my back, nearly ripping the seams of my worn jean jacket.

"You can't blame me for any of this." Rose waved her manicured hand saucily in the air. "This one is all on Marissa. This, like every other unthought-out plan, is Mar's fault."

"Plan schman . . ." I sighed. "You can't plan life; no one knows what's going to happen in five minutes, let alone five years. You might as well enjoy the ride. Your lives would be boring without me. Admit it."

"I'm fine with boring," Faith grumbled.

"Don't worry, we *will* get you back." Rose raised a perfectly shaped eyebrow.

The three of us stepped into a room bathed in red light. Chains swung back and forth from the ceiling. The lit window to the right had bloody handprints smeared on the glass.

It had been my idea to drive an hour to Clifton, Idaho for a girls' night at the Fall Festival. The rule of the night—do something we normally never would.

I was sick of life feeling repetitive in our hometown of Hillsdale; same job since high school, same two restaurants, and the same small-town gossip about anyone and everyone. There is good and bad in growing up in a small town. The good, everyone pulls together in a crisis. The bad, everyone thinks they know everything about you, and after a while, you believe they might be right.

I wanted an adventure, even a mini one. Tonight was full of fall magic. The smell of the dirt under my feet, the crisp air in my lungs, and the scratchy hay in the air, coupled with the promise of being in a new city, with new possibilities, I felt like a new me. Just for tonight, Clifton, held all the potential in the world.

Faith peeked over my shoulder at the swinging chains and whimpered. "I've earned all my irrational fears and don't have to prove anything to you. You're worse than my second graders with your peer pressure."

A crooked hung door screeched as I pushed around it. Stepping past the door and over a protruding two-by-four, I made sure Faith stepped over it too. The black light glowed purple off my Vans white laces. Metal clanged somewhere nearby, and I flinched, a quick scream escaping my lips. Whoops.

Faith slapped my back, hard. "Not funny, Mar!" She gripped my jacket tighter. "I swear, if I see a clown, you're dead."

Faith was shaking behind me more than the leaves blowing on the trees outside. The least I could do was provide a human shield. That she could hide behind me at all was proof of how small she was. I was five-five in heels. At least I assume I would be if I ever wore heels. I was more of a tennis shoes, t-shirt, and jeans girl.

Faith had short blonde hair, blue eyes, and the love of every second grader she taught. She even baked them a special cupcake on their birthdays. That's who Faith was, sweet and kind. Although tonight she was feeling anything but sweet towards me.

Rose's heel caught on a loose floorboard, and she stutter-stepped in her heeled leather boots. "Seriously, Mar, if I ruin my nails after I just got them done, you're paying for the redo!" she snipped at me.

Rose and I had been friends since my sophomore year of high school when I came to live in Hillsdale. Faith came a few years after graduation, and she became our third bestie. Together, the three of us were the musketeers. Tonight, I was really putting the "all for one, and one for all" thing to the test.

I heard clicking to my left and fog-crawled across the floor, assaulting my nose with its sweet, damp smell.

"Let's make a run for it," Faith's voice was shaking.

"Run? Are you joking?" Rose put a hand to her stomach. "After that stupid pie-eating contest I had to enter, the only place I'm running is to the bathroom. I'm still surprised I didn't puke."

I wasn't. If she had puked, she wouldn't have won, and Rose always had to win. Even at a pie-eating contest she didn't want to enter. Rose was a feisty goddess with dark eyes, thick hair, and curves she knew how to flaunt. She was a bit like playing with fire —amazing, so long as she was on your side.

A tall blond man stood behind a large metal table. Fake blood matted in his hair, and white teeth gleamed in his sinister smile. He raised a chainsaw and revved it to life with a crazed laugh.

I caught myself from falling backward as Faith pulled on my jacket. The loud noise of the chainsaw almost covered Faith's blood-curdling scream, but even a chainsaw could only do so much. My ears would ring for a week. She bolted for the exit.

Yep. She's gonna kill me.

I rushed after her, with Rose at my side, swearing at me in Spanish and holding her stomach. I couldn't stop laughing. Faith had done amazing. They both had. This was so much fun.

Outside the exit, I found Faith gasping.

"This idea . . ." she inhaled deeply, "was stupid." She placed her hands on her knees. "I think I peed my pants. I need to sit down, and someone needs to get me chocolate."

Rose gagged. "If I smell more sugar tonight, I'll throw up."

"No, seriously, guys," Faith said, leaning over. "I need to sit down. Now." She pointed to some hay bales lining the outskirts of the fair. We crossed behind her. She plopped down and put her head between her knees. I sat beside her, bumping her with my shoulder.

"You did amazing. Wasn't that exciting?"

"No! It was torture." Faith's hands were shaking.

"Torture? Come on, it was an adventure."

Faith leaned back, looking at the stars and taking deep, slow breaths. "I'm not looking for adventure, Marissa. I'm not like you."

My stomach tightened. Maybe I had pushed her too hard.

"Mar talks big about going on adventures." Rose stayed standing and eyed the hay bale, unsure if she should sit and risk getting her pants dirty. "Not that she knows yet."

I felt a stab in my chest. Were we going to talk about my lack of chasing my dreams again? "Look if this is about London—"

"It's not." Rose's glare softened. "Promise." She looked around the fair. "I'm referring to the fact that it's your turn for a challenge tonight."

"Right. Challenge. Fair." I sighed and looked around the

grounds. It was full of kids in costumes and the smell of chocolate and pumpkins.

I had always planned to visit London. I had been saving for years, saying I would go. But I never did.

London was where my parents went on their honeymoon. I loved the pictures of Mom with her bright smile and Dad's stupid goofy grin in the jean jacket I now wore. It seemed like a fairytale. A different life, a simpler one. We were all going to go for a summer after I graduated high school. I applied for my passport for my seventeenth birthday, received it, but still no stamps. It never felt like the right time. Besides, I had been talking about it for so long, what if it wasn't what I expected? What if it didn't fix me? I tugged on my undershirt, making sure it covered my scars.

Plus, I needed to help take care of Nan now. It couldn't have been easy to raise a teenager in her seventies. I owed it to my parents and to Nan.

Faith leaned next to me, her fire gone. "It'll happen Marissa. I know it. Let's put it out in the universe that you are going to London this next year. I believe it will work out. Fate."

I chuckled. "Sure, Faith, put in that order for me."

Fate. Only someone as pure as Faith would believe in Fate.

"Enough with all that Fate garbage." Rose put her hands on her hips. "It's your challenge now, Mar."

I looked around the festival and tried to imagine the worst potential challenge my friends could come up with. After what I had put them through, this adventure was likely to bite me in the backside, and soon.

Rose stood up on a nearby hay bale and leaned to the left, taking in her surroundings. She grinned, showing her perfect white teeth like a wolf that targeted its prey.

"Found it," she added in a singsong voice, gesturing to the crowd of women behind food truck vendors in the middle of the fairgrounds. They were cheering at something, and they ranged from their twenties to their eighties.

My stomach dropped, and I felt a spike of adrenaline. "What is it?"

Faith jumped up on the hay bale next to Rose, peering around the trucks, and giggled. "Yes, this is perfect!"

"Wait, what?" I tried to imagine the worst thing I could. Maybe pig wrestling or kissing a cow? What if it was a talent show or singing karaoke?

I scrambled up next to them, and stood on my tippy toes, and leaned as far as I could to peer around the food trucks. My breath caught in my throat.

Nope. This was so much worse. I would happily kiss a cow, and that's saying something.

Men were lined up on a low platform trailer with numbers pinned to their chests. The butcher paper sign along the bottom read "Blind Date Raffle—Save the Animal Shelter" in bright red lettering.

"No . . . No way . . ." My throat felt as dry as the sagebrush desert. No, no dates. I promised myself no more dating. It always overcomplicated everything. Dating led to making plans and talks about happy futures. Two things I wanted nothing to do with.

Rose and Faith hopped down, each grabbed one of my arms, and pulled me toward the crowd.

"Oh, this is happening." Rose's grip tightened.

"Guys, but my rules! Remember?" I was pleading now. I would beg, borrow, and yeah, I might even steal to get out of this one. What are the odds there would be a dating event at a fair? Ugh. I tried to slow our steps. I needed to think.

"Yeah, we know," Rose smirked. "You don't date . . . and I don't eat junk food, and Faith hates all things scary and crowds." She glared at me. "This was your idea, Marissa, and remember . . . 'No backsies'." Rose emphasized with air quotes around my stupid rule.

"I didn't know a date would be an option. If I had, I wouldn't have done this."

Rose shrugged but showed no signs of weakness. "Maybe if you planned, you could've avoided it. I'm sure they listed it on the schedule, but we know how you feel about plans."

I searched my mind for any other option, my knees aching from my stiff steps. "Maybe I can try seafood instead?" I asked.

Faith shook her head. "Marissa, you're allergic to seafood."

"Not happening." Rose tugged me forward through the crowd.

A woman in khakis and a blue polo yelled into a megaphone. "Help save our animal shelter and win a hot date in a corn maze." She gestured to the lineup. "Come on guys, let's give them a show."

Men were flexing, blowing kisses, and showing off the backside of their jeans that were tighter than mine. Then there was the man at the end. He just stood there in a suit, straightening the paper with his number.

Yikes! Did he dress in a suit for this? Desperate much?

"I don't know about you, Faith, but I have this sudden urge to save all the puppies." Rose sauntered over to the ticket booth manned by a guy wearing dog ears and a tail.

"Oh, don't pretend like this is for them. You hate animals," I called over the crowd.

Faith gave me a side hug. "This was your idea . . ."

"Yeah, but my rules. No dating, especially since Tyler—"

"Tyler and his mom are stupid, and it was like four or five years ago." Faith reached down and squeezed my hand. "You might not get picked, and if you do, you'll never see the guy again. I think you are getting off lucky after that haunted house."

Faith was right. At least here no one knew me. I could pretend to be anyone for a night. No pressure, no second dates.

And maybe I wouldn't even get picked.

"Hot date for charity! Hot date for charity!" The dog-eared man jumped up and down, chanting behind the ticket booth.

Some old ladies punched their canes in the air as the crowd latched on to the chant. I felt like I was going to be sick.

I met Rose's eyes as she turned and flashed me a huge grin over an enormous pile of tickets.

"The odds of me not getting picked aren't looking great . . . I think Rose might have single-handedly saved the shelter."

Faith chuckled.

"Before I draw our winners," the woman in the polo shirt said, "the prize for the winning couple is two twenty-dollar gift certificates for Bella's Cookies, tickets for the petting zoo, and fifty dollars off any pet adoption and supplies at Clifton Pet Rescue. The first team to make it to the center of the maze and bring back the doggie treats, wins."

I still wasn't happy about the idea, but if I had to go through this, I wanted to win those cookies.

Deep breaths.

Cookies with sprinkles.

Never see him again.

Maybe not even picked.

Rose handed Faith half of the tickets. "Here we go!"

Chapter Two

SCOTT

FRIDAY DATE NIGHT WAS NOT ON THE AGENDA. NEITHER was being auctioned off as some animal shelter raffle prize. I was supposed to be in the office completing the numbers on the Smith case. I straightened my suit jacket sleeves and tried to not fidget. You never know when you might meet a potential client.

Professionalism is key.

Nothing about my current situation was professional.

This was ridiculous, even if I was helping James.

I looked over at him with his floppy ears and chuckled. The man was all action, no forethought. If he wasn't my only friend since high school, I would've dropped this whole ordeal, like I often do.

According to this month's financial magazine, "Social sacrifices often must be made in pursuit of greatness." My mother believes I take the advice too far. But I was here now for James, and that would make her happy.

Last time James asked out a woman, he was in a chicken suit saying, "I've been CHICKEN you out." That woman and her college roommates had shamed him on social media for weeks. We were currently on a strict no-costume policy. So, when James texted me the photo of himself in a dog costume with ears, a tail, and a shirt that said, "I WOOF YOU" in front of the fall festival entrance, with a thumbs up and a message that said, "wish me luck," I rushed from work to save him from himself and his big gestures.

Well, I tried. I at least convinced him to turn the shirt inside out, but the tail and ears were apparently non-negotiable.

Anna, who oversaw the fundraiser for the animal shelter, laughed as she flipped his ear out of his face. Seemed like she didn't mind them. *Strange.*

What I minded was when they needed more volunteers, and somehow, I ended up auctioned off for some ridiculous blind date.

I watched the other men on the flatbed trailer. They were flexing and showing off. That just wasn't my style. I often found those types to be more show than substance, anyway. I re-adjusted the paper that was safety pinned to my shirt. I couldn't seem to get it to lie flat across my chest.

Should I take off the suit coat? And do what with it, lay it in the dirt? This was my favorite jacket, the suit coat would have to stay.

I watched as Anna pulled the ticket for the first man. James started jumping with excitement, his dog ears flapping with the movement. You would never know that the man is a genius. He was the only one in our high school who scored higher on the SAT than me. Also, I was pretty sure he got a C on the final in advanced calculus so that I could be valedictorian. He said he must have failed and never cared for the label anyway. Now he's a computer genius, and jumps between small businesses, saving their financials and investing in all the right things. The man is loaded. Even in dog ears and a waving tail, he is the best guy I know. He is an amazing friend. One I don't deserve with how often I drop off the face of the earth with my studies and work schedule.

Which is why I don't just run off the flatbed trailer. I owe James more than this.

The auction continued down the line, each contestant receiving screams of excitement when their date was picked. I looked down at the paper safety-pinned to my chest, the number 106 written across it with a sharpie.

I wondered if I would get one of the old ladies with a cane. It didn't matter who it was. I was here for James and nothing romantic. Romance takes time, and that was something that was not in the plan for at least two more years. If it all went according to plan.

Not if, when.

Anna hollered 106, bringing my attention back to the present as she reached into the bucket and pulled out a red ticket stub.

"520402."

I watched as a dark-haired woman in high leather boots clapped. "That's me!" she shouted, and then shoved the ticket at her friend in a faded jean jacket. "Well, I mean it's her."

With a woman on either side, they began pushing my date toward the stage. She looked like she might throw up. Well, that didn't improve one's confidence. I adjusted my tie, making sure it was straight.

She had long straight brown hair, red Vans shoes, a Beatles t-shirt under her jacket, and was barely over five feet tall. She was cute, not my usual type of woman in a business dress and hair in a tight bun, but cute.

I lowered my hand to help her up on the platform. Her hand shook as she placed it in mine. I was no muscle man like the guy down the line, but my hand dwarfed hers.

My twin had used his six-foot frame and large palms to become the basketball captain and most popular guy of our high school. Mine were used to push up my glasses on my thin nose as I led the debate team to victory.

Not nearly as sexy.

The top of her head reached my chest and her hair smelled fruity, like apples maybe.

I leaned down close to her ear, so I didn't have to shout over the crowd. "Hey, I'm Scott."

She squeaked and raised her palm to her heart.

"Sorry, I didn't mean to scare you." I smiled down at her.

"Nope, I wasn't scared." Her voice was scratchy, and she cleared it.

I raised an eyebrow in question.

She had a slight raise to one corner of her bright pink lips and shrugged.

"Hey, I'm Mar . . ." her nose scrunched. "I'm Mary," she drew it out long and unsure.

"You positive?" I could tell when I was being lied to, an occupational hazard as a lawyer. Although it wouldn't take any training to tell with "Mary" she was a terrible liar. Her cheeks had flushed, she refused to make eye contact, and I'm pretty sure she squeaked when I asked if she was sure.

"Yep." She stared at her shoes.

Okay, whatever. Mary it is. I don't care either way.

Anna cleared her throat through the megaphone, bringing my attention back to her. "Each team head to your starting zones. They match the numbers on your leading man's shirt."

106, got it. I looked at the boxes stacked near the different corn maze entrances and noticed ours off to the left.

"And you'll need to hold hands," James leaned over and yelled into the megaphone.

What?

I shot him a glare as he winked at me.

"That way, you stay together," he added through the megaphone, looking at Anna for confirmation.

Anna looked at the lady with the cane. "Or lock elbows or something."

Great. Thanks, James. Like this wasn't already awkward enough. Let's add physical contact into the mix.

I hopped down off the trailer and held out my hand to help Mary. She took a deep breath and put her hand more confidently on mine. We headed toward our entrance.

"Do you always wear a suit on a first date?" She tipped her head to the side. "It seems fancy for a corn maze."

Did she think I dressed like this for a blind date with a random stranger?

"I came here straight from work to help a friend." I pointed at James. "I was coming to help him get a date, still not sure how I ended up with one." We walked to our entrance.

She looked up at me. "You didn't want a date either? So there isn't a lot of pressure on us or anything?"

I got my first good glimpse of her eyes. They were green with a dark line around the edge. I had never seen eyes like hers before.

"Zero pressure," I said.

Anna asked through the megaphone, "Everyone ready?"

"Well, maybe not zero." Mary placed her free hand on her hip.

My face must have showed my question because she continued.

"If this isn't like a date-date, let's win those cookies. Bella's is the best!"

She hopped on her toes, bursting with energy.

I grinned. Between my car payments and the low salary I took while paying my student loans back to my father, I was on a strong diet of tuna pouches, PB&Js, and cereal.

"I'm always up for winning free food." Looking down the lineup, our odds seemed good. There was the lady with the cane, two other women in high-heeled shoes, and two more serious contenders who looked like they may put up a fight.

I felt her grip shift in my hand.

Was my hand getting sweaty? When was the last time I held a woman's hand?

It would've been Brooke's hand in law school. We were pretty good together, but then I needed to study for the bar, and well, she was a distraction.

Mary nodded back over at James; his tail wagging was in full effect. "I've got to know, was the tail your idea?"

I laughed. "Definitely not."

She nodded. "I think it's kinda cute. It seems like *she* doesn't mind." I felt her squeeze my hand softly, and I wondered if I'd imagined it.

"Go!" Anna hollered through the megaphone. "The first team back with dog treats wins!"

My date pulled me off my feet as she lunged for the maze.

Wow, she wasn't joking about those cookies.

We rushed through the tall, dry stalks and as we reached a T in the maze, I tried to slow down, but Mary ran full speed to the right.

"Let's formulate a plan. We need a system," I added, trying to pull her back.

"Plan?" She leaned away from me like I might be contagious. "It's a maze . . . How about our plan is, go fast and win cookies?" She started ahead.

That was no plan. How could they remember which corners they took? They would end up going in circles.

"Wait. We can't just randomly take corners." I pulled Mary to a stop. I couldn't think and run at the same time.

She scowled up at me.

"Wait a second, let me think. I remember reading something once about maze strategy."

Her face scrunched. "Plans aren't my thing."

I nodded. Very few people loved plans as much as I did.

"Maybe not, but I think cookies are, and I read somewhere that if you use a strategy with mazes, you're more successful. Let's go right at every intersection. If we hit a dead end, we circle back, take a left, and continue right." I nodded my head. It was a solid plan, a good plan.

Mary groaned. "I don't know what you've been reading, but that sounds terrible."

I chuckled. "It's not terrible, it's logical. Just like plans are."

Planning was a main guidepost for success. Life is busy and if I don't have a plan, how would I ever know if I was heading toward my goals? Everything in my life had a plan. The car, the penthouse, the prestigious job.

I was going to become a partner at Raymond & Johnson Law in four years. I had an offer, once, but then life got in the way. Dad had put me through law school and saving his firm had to come first. Now that it was out of the red and we had hired a few junior lawyers, it looked like things were turning around.

It would require diligence, perseverance, and getting employed at Raymond & Johnson Law.

One step at a time.

Mary let out a long sigh. "Corn mazes aren't very exciting as it is, but going right every time is going to be torture." She formed a little pouty lip. "Come on. Let's run and choose at random." She shrugged. "Let Fate decide."

"Fate is not real. If you don't have a plan or a system, you won't get where you want to go. Besides, Benjamin Franklin said, 'Every minute spent organizing is an hour earned.'"

Mary tugged my hand to the left. "Tonight I have an order placed with Fate, and I'm hoping for the best. Come on." She squeezed my hand and leaned her shoulder into me. I felt a rush run up my arm and she looked at me pleading. "I think you should try to go with no plan. They rarely work anyway."

This would not lead to efficiency.

She groaned and reached into her pocket and grabbed out a quarter. "Fine. Compromise?" She raised an eyebrow and showed the dirty quarter.

"How so?" I guess it was just a date. Surely it wouldn't be dangerous to have one night with no plans. I could let go a bit.

Her face lit with joy, like she radiated sunlight somehow. She must really want those cookies.

"I'm listening. Is this the magic Fate quarter?"

She grinned and nodded. "Yep. And it says heads, we go left, tails, right."

I rolled my eyes but couldn't stop smiling. "You know, technically, this is still a plan, right?"

"Shhh, don't ruin this for me." She charged into the next intersection.

We continued through the maze, heads left, tails right. Mary dropped the magical quarter three times in the dark, and we had to find it with our phone flashlights. We decided a dramatic shaking system with a grand reveal worked better.

"Tails. Right it is." I squeezed her hand and headed to the right. Tonight was turning out to be more fun than I expected. "Tell me. How did your friends convince you to go on this date?"

She jumped over a fallen stalk. "I told them we each had to do something that was out of our comfort zone." She shrugged. "This is mine."

"Blind dates?" We stepped around a large mud puddle.

"Dating in general," she added.

Well, at least she wasn't disappointed to be with me specifically. I brushed against her shoulder. "Well, hopefully it hasn't been too terrible so far."

Okay . . . I guess I'm flirty now?

"Just shy of it," she shot back a wink. "What do you do for work?" She eyed my suit.

"Lawyer," I added. She would probably imagine my life as one of prestige. Not that I was living off ramen, debt, and dreams.

We reached another fork in the maze.

"Why law?" Mary placed the quarter in my hands. Her fingers

brushed against my palm and my stomach dropped. I tightened my grip on her hand involuntarily.

"Left." She looked away and took the quarter.

"Why not, I guess." I shrugged. "I knew the schooling was something I could excel at, and it would provide the type of lifestyle I wanted."

"I work as an office manager at a small law firm." She went rigid and nearly tripped.

It was the truth, but it slipped out. She must have forgotten she was playing as "Mary" tonight.

"Small world." I stopped at the next corner and waited for the quarter's divine answer. "Why an office manager?"

She deflated a bit. "It has always been a means to an end. The end is taking longer to reach than I hoped."

"Sounds like you need a plan." I winked, rubbing small circles on the back of her hand with my thumb. This was fun. Not at all what I would ever plan, but fun. I felt her hand squeeze mine back affectionately.

"Plan. Gross." She mimicked vomiting. "This might be a shock, but not everyone reads planning material for fun." She kicked a rock to the left of the path. "The more I plan for something, the more it feels like it will never work out." She pulled on her shirt, lengthening it with her free hand. "Better to just keep it in the moment, you know?"

"Are you cold?" I dropped her hand and shrugged out of my suit coat and held it out to her. The jacket she wore looked threadbare.

She looked down at her free hand. "Oh no! Are we going to be disqualified now?"

"I won't tell if you don't." I smiled in her direction. I must have stolen my twin brother's persona for the night because this comfortable flirting and talking with a woman was not a me thing. I wondered if Micheal was somewhere randomly rattling off statistics.

She draped my jacket over her shoulders. She held her hand back out for mine and I took it.

"Deal. If they ask about the jacket, it was autumn magic."

"What's autumn magic? That sounds dangerously like Fate."

She laughed. "No, autumn magic is real. You can feel the power of change even in the air. The crisp air, the leaves changing colors, all of nature feels like magic."

"So, what are you hoping for, eventually . . . but without a plan?"

"Nope. Tonight is not about that; tonight is about cookies."

The conversation was closed, but my curiosity about who this woman was wouldn't leave my mind. She had bright green eyes, was a horrible liar, believed in magic, detested plans, and had a fierce love for cookies. I was sure I would never meet another woman like her.

Mary squealed. "Look it's the dog treats!"

Chapter Three

MARISSA

Pretending to be Mary for the night was fun. There were no expectations or pressure. Just fun.

I leaned down and grabbed the little bag full of doggie treats.

I couldn't wait for my share of the cookies. That's what I needed to put all my focus on, not the little circles that Scott rubbed on the back of my hand, or how his jacket smelled like cinnamon. I raised my shoulder for a quick, hopefully non-noticeable sniff. Yep. Cinnamon. Scott's hand dwarfed mine as he led me around a corner in the maze, watching to ensure I didn't trip over the dips in the dirt.

Cookies. Focus on cookies.

"Cookies for the win!" I leaned against Scott with my shoulder. "And we didn't even need a plan."

I could tell it wasn't easy for him to let go of his plans. It was sweet that he had compromised.

Scott sighed and chuckled. "We still had a plan. What's your favorite cookie?"

"I like sugar cookies, bonus if it has sprinkles." We headed back through the maze. "Let me guess. You're an oatmeal raisin guy?"

I should have given him his jacket back. With all this hand holding and his stormy eyes searching mine, I was no longer cold . . . at all.

He chuckled. "Why would you say that?"

"Oatmeal raisin is the most somewhat-healthy and sensible cookie there is, and that seems like it fits." We reached a fork in the maze.

"Which way?" He looked at my pocket with the quarter.

I no longer cared. "I already proved my point. It's more fun when you don't have a plan. You can lead from here."

He shook his head. "It was fun, and yes, I do like oatmeal raisin."

"I knew it!" I tried to withhold my victory dance but ended up with a little skip anyway.

Scott raised the left corner of his mouth in a grin. "They don't get enough love, you know. Everyone goes for the chocolate chip, but a soft oatmeal raisin, that's where it's at."

Gross. Why put raisins in anything? "Well, enjoy those boring oatmeal cookies. I'm going to get something with sprinkles."

Scott rubbed the back of my hand with his thumb. "You seem like sprinkles. Bright and fun."

Ah, how sweet. Good thing this was all temporary or he would have me running for the nearest exit with those gorgeous eyes.

"You know, sprinkles might be growing on me." He winked so quickly I questioned if it happened at all. "I might have to try some." His eyes flicked to my lips.

Heat ran from my stomach up to the tips of my ears. What did he mean by that? We were still talking cookies, right? Warning bells went off in the back of my mind, but I reminded my bells that I was Mary. I would never see Scott again.

No real future risk.

"If we followed the original plan, finding our way out would've been faster because I would know which way to turn." Scott smiled, trying to prove once again that plans were important.

I shrugged. "We've already won. Why does it matter how fast we leave? Out of the maze, it's back to real life, and this isn't so bad." It had been fun.

"In that case . . ." Scott slowed his pace to a crawl.

Laughing, I pulled him along. I was not ready to stop in this maze with the way he kept glancing at my lips. Besides, what if they ran out of cookies?

"If sprinkles make me bright and fun, what does being an oatmeal raisin guy make you?"

He pulled me to the right and watched as I stepped over some fallen corn stalks.

Scott scrunched his nose. "Underrated and gooey?"

I laughed. "Oh, you are fun," and let my head lean against him.

"Not usually." Scott sounded genuinely surprised.

We continued in silence for a bit, him rubbing the back of my hand with his thumb. It was soothing. I haven't allowed myself to have any physical contact like this since Tyler. Would it feel this comfortable with anyone? Maybe I should start holding random stranger's hands and test the theory. I shook my head at the absurd thought.

"This was fun. Maybe we could try it again sometime." Scott squeezed my hand.

My body went rigid and sweat started ramping up right on cue. Nope. "What do you mean? I thought this was all just for fun."

"It has been fun, and I just meant we make a good team." Scott shrugged noncommittally, but I watched his eyes. He was nervous. He wanted to see me again. Like after tonight.

Crap.

"We could go pick up the prize cookies together." He raised his left shoulder.

I bit my bottom lip to stop it from trembling. I had rules. This was supposed to be safe. Why was he ruining it? Why had I let Rose and Faith talk me into this stupid date, anyway?

"Um, yeah, I don't do the whole dating thing. Remember?"

"Why? Was this so bad?" Scott gestured down to our linked hands.

"It's complicated. This was for a challenge. I have these rules . . ." I felt the weight of my real life rush back in, threatening to crush me.

I'm not Mary.

I fought the urge to run and caught myself as I pulled on my green undershirt again. "Look, you've been great. Best pretend date ever."

His head tipped in confusion, and I had to close my eyes. He had been great and felt nice. Ugh.

"This is a one-time thing for me," I said, grasping at straws for an idea why. "Besides, I'm not from Clifton." Then I remembered Faith putting in my order for London. "And I'm leaving the country."

Scott leaned away. "Thanks?" His voice sounded anything but grateful. "I don't think you need to flee the country. It's not that big a deal."

"No, it's not because of you. It was Fate who decided." I was making everything so much worse. I needed to stop talking.

Scott bristled. "Okay. Whatever, I got it. No more dates."

I stared at the ground. My hand, once comfortable in his, began sweating profusely. The circles had stopped. *I needed to get out of the maze and drop his stinking hand.*

The exit now loomed in front of me, and I fought the urge to leave at a dead sprint.

"Team 106 has won!" The woman in the blue shirt called out from the trailer. "Nice job!" She hopped off the trailer and came to us with the dog-ear man following right behind her.

I handed off the dog treats and dropped Scott's hand like it had burned me. I wiped my sweaty palm on my jeans. Remembering that I was wearing Scott's jacket, I ripped it off and thrust it back at him. When I spotted Rose and Faith off to the side, I shot them the worst glare I could muster.

"The prize is near the front entrance," the woman continued. "Follow me and we'll go grab it."

We started for the front of the fairgrounds. Scott's friend was at his side, his tail wagging behind him as he whispered, "You owe me for the hand-hold thing. Genius right!"

I didn't want to hear Scott's response. I put more distance between us.

Once we reached the booth, she went inside while I waited awkwardly, refusing to make eye contact with Scott or his friend. If it wasn't for the cookies, I would've bolted.

"I think we're gonna do the hayride in twenty minutes," Scott's friend said. "Do you wanna come?" He looked between Scott and me.

Oh, I was going to be sick. This is why I have my dating rules. This was so awkward.

"Thanks, man, but I'm calling it a night." Scott's reply was quick.

"Um, yeah. I'm calling it too. Thanks though." I felt my shoulders relax a little. At least Scott had been civil about it all.

"Thanks, guys." The blue-shirted lady smiled at us both and handed out the envelopes as she stepped out of the booth and shut the door behind her.

"Thanks." I took my envelope and hurried away from the group, wanting to put distance between myself and the entire situation.

Wait. What if she forgot the cookie coupon?

I stopped and began thumbing through the few coupons. I needed cookies, and fast. A little boy in a cowboy hat yelling about pumpkins bumped into me hard, knocking the envelope and its contents out of my hand. And, of course, a gust of wind picked the coupons up over the hay bales behind me into a field.

I no longer believed in Fate. And if she was real, I hated her.

I had come too far to not get cookies. I rushed over the hay bales behind me and pushed decorative caution tape to the side.

I chased after my little papers on the field of pumpkin guts. Seeing one to the left, I grabbed it. Please be the cookie one . . . Nope. Animal shelter. Ugh, slipped on the pumpkin guts in the next rut as I rushed over and picked up another paper. Cookies . . . Nope. *Ugh, where is that stinking cookie one?*

"Mary! Look out," I heard someone hollering. I wanted to check what was going on, but then I saw it. My last coupon was stuck in a gooey pile of pumpkin further into the field. I rushed toward it.

"Mary!"

The voice seemed closer now, but so was the coupon. I reached down to grab it just as a force hit me from behind, sending me flopping onto a pumpkin stem that struck me right in my gut. The back of my head collided hard with something from behind.

Air rushed from my lungs and refused to return, and my vision blurred. There was something heavy on my back, and gray arms wrapped over my head.

What?

Where?

I tried to clear my vision, but nothing would focus. I tried to push myself off the pumpkin that was crushing me. Someone let out a stream of curses as they rolled off my back onto the field. Scott was next to me. His eyes were closed tight in pain. I couldn't connect the dots as the air scorched through my lungs.

Scott was sprawled out on the ground, covered in orange pumpkin goo and seeds. His hair was matted, and his large hand that had been holding mine was clenched around his shoulder. His suit . . . well, it would need dry cleaning, to say the least.

"What are you doing?" I asked. Why had he leveled me to the ground? Was he that upset about the date thing? I rubbed the back of my head, trying to ease the pain.

"What am I doing?" Scott growled. He opened his eyes and gestured around the field of pumpkin guts, flinging orange pumpkin strings from his hand. "What in the world were you doing?"

My breath caught as I remembered my cookie coupon. I looked to where it had been. It was gone.

"I dropped my cookie coupon." Dang it.

That's when I saw it. The pumpkin cannon at the front of the field. The smashed pumpkins everywhere made more sense now. This was a pumpkin chucking zone. Oh . . . Scott saved me from a pumpkin . . .

"Why didn't you come back when I called?" Scott asked, rubbing his shoulder.

"I didn't hear you call my name . . ."

"Right, because your name isn't Mary."

Oh, I was Mary. Right . . . Whoops. Should I tell him my real name?

Scott sat up, groaning. Large sections of pumpkin were falling off his jacket.

"Uh, Scott. Did you just take a pumpkin bullet for me?"

Why would he do that?

"Pretty sure I took it for Mary." He looked at me, annoyed.

I flinched. "Umm, yea . . . sorry. Are you okay?" He was gripping his shoulder and breathing through his clenched teeth and the bruise forming under his right eye looked like it would be black by morning. From the knot forming on the back of my head, I was guessing my skull was the culprit.

"Yep, never better." He tried to move his left arm, which was followed by a round of curses. "Did you get the coupon?"

"No." I couldn't keep the sadness from my voice. After all, it would be wrong to be sad about cookies when he just got hit with a pumpkin. Well, at least I shouldn't be.

He grabbed his envelope from his pumpkin-flavored suit

jacket. "Here, take this. I'm pretty sure I will have plenty to remember tonight by."

There was a surge of people running toward us now, a lady in an EMT coat and a man bringing out a stretcher among them. Nope. I was not doing that.

"I think we need to have you both checked out." A lady with a vest started shining a bright light in my eyes.

No way I was leaving this field on a stretcher.

"Nope. I'm good." I stood and stepped away from the stretcher. "I wasn't hit. He saved me." I pointed to Scott.

"Thanks a lot," he grumbled.

The EMT lady scowled. "I at least need you to sign a form saying that I offered you care."

"Will do," I nodded.

With that, Scott's puppy friend swooped in and tried to help pull him up. Scott yelled in pain.

"Other arm, James!" Scott closed his eyes and his face turned white.

"Um, thanks again?" I felt terrible, but there was nothing I could do at this point. If I ever saw Scott again, it would be too soon. I ran from the field.

Chapter Four

SCOTT

One night of chaos with "Mary" and I found a renewed passion to get back on track with my plans.

I had lost focus and was going nowhere fast. It was time to refocus and prove to myself what I could achieve.

Time to email the letter to the Raymond & Johnson Law Firm. I had rewritten it a million times. Time to tell my dad I was ready for a change.

A few years of long hours and careful planning, and my dad's law firm was out of the red.

My father, Ron, was a great man, but a horrible business owner.

I switched from the office email to my personal account and began sorting and deleting different messages I'd received that day. The best inbox was clutter-free and organized.

I shuddered when I thought of my dad's work email. Pages and pages of spam mixed in with invoices and inquiries. I showed him how to sort and block different senders. It took me a full weekend to clean it up and set up how I thought it should run. Six months later, it was back in chaos. He swore he knew where everything was, and it didn't bug him.

After cleaning up my inbox, I went to my drafts and opened the email to Clyde Johnson at Raymond & Johnson Law.

Mr. Johnson,

If the offer is still available, I'm interested in the position offered me previously with your law firm.

For the last several years, I've added commercial law, marketing strategies, streamlining office practices, and management to my resume. These have been paramount in saving my father's law firm and with your consideration, I'm certain it would add to profiting Raymond & Johnson Law as well. Resume attached.

Thank you,

Scott Elliot

With three more read-throughs and a deep cleansing breath, I hit send and prayed he remembered me.

I did it; I sent the email. A combination of nerves and excitement rushed through my veins. I stood up and stretched, my shoulder still stiff from the pumpkin incident. After it got popped back in place, the nausea and pain mostly vanished. My eye, however, had quite the shiner.

The office Dad and I shared was filing cabinets, law books, and florescent lighting. Family photos covered every inch of his desk. The room felt stuffy and dusty, regardless of how I organized it.

I wouldn't be sad to trade it all for a big corner office with a view.

The front door dinged. Did I forget to lock it?

It was Saturday morning and there was no one at the reception desk since we were closed. I reached behind me and put on my suit jacket, ignoring my protesting shoulder. I stretched the sleeves, trying to lengthen it. Yep. Still too short. The other one was at the cleaners with pumpkin guts and may never recover. I had to find garbage bags to cover my car seats before I could even drive home last night.

"I knew I would find you working today," my father's voice called from the hallway.

He walked in wearing a Hawaiian button-up shirt and an enormous smile. "We both know your salary doesn't cover this extra time. Now that things are slowing down, you might want some hobbies . . . or a girlfriend." My father's steps slowed as he took in my puffy left eye. "Or maybe you have picked up a hobby?"

"Hey, Dad." I closed the distance between us and gave him a one-armed hug. I pointed toward my eye. "This was a one-time occurrence. No need to worry about further injury."

He nodded.

This was good. I needed to talk to Dad about switching jobs. I had a plan all laid out for him to follow. It would be simple.

Everything would work out.

My dad scanned me, looking for further injury. "Your mother was wondering if you would come for dinner next Sunday." His lips turned down. "Looks like you're gonna have a real shiner."

"I'm blaming James for it."

Dad winced, probably wondering what disaster James had gotten me into this time.

"You could've just texted about dinner," I offered. It was easier to avoid a text.

"Yes, but I thought I might get a different response if I guilted you in person." He bumped my shoulder good-naturedly. Dad went over to the plant in the corner and tested the soil for water. I suggested plastic plants, but Dad was happy to water the few plants that survived this long. The fact that Mom had given them to him was evident in his care for them. He loved pleasing her.

My family was persistent. I would give them that. I loved them, I did. But, I also felt unsettled there as well. Everyone else seemed content with the life they were handed. Everyone but me.

I wanted something different. Not hand-me-downs and left-over casserole lunches.

My dad owned a law firm but was still more of a family man

than a true lawyer. Growing up, there was a constant stream of strangers at the dinner table, and my parents seemed to adopt every charity case they came across. They gave to everyone, but it wasn't like they had excess. If they kept some of that for themselves, I might not have to be here saving their company. I rubbed the back of my neck.

I loved them, I did, and I knew they loved me. I just didn't always feel like I meshed.

"I don't know . . ." I said, running a hand through my hair. "I thought I might catch up on some reading, those financial journals don't read themselves." The excuse sounded boring even to my ears. I thought about Mary and her comment on my boring reading material.

"Come on. The boss lady would love it and you know what they say, *Happy wife . . .*"

"*Happy life,*" I completed my dad's familiar saying.

"So . . . ?" He grinned, crossing back to me. "What do you say?"

"I was at dinner two weekends ago. Remember the one when Mom and Jessica invited any single adult women they could find?"

Mom decided that one of her recent charity cases was me and roped my older sister into the scheme. Mom wanted me to relax, get a girlfriend, and change my priorities.

I know she means well.

My father laughed. "She just wants to see you happy. You could always volunteer to bring your own date . . ."

I gestured to my swollen eye. "This is where one date got me. For now, I'm going to pass."

Dad tipped his head to the side. "Sounds like there's a story there."

I didn't want to give him false hope to send to my mom. "Not much of one, just a blind date. Besides, Michael dates enough for the both of us."

My dad shook his head. "Michael doesn't date. He runs

through a different date each night, no commitment, and no strings." The corner of Dad's mouth pulled down in a frown.

I didn't want to get into a dating conversation.

"I'll come to Sunday dinner alone and please tell Mom I'll leave alone." I smiled. I hated to see either of my parents unhappy. They were as inseparable as peanut butter and jelly. Some kids grew up in houses where they never saw their parents kiss. I used to be envious. I was glad my parents loved each other, but I didn't always want to have a front row seat to it. I realize now how lucky my parents were to have someone that complimented the other so much.

"Good man." Dad patted me on the back. "We're happy you'll be there." His grin fell once more, and his shoulders sagged with an invisible weight. "Wondering if I could bend your ear a bit while I'm here?" He nodded at the cracked black leather couch. "Mind if we sit?"

Oh no. What happened?

Dad rarely asked for anything from anyone. The only reason he let me help with the firm was because I convinced him it was a trade, because he helped pay for my schooling. Holding my breath and questions, I followed him to the leather sofa in the corner and sat.

Dad let out a sigh as he sank into the cushions and ran a hand down his face. "I appreciate all you have done for this firm. It wouldn't have survived without you." His eyes looked around the room with what looked like pride.

"Of course, Dad. I was happy to do it." We had a deal. I never even told Dad about the very lucrative offer I'd once received from Raymond & Johnson Law.

Dad leaned forward, placed his hands on his knees. "Happy enough that you wouldn't mind taking on another project?"

Great. What charity case had he gotten involved in now?

I leaned away from him, waiting.

"I have this friend, Harry, back from law school." Dad rubbed his hands together. "He has fallen on hard times the last few years. His wife Sal's been sick with cancer. They have all sorts of medical bills." He pushed his silver hair away from his blue eyes.

My stomach sank, trying to connect the inevitable dots.

"We talked about merging off and on through the years, but time can be a tricky thing." Dad's shoulders dropped forward, and he nodded. "Your mom and I talked . . . we merged with his firm to let him retire early. He won't have time to train a replacement, but he isn't sure how much time Sal has. I thought maybe you . . ."

Wait.

I placed my hands in front of me, trying to stop the momentum of the conversation. "You're merging with another firm?" My eyebrows flew up.

Please, say I connected the wrong dots.

"Well, the more correct term is merged." He watched me cautiously from the side.

"Merged. Like it already happened?" I stood, the seat no longer able to ground me and the anxiety pulsing through me. "How did you even get it all approved?" There wasn't very much extra cash flow. The business could not possibly cover it.

My dad shrugged. "We took out a loan on the house."

"You guys mortgaged your house to fund someone else's business?" I paced the five feet of space in front of me.

No. No. No. Maybe it's not too late. I can still fix this.

"I need to see the contract. Can you still get out of it? Why did the bank even approve?"

"Wasn't too much paperwork with Harry, plus we shook on it. He will pay it back, or whoever takes over the firm will. I trust him." Dad sat up and watched me pace. "Things will work out."

Great. No contract . . .

"As for the bank, Norm knows I'm good for it. Plus, he owes me for helping his son-in-law a few years back. He'll work with me and he gave me a great interest rate. Your mother and I agree that as long as we have each other, we can make it through anything."

My idea of "making it" once again differed from my parents. "Is there any way you could get back the money? Are you sure you want to do this? Mom loves that house."

"I know," Dad sank into his seat, "but this is the right thing to do."

His mind was made up. *Great.* The dread in my stomach was lead. Solid and immovable.

"I wanted to give Harry a chance to help his wife and spend time with her. Your mother means everything to me, way more than a house. If I needed this, I would hope he would return the favor if he could." Dad rubbed his calloused hands together. "Good comes back around. It'll work out."

That was that.

Dad's generosity had no bounds. Unfortunately, his bank account did.

I sat back down, pinching my nose, and closing my eyes. "Please tell me you at least looked at the financials? Are they even profitable?"

"Well, that's where you come in. I looked at the numbers and it won't be easy, but Scott, you worked miracles with this place." Dad gestured around the office; his eyes shined bright.

It was hardly the vision of a miracle.

"I'm sure you can do it again." Dad gave my left knee a little squeeze. "I know that you've sacrificed a lot for this place already. You don't need to do this. If you're ready to move on to something else, I can figure this out."

Could I do that? Could I walk away and let my dad solve his own problem?

I steepled my hands in front of my mouth.

"I'm pretty sure I can handle it if necessary." Dad nodded. "I bet the new guy you hired, Adam, could help me. You more than paid me back for law school with the work you have done."

I liked Adam and all, but there was no way I trusted him this much. My parents could lose their house and the firm. I had no choice. I needed to save them again, but this would have to be the last time.

My stomach dropped. The email.

I just sent that email to Raymond & Johnson Law. What if they came back and offered me a position? Could I turn it down . . . again?

I took a slow breath and pictured my mom and dad out on their front porch swing. She loved everything about that house. She fought the city and turned the whole area into a historical district. That was the story of how my parents met, Dad a young lawyer, and Mom a stubborn conservationist.

"No, I'll figure this out." I couldn't trust anyone else to do it right. Saving a law firm would be faster the second time around, right? Then, I could move on to a more prestigious career. "Where is it, and when do we start?"

"Hillsdale."

"Where?" I searched my mind for any recollection of the city.

"It's a small farming town a little over an hour south, and I was hoping you could start on Monday? See what needs to be done? Harry is itching to leave." Dad stood from the couch and walked over to me and gave my shoulder a squeeze. "Who knows, maybe it'll end up being an excellent investment, and then both of us could go in on it together." I heard the hopefulness in his voice. I was not having the family business conversation again.

"Dad, look, I know you love what you do. You love the smaller firms and deep connections with the people you help. And I'm proud of you and the difference you make." I looked around the cramped office with no windows pushing down on me on all sides. "But it's not for me. I want something with bigger margins, I want a big corner office with a view, and to win a big case with high publicity . . . . I want more. I'm trying to secure a position at Raymond & Johnson Law." I felt myself shrink. I didn't mean to hurt him. My dad was great. We wanted different things.

Dad's lips pulled down in a momentary frown. "Raymond &

Johnson's, huh?" He looked like he was about to bring up something more, then shook his head. "That's great, son. Understandable, the tight margins aren't for everyone."

I felt sick as Dad stared at the floor in thought.

"This isn't what I planned for my life, you know."

Dad smiled. "It'll all work out." He said it softer than before, as if trying to reassure himself. "Life has a funny way sometimes of making better plans for us than we make for ourselves. You go ahead and start that big career. I've got this." Dad nodded and reached to give me a hug. "Thanks, son. For everything. Don't let me hold you back any longer—"

"No, Dad. I'll help with this Hillsdale situation, but then I will look for other employment." It was good for us to have clear expectations.

"I appreciate you and all the work you've done. You're a wonder." Dad pulled me in for a hug. "If you are ready for something else—"

"I am, but I'll help get things situated first."

Dad nodded and headed toward the door. "If that changes, let me know. Now don't forget."

"Dinner, next Sunday. Got it." I waved goodbye.

I sighed and melted into the couch. Just when I thought my plan was getting back on track.

Chapter Five

MARISSA

MONDAY, GROSS. I REACHED UP AND FELT FOR THE goose egg on the back of my head. I think it shrunk enough to brush my hair without flinching . . . at least I hoped it did.

I wondered how Scott's injuries were healing. Silver lining: if he got a concussion, he wouldn't remember anything about the night we met. If I could erase that date from existence, I would. At least I didn't have to worry about seeing him again.

I pushed back my worn patchwork quilt, sat up in bed, and reached for my phone, silencing the alarm. My screen was flooded with notifications of texts from Rose.

Rose: Morning! I thought you might like a copy of these . . .

I looked through the pictures that she took of the girl's night; it was an epic evening. The last photo popped up, and I groaned. Of course, she took some with me and Scott. I zoomed in on the picture. Scott was reaching down and pulling me up beside him. He was smiling, and I was blushing.

Okay, certain parts of the date were worth remembering. His gray eyes were gorgeous. He was funny, and when he rubbed circles on the back of my hand with his thumb, I melted. Not like the classy, smooth melty chocolate, but more like the kind when you find an old candy bar in your car, all messy and distorted. Not bad, but maybe not good either.

I laid back down on the pillow, studying the next picture longer than I would ever admit to. It was me standing next to Scott on the trailer, his lips hovering dangerously close to my ear.

I can't believe he asked to see me again . . . before my overreaction and almost-killing-him thing. I closed my eyes. I had dating rules to protect me, but never considered them to be for my date's protection too. No one could have planned those chains of events for sure. I shrugged and set down my phone.

I crossed my small bedroom to the closet and pulled off my PJs and grabbed my Lucky Charms shirt off the hanger. I pulled it over my gray tank top and tucked my tank into my faded jeans. The scars on my stomach from the car wreck with my parents never healed properly. The constant tank tops were dual purpose: to keep the scars from rubbing on my jeans and so people could stop giving me sad looks. Most of the town gossips had moved on to more recent stories years ago and I was fine without the reminders.

Okay, no more dwelling on the past. Today was a gift, each day was. I didn't want to waste it reliving old nightmares.

"How's the noggin?" Nan eased into my bedroom, her hair in tight curlers and wearing her worn pink fuzzy bathrobe.

"I'm great, Nan." I pulled on my tennis shoes, glancing at her as I tied the laces.

Worry lines formed around Nan's mouth.

"Honest, just had a bit of a headache yesterday. No worrying about me. You need to focus on your own recovery. How's your hip?" She huffed, waving away my concern. I eased past her, heading through the living room towards the kitchen. "I mean it, no more ladders," I said over my shoulder. "Ever."

"I'm fine. Just set the ladder up wrong, plus I got a nice new hip."

Nan grinned as she wiggled her hips from side to side. "I wonder if I could have a job as a magnet tester or something." She giggled at her own joke. She leaned against the kitchen door frame, tired from her efforts.

I loved Nan and her ability to joke about anything. I had watched Nan work extra shifts and long hours for years as she raised me through high school. It was my turn to take care of her. "Speaking of jobs, I better go, or I'm gonna be late."

I grabbed a granola bar from the pantry, gave Nan a quick peck on the cheek, and ran for the front door, stepping over the patch of raised linoleum I needed to still fix. "No beer, boys, or broken promises," I hollered over my shoulder. Nan chuckled at the saying she used on me in high school. "And no ladders," I added.

"I'm old enough. I can have all the boys over I want," Nan shot back and waddled to her favorite rocking chair as I rushed out the door. The screen door flew back with a loud bang, reminding me of another thing I needed to fix.

I headed in the direction of the Hillsdale Law office. It was only a little over a half-mile away and I intended to enjoy every minute of the fall air. I started my job when I was a sophomore in high school, but never meant it to last this long. Harry gave me the manager position once I graduated, but nothing changed but the title. I think it was his way of showing gratitude.

I was going to leave this town right after graduation for my three months in Europe. But one thing led to another, and I'm grateful I've got a job.

Hillsdale wasn't all bad. There were people here I loved, but I did not love Hillsdale. I wanted to fulfill the plans I had made with my parents. To travel, see different cultures, and taste different food. There wasn't a decent Indian restaurant within an hour's drive from town. In fact, it had little of anything. A few gas stations, two competing churches, a questionable bar or two, a pawnshop, a few school buildings—that was basically it. A new stop light was hung a few years ago. The whole town came out and watched it being installed.

I walked down a sidewalk lined with maple trees. The leaves had just started turning colors. Fall was a season of magic, change, and possibilities. Plus, pumpkin-flavored everything was always a plus. I cringed as I imagined Scott's pumpkin-flavored suit as well.

Whoops.

"Hey Marissa," a sweet, quiet voice startled me from my thoughts. "How's your grandma doing?"

Arlene smiled from under her floppy gardening hat. She wore her usual flannel over-shirt and worn gardening gloves. The old lady was as sweet as her voice. She was always welcoming, and I never heard her gossip, which, for Hillsdale, was saying a lot.

"She is doing much better. Thanks. Almost fully recovered." I stopped near the white picket fence. "Got to keep her feet on the ground."

Her eyelids crinkled. "I'm glad. I'll try to visit her today while you're at work."

"Thanks, I'm sure she'd love that. And I'd love the added surveillance," I laughed. "I locked the ladders in the shed, but I'm not sure that'll stop her."

She chuckled. "I think Bert is helping her take it easy . . ."

Bert.

My stomach felt uneasy. I couldn't decide how I felt about him, or the way his infrequent visits had become . . . well, frequent. What would happen if that became more permanent?

"Okay, well, I need to go. Running late."

"Have a great day, dear." She eased over and picked up her metal watering can on the porch and turned back to the mums in her flower boxes. Nan had taught me about watching for angels on earth. I was pretty sure Arlene was one of them.

Two streets over, I crossed the road and saw Ashley waiting by her fence, and all thoughts of angels and kindness fled. Ashley's hair was in a tight ponytail and her makeup was perfect. She had always reigned as the town princess throughout high school and clung to the title years later.

Why she had hated me from the start, I had no idea. Rose thinks it was because I was Jr. Princess my sophomore year at Homecoming, and I stole the spotlight with all my "orphan drama." I would've given up either title. The princess garbage was just because the town felt sorry for me, anyway.

Ashley wore a pink floral dress, high heels, and was standing on her manicured lawn holding her awful cat. Was it too late to avoid her?

"Mar. How lucky that I caught you this morning!" Ashley grinned and called out to me. She waved me over. It was people like Ashley that made me want to run far away from Hillsdale and never return. Her third marriage was already down the drain if the rumor mill was to be believed. I had to assume not very many people could stand her or her cat.

No point running now. She would chase me down. The cat looked at me and hissed. Ashley always pretended to have a southern drawl. I knew it was fake. She had lived in Idaho all her life.

"Morning Ashley, I'm running late . . ."

"I heard you were in Clifton a few nights ago. How was the fall festival?" She leaned forward, but instead of a sweet tone, hers sounded like rotten milk.

How did she already know? "It was fun. Thanks." I kept walking along the fence, with Ashley following in her yard beside me. Only a few more steps until Ashley would run out of real estate.

Ashley's lips pinched. "Now darlin', I sure hope you weren't leading some boy on. Dating in high school was one thing, but now they ought to know about," she leaned in and whispered, "your condition."

Whoa.

Nope. I stopped and faced her.

The whole town knowing about my infertility from the car accident was one thing. The way they felt they had a say in my future choices was quite another.

"I wasn't there for a guy, and if I was, it would be none of your business." I stood my ground.

"I know, but I'd hate for you to get hurt again. I know how much it must have hurt when Tyler's mom—"

"How about you worry about your own life, Ashley?" I challenged.

"Well, I never . . ." she gasped and put a hand to her Barbie-pink lips. Her eyes flew wide, her mouth dropped open, and she stepped back. She looked like a fish. Ashley glared, no longer hiding behind her beauty or southern charm. "I only meant it as a kindness," she snarled.

"Spare me your kindness. I don't need or want it. Have a nice day." I stormed off, no longer feeling the autumn chill. I knew my Nan was going to hear from Ashley's mother about my rudeness within the hour, but Nan would be on my side. *I needed to get out of this town.*

The front door chimed as I stepped into the office. "Sorry I'm late, Harry," I called out to his closed office door. The office was small, with a little square foyer, a water cooler, a mini fridge, and a wall of filing cabinets.

Crossing the foyer, I went to my desk and hit the power button on the old PC. I began sorting through loose papers on my desk about the recent complaints about Coach Peters and put them into his blue file, knowing full well it would take five minutes before the loud humming stopped and the dinosaur would be ready for a password. I needed to get Ashley out of my head. I wouldn't let her ruin my day. I took a deep breath and focused on the office around me.

Sal, Harry's wife, had decorated the space with mini paper pumpkins, window decals, and candy corn vases. The pumpkins reminded me of Scott. I picked up the paper pumpkin from my desk and moved it behind the water cooler.

Once Harry was done with whoever was in his office, I should ask him if someone can press charges from Friday night's pumpkin maiming. Just to be on the safe side.

Harry's office door opened, and he came out whistling. Sal must have been feeling well. I hadn't seen him this happy or relaxed for a while, maybe since before they diagnosed Sal with cancer.

"There you are, Mar." He turned, gesturing behind him. "I want you to meet someone."

I sat up straight. Meet? I knew everyone in this town.

"Scott, come here, please. I'd like you to meet our office manager and resident know-it-all, Marissa." Harry joked. "She has this crazy memory. She'll be a lifesaver for you."

Scott? Scott who? Not my blind date, right? Was he here to file charges?

Scott stepped out wearing a too-small navy suit and a purple left eye. Not just any Scott, my Scott.

Well, not my Scott.

"Holy—" I muffled. I pulled a folder from the desk up to cover my face. *Shoot, shoot, shoot. What are the odds?*

Maybe he didn't recognize me? I peeked over the folder to find Scott staring at me, his left eye puffy and purple, his mouth open.

"Mary?" Scott's eyes opened wide. Well, the one without the bruise did. He took a step back and gawked at me. "Is this some kind of joke?" He looked toward Harry.

Smiling awkwardly, I lowered the folder and shrugged. "Is your eye okay?" I bit my bottom lip.

Why was he here?

"Not Mary," Harry said. "Marissa, but it was a good guess since everyone calls her Mar." Harry shot me a quick questioning glance, and I shook my head no. He would be back with questions, but not now.

Scott groaned. "This is the office manager you've been going on about?" he asked, gesturing at me.

"Have you two met?" Harry leaned up against my desk, crossing his arms.

"Nope," I replied.

Ugh! Why did I say no? Deniability for the pumpkin? He clearly recognized me.

Scott rolled his eyes. "Yes."

Well, at this point, I was committed. *Full steam ahead.*

"I'm pretty sure you met Mary." I bit my bottom lip.

Why? Why don't I just apologize now?

Scott's dark blue tie was matching the color of his swollen eye. "Well, Marissa, I must have met your identical twin. I swear it was you at the fall festival on Friday night?"

"Nope."

Abort. What am I supposed to do now?

Harry raised his eyebrows in question. "Huh? Crazy."

Yep, he wasn't buying it. I needed to learn to not lie to lawyers. My cheeks flushed with embarrassment. I tried my best to look busy with stacking papers on my desk.

"Well, hopefully you two *strangers* can work together. This town doesn't always take to newcomers. This transition might be a little tricky." He turned to Scott.

"I'm sure we will get along as well as I did with her identical twin." Scott said. I scowled at him.

He knew the pumpkin thing was an accident, right?

Wait.

"Transition? What transition?" I came around the desk in front of Harry, keeping my back to Scott. "What are you talking about?"

He reached out, pulling me into a tight hug. "The merge went through ahead of schedule. I'm taking an early retirement!"

Harry had talked about the eventual merger for a while, but I thought it was still a few years out. Harry motioned toward Scott, over my shoulder. "This is Scott Elliot, your new boss."

I died inside a little. "Wait, you're Scott Elliot, like from the Elliot Law firm in Clifton?" I'm so getting fired. "Wow . . ."

Scott nodded with no emotion.

"He'll be running the place for the foreseeable future. The firm is now merged with his dad's firm in Clifton."

I let out a tight breath and covered my face with my hands. Perfect. Almost killed my boss, then I lied to him. Twice.

"Oh, don't worry darling," Harry rubbed my back. "His dad guaranteed your job. Besides, this city guy won't get far here without you." He gave my shoulders a soft squeeze.

"Clifton hardly counts as a city." Scott rubbed his forehead.

Harry chuckled. "Well, compared to Hillsdale, it's massive." Harry nodded back at his office. "Lots to cover today. What'd you say happened to your eye again? Something about a pumpkin?" Harry tipped his head at me, and I felt myself turn an even darker shade of red.

"Hey Mar, would you order us lunch from Merritt's later? We have a lot to go over." Harry chuckled. "Sal was so excited. She already booked us a vacation at an all-inclusive resort."

"You're leaving town already?" Scott asked. The panic was clear in his voice, though his face showed no emotion.

"Oh, I'm sure you'll do just fine picking up where I left off. Your dad swears you're a genius. Besides, Marissa knows everything that goes on around here."

They headed into Harry's office and closed the door behind them. I walked back to my seat in a haze and plopped down in my chair. I was going to die from embarrassment.

Would he still sue me? Was he going to tell everyone what happened with the pumpkins? It would be all around the town by lunch, then the *good-natured* nicknames would start. Once you got a nickname in Hillsdale, it took years to clear it. I could already see it. "The Pumpkin Maimer" or maybe "Jack-O-Slammer."

I grabbed my phone and opened the group text with Rose and Faith.

Marissa: Umm, you guys wanna guess who my new boss is?

I waited and saw three dots appear as Rose typed her reply.

Rose: Wait . . . WHAT . . . Did Harry sell the law firm?

Marissa: Merged apparently . . . this weekend. It's been in the works for a bit but got expedited, I guess. New guy is here to take his place.

Rose: Oh guy, FUN. Is he hot?

Marissa: Yes, hot.

Rose: Single?

Marissa: Grumpy.

Although I didn't blame him for it. He had lots of reasons to be grumpy. All those reasons pointed at me.

Rose:?

Faith: Wait, I just sent my kids out for recess and only have a few minutes before I need to prep my next lesson. What's going on?

Rose: Marissa got a new lawyer boss, and he is hot, but grumpy?

Faith: Oh, I'm happy for Harry. He has been wanting to spend more time with Sal. She must be so excited.

Rose: FAITH, you missed the point. New boss . . . HOT.

Faith: Ha ha. Right, that too, but why grumpy?

Marissa: Remember how the guy from the corn maze was a lawyer . . .

What were the chances?

Seriously.

So much for Fate being on my side.

Rose: NO WAY! Pumpkin guy!

Marissa: I'm still not sure I'm at fault for that. I mean, he didn't have to come after me, right?

Faith: OMG! For reals!!!

Marissa: Yep . . .

Faith: Oh my gosh! I'd be mortified.

Rose: Girl, he is HOT. Who cares?

Marissa: Ha ha, thanks for the help.
Faith: Time's up. I'll check in with you guys later.
Rose: Yeah, dessert soon at Merritt's and I want EVERY detail!
Faith: Yes! Girl's Night!
Marissa: Deal. Hopefully, he doesn't fire me first.
Faith: Wait. OH MY GOSH!! Marissa! It's Fate!!!
Marissa: . . .
Rose: Oh boy, here she goes.
Faith: No, I'm serious! Think about it!! Nan has a BF and Harry doesn't need you at the law firm now . . . you know what that means?

I tilted my head and thought about what Faith was saying. Both the ties that held me to Hillsdale were dissolving. Maybe her order to Fate was coming true. Time to start over. Time to be anywhere but here.

Rose: It means it's time for her to get a boyfriend.
Faith: No, Well . . . I mean, a boyfriend is always fun, but I was thinking
Marissa: London!
Rose: Foreign men!
Faith: LONDON!

We answered at the same time, and I laughed.

Rose: I bet guys in London are hot. Plus, think of the accent. She used a kiss emoji.

I rolled my eyes and sent back the emoji of money and tears. If only I could afford it. I was getting closer, but my savings account took a hit when a tree fell over in the yard during the last rainstorm.

Chapter Six

SCOTT

THE OFFICE WAS SWELTERING. I SHOVED THE WINDOW open, and it groaned in protest. I wanted to scream along with it. How had I convinced myself this would be a quick project? I looked around the office with its stacked cardboard boxes and filing cabinets. If my dad's office was antique in its processes, Hillsdale was archaic. Harry didn't even have a computer. Apparently, if he touched one, it got a virus.

I wiped a trail of sweat from my neck collar. I felt trapped and my life was rolling further off track. My suit jacket was too small and hot, but it stayed in place. I needed a good first impression with any potential clients. One accidental whiff of my underarms would not add to my professionalism. I should've put on an extra layer of deodorant this morning.

Today was my first official day without Harry and I wanted to ensure that everything ran smoothly. I walked around the large particle board desk and sat in the black office chair. It made a cracking sound as I leaned back. I quickly righted myself.

I looked at the blue folder on my desk. It was full of pages that were falling apart, sticky notes, and old letters. Everything was out of order, and I was pretty sure Harry must have used some sticker system. His desk drawer looked like an elementary school teacher's. Every square inch of the table was covered with random papers, pens, and highlighters. *What did he even use the gold stars for?*

I flipped through the papers. This case's start date was in 1985, surely it was closed by now. All I could make sense of was that it was about a cow named Betsy and some long-standing family dispute of ownership. The current *custody arrangement* split milking days as they moved the cow, and now her calf Betsy 2, back and forth to each other's farm once a week so that the animal felt at home and safe in both places.

I thought my dad's firm would help me in Hillsdale, but I'm beginning to wonder if nothing could have prepared me.

Marissa must have sensed my overwhelm through the door and walked in with a large cup of coffee. What were the odds she was the office assistant. Actually, it was a great question. *What are the odds?*

Small world. She had on the same jean jacket she wore at the corn maze. Her long brown hair was in a high ponytail and her cheeks flushed red.

Were we finally going to talk about things then? Mary/Marissa had avoided eye contact with me for the last two days, and I didn't have the energy or brain space to pry. Keeping things polite and professional would be best between us anyhow. Thankfully, she had ended the possibility of a second date before it even began. It would look terrible if I just started here and was already dating the only other employee.

Looks like I dodged a bullet, but not the pumpkin.

"Good morning . . . Mary." I drew out her fake name as I grinned to show her that I was playing. I couldn't help but tease her a little. It seemed only fair with my bruised eye. The skin beneath it had gone from black and puffy to the color of mustard.

She closed her eyes and scrunched her nose. "About that . . ."

"Why didn't you tell Harry the truth?" I smiled to let her know I didn't mean any venom.

She shrugged her right shoulder. "I'm still not sure. I panicked I guess." She walked over to my desk and sat on the corner. I glanced to the foyer. This would not look good if someone were to walk in, they would have gotten the wrong idea.

"Plausible deniability in case you tried to sue me?" Marissa handed me the cup of coffee with a sweet smile. *#1 Boss* was printed on the mug. "Plus, you took me off guard a little." She bit her bottom lip, and my gaze followed the movement before I glanced back at her eyes.

I grabbed the cup from her outstretched hand. "I'm not going to sue you. Besides, it would never hold up in court. I went into the pumpkin patch willingly." I nodded to the cup. "Thanks."

She nodded back but seemed far away in thought. "Why?"

"Why what?"

"Why did you help me after I was rude to you?" She tugged on her shirt. I remembered her doing it before; it must be a tell when she was uncomfortable. "I feel so awful. I can't believe you got hit by a pumpkin. I should've paid better attention. Your eye is looking better though. You're wearing a different suit coat. Did I ruin the other one? I panicked and I really don't date, that at least wasn't a lie. Even though that night was fun."

Wow, she's not beating around the bush. Marissa was spewing out everything she had held in the last few days.

"If you would've given me your real name, I might not have had to, but when you didn't see the danger . . . I did what anyone would." I set down the cup, avoiding the Betsy cow case.

"Probably not *anyone.*"

True, being a lawyer had shown me sides of the human character that I wanted to forget. "Well, my mother would've never forgiven me."

Her eyes seemed to soften, and she gave me a small smile. "Start over?" She held up her hand to shake on it.

"Gladly." I grabbed her hand. I was reminded of our size difference and the gentle way her hand felt in mine. The past sparks shot up my arm and I reminded them we were now co-workers. Worse, I was her boss.

She glanced down at my desk, shifting her weight further onto the desk. "Yikes, are you starting with Betsy?" She exhaled. "You're going to need more coffee." She slid off the desk. "And maybe chocolate, or are you more of a salty guy?"

"You know about this case, just by glancing at it?" I had been staring at the file for over an hour and could not make heads or tails of it . . . pun intended.

She shrugged. "I imagine I know about quite a few cases, but I think everyone in town knows about *that* case."

"Does the town talk openly about most legal affairs?" That could complicate some situations.

"Oh, the town talks openly about everything." She flinched. "Although, don't believe everything you hear."

"I'm a lawyer. I rarely believe what I hear." I grinned.

She chuckled. "That's fair." She nodded toward the file. "Betsy goes back generations. If you want to make sense of the files, I would start with the yellow folders." She pointed to the left corner of the room. "They hold less, so they are less complicated. Avoid blue unless you are ready for a mess. Especially *that* one." She grimaced. "Think Romeo and Juliet family feud, but over a cow."

"Thanks for the tip." I felt my lips lift; I was happy to be on friendly terms with Marissa again. This place would be lonely with no one to talk to, but I needed to remember to keep it *only* friendly. I was already thinking of dates with sprinkles and a magic quarters redo.

"Do I have any appointments set up for today?"

Marissa tipped her head to the side. "What do you mean?"

How could she not know?

"Do I have any scheduled appointments with new or existing clients to go over any legal matters today?"

She sighed. "Harry didn't tell me if he did, but everyone would show up here or his house, or catch him at the grocery store for most things, and schedule meetings while he was out. He tried keeping a schedule at the office for a while, but it never seemed to work out. He might have written something down in that notebook he always carried. I will see if I can find it." She turned to leave.

"I have it, but his handwriting is horrid." I pulled out the blue spiral notebook filled with chicken scratch in different colors and more stickers.

Marissa laughed. "Yeah, it is. I tried to add meetings to his Google calendar attached to his email. He never checked it anyway and would cancel appointments without meaning to. Electronics and Harry were rarely on friendly terms."

I chuckled. "Can you decipher his hieroglyphics? And what about the stickers?"

"Yep, I've got you." She came back and sat on the desk. There were chairs right across the table. She leaned down over the notebook and her apple-scented hair fell across her shoulder. I wondered how soft it was. I put my hands in my lap. I needed to set some clear boundaries. I stood and offered her the chair.

"I'm not sure that desk is safe to sit on."

She waved me off. "I've always sat on it. I think it might be safer than that chair." She flipped the page. "Looks like a few coach complaints at the Merc. George stopped him at church, but they didn't set a time. And Mrs. Bates came by his house too . . ."

"People would show up at his house and talk about legal affairs at church?" *Yikes*.

Marissa nodded. "Things work a little differently here than what you are used to, I'm sure." She pointed to the gold stickers. "Harry used these to show if someone needed—"

"Well, that is *not* going to happen anymore." I was still thinking about how this town would catch Harry whenever and wherever. It was the opposite of professional. "Is there an office phone line?"

"Yep, I don't know if anyone knows it." Marissa grabbed her cell out of her back pocket and started scrolling. "Actually, I don't even know it." She smirked and let out a little chuckle. "Do you want me to start giving out your cell number instead?"

"Are you asking for my number?" I leaned towards her.

Her cheeks flushed pink. "Wait . . . no . . . I mean, maybe?"

That sparkle of mischief lit her eyes, and she looked more like the woman from the corn maze, and I liked it.

I shook my head. What was I thinking? *Be professional.*

"From now on, I will need to only see clients who have scheduled an appointment with you, and I will need at least twenty four hours notice. Let's see if we can figure out the office line as well." I didn't know where to start with the mess of paperwork, but I could at least begin with establishing procedure order.

She leaned away from me. "Okay boss, if you're sure . . ." Her nose scrunched. "I'm not convinced that will work well here—"

"If my current practices add efficiency on a large scale, they should be equally effective here." I nodded. "I know how to run a firm."

She flinched and stepped away from me. "Well, you're the boss. Enjoy the coffee." She left the room without giving me a second glance. Marissa was angry. I might have come off harsher than I intended. I wouldn't take it back though. I needed to establish order and expectations for this place to succeed. I had too much riding on its quick success to do it halfway. I was certain the way forward needed to be professional and streamlined. I grabbed the stack of stickers from Harry's desk and threw them away.

And no more stickers.

Turning back to the blue folder, I groaned at the mess. I closed it and peeked out into the foyer to see if Marissa could see me as I crossed my office. I quietly exchanged the blue folder for a yellow one and crept back to my desk. No need for her to see how over-whelmed I felt.

My chair groaned loudly as I sat, and I cursed everything in this office. So much for being sneaky.

I opened the folder. Divorce. Perfect. Ashley and Sam and a cat.

I used my phone and laptop to take pictures of the documents, load them into the software, and organize them in the right folders.

I began tabbing through the different sections in the software and added files into the proper spots. The upload speed here was terrible.

"Is Harry in?" I heard a woman wail through the open door. "Letty said he sold. That can't be true! Is that true?" She spoke, rattling off questions before Marissa could answer.

"Sorry, it's true, Mrs. Bates. The firm merged with the Elliot Law firm in Clifton, and Harry is spending some time with Sal," Marissa answered. "Mr. Scott Elliot is here now and taking over Harry's clients."

"But Harry said he'd meet with me. It's happening again with the gnomes." The last part of the sentence came out as a whisper. "How do we know this new guy can even be trusted?"

"Harry must've trusted him," Marissa said. "Or at least he trusted his dad."

I stood up and straightened my jacket. The first potential client—I needed for this to go well. Harry mentioned how fast word spread in this town. I went through the office door and saw a petite older woman with short brown, fuzzy hair and a huge purple bag slung over her shoulder. She was pacing back and forth; her face was flushed.

Crossing the foyer, I held up my hand. "Hello, my name is Scott Elliot. I assure you I'm trustworthy and qualified to handle your legal affairs. And you are?" I smiled and I waited.

She looked at my hand, her eyes pulled wide in shock as she took several steps backward. "Well, I never!" She turned to Marissa.

Marissa twisted her head away from me and cleared her throat, suppressing a chuckle. "Mrs. Bates, forgive Mr. Elliot. He is unaware of your feelings about hands and their potential germs."

I let my extended hand fall awkwardly to my side.

The lady's eyebrows drew together in a scowl. "Exactly my point," she whispered to Marissa. "He doesn't even know us. Not like Harry does."

"I assure you, ma'am, I have excellent references and graduated top of my class. If you make an appointment with Marissa, I can see you at my next opening." I put my arms behind my back and tried my best to look professional.

The woman scowled and peeked around my shoulder toward my empty office. "It looks like you have an opening now." Her large purple bag followed the movement.

"Yes, though I prefer my appointments to be scheduled in advance so I can offer my clients my full attention. You're welcome to call later if you are unsure what time would work best for you." I nodded at Marissa. "Have we located the office number?"

"You want me to give personal information over the phone?" Her eyes somehow bulged wider, and she took a step back. I looked to Marissa for the information I was missing once again.

"Mrs. Bates has evidence someone tapped her phone after watching a spy movie a year ago. She doesn't use a phone anymore. She prefers in-person conversations." Marissa's eyes twinkled.

Was she just messing with me?

I fought the urge to roll my own eyes. I could not afford to make enemies in this town. I let out a breath slowly.

Ugh, so much for order and rules.

"Very well. If you have your payment information on file, I will visit with you now."

The eccentric woman held on tightly to her purse. "Oh. You're not getting a dime of my money. What have you done to earn it?"

"Besides attending law school and passing the bar?" I muttered under my breath, clearly not quietly enough, because Marissa snorted.

I put on a polite smile. "Very well. Let's do a free twenty-minute consultation. Then you can decide if you want to continue with my services."

Eyeing me, she stormed past me to the office, muttering. I watched as she reached into her purse and pulled out a container of antibacterial wipes. Not the mini size, but the large full-size container. She wiped down the seat before she sat.

"I'll time the twenty minutes, if you don't mind." She pulled out a board game sand timer.

I itched to start a timer on my phone, but she eyed the device with a glare. I moved it out of sight. Best to not fight this one. "Yes, of course. Your timing this meeting would be most helpful. What can I do for you?"

She settled into the chair and let out a slow exhale as she looked side to side. "Last night it was raining," she leaned in closer to whisper. "They came to life again."

"What came to life?"

Is this some kind of prank on the new guy?

"The gnomes," Mrs. Bates whispered.

What on earth? I reminded myself to show no emotion. "Gnomes?"

"The garden ceramic ones in my yard. I have thirty of them. It happens every time it rains." She pointed her finger at me for emphasis. "They move."

I held her gaze.

Did she believe this?

She glanced around the office nervously. She believed it or she was a great actress.

"Why do you think they came to life?" This woman didn't need legal help, but a mental health professional. Why had she even come here? Unless she knew that the gnome animation was a prank and wanted those responsible prosecuted.

"*Think*? I know they did. They were all moved. Again. They are sending me a message . . . with letters this time."

Oh dear. "What are you hoping to do legally against . . . the gnomes?" I was glad that I had kept some of the sarcasm out of my voice. Maybe I could humor her for a few minutes, just to be nice. Make a good impression.

"Well, you are used to working with unsavory types, and I don't know their intentions." Mrs. Bates rubbed her arms, fighting a chill. "I want you to talk to them. See what they are trying to say. Maybe they have demands." She moved in close, nodding.

"Demands? The garden gnomes?" Nope, this was not for me to fix. "I don't speak gnome. If you would like to open charges against the *people* who are messing with your yard gnomes and property, that is something I may help with."

"What do you mean, people? The gnomes are moving by themselves," she emphasized.

I was not the one who could help this woman. "I'm not sure I'm who you need to see about this, Mrs. Bates. Is there perhaps a mental health counselor in town?"

"What do you mean?" She leaned back in her chair, her eyes guarded.

How could I put this without offending the woman? "I don't feel as if you would profit from legal advice, but maybe some mental advice or a great counselor." I was doing her a favor. I didn't want to waste her time or mine. Why did she look at me like I was a monster?

She stood. "Well, I never!" She grabbed her timer and thrust it into her bag. "You don't believe me." She stepped away from the chair and looked both embarrassed and small. "Harry always believed me. He would always listen." She threw her shoulders back, determined. "You aren't getting a dime from me."

I felt my stomach drop as the woman held back frustrated tears.

"No wait," but I wasn't sure what to say. I wasn't going to go talk to garden gnomes, and I really thought she could use help.

"Just wait till I tell Letty about this." She stormed out of the room. "Marissa, if I have any other appointments with this lawyer, cancel them."

I stood and went to the office door and watched Marissa rush around her desk to pull Mrs. Bates into a hug. Marissa scowled at me. *If looks could kill.* What did she want from me?

Marissa leaned close to the older woman and began leading her outside. "Hey, are you okay? Do you wanna talk about it?"

There was nothing wrong with getting mental help. It would be a waste of time and resources to pretend like I could help her.

Seconds later, Marissa stormed back in with fire in her eyes. All five feet nothing of her marched right up to me and pushed me in the chest. "Would it have killed you to listen to her?"

I stepped back, getting a better stance. "What do you mean? I did listen."

"No, you didn't listen. You dismissed her as crazy and went right to suggesting she meet with a mental counselor." Marissa stomped her foot and huffed.

"And that's . . . bad?" Wasn't that what she had come here for?

"No one likes to be talked down to. You could have shown her a little compassion. She's a widow, and she's lonely. Her kids never visit, and she needs someone to pretend like they care." Marissa turned to grab her phone and jacket from her desk. "Harry always cared and had time. He would listen to her for twenty minutes and she would leave smiling."

"If I pretended to help her, it would be a waste of her money and our time. Compassion is not the best business practice," I whispered. There was a reason I had to come in and save Dad's business, and now this.

I didn't love it, but time was money.

Marissa gestured to the outside door. "Do you think that is going to help your business?" She huffed. "Look, I know you're experienced, but things are different here. To Harry, everyone who walked through that door was someone he cared about and knew." She pulled her jacket on with force. "If you want to get anywhere with the people in this town, you had better start looking at them more as people and less like numbers." She charged to the door.

"Where are you going?"

She growled. "To eat a cookie and go check that Mrs. Bates gets home alright."

I was not going to come between her and cookies again. She stormed out.

I stood rooted to the spot in the empty office and pulled off my suit jacket. So much for a good first impression.

Chapter Seven

SCOTT

I WENT TO THE FILING CABINET AND SEARCHED FOR A folder on Mrs. Bates. When I lifted the yellow folder from my desk, a few sticky notes fell out. I reached down and grabbed them off the floor. "Handshake/germs" was highlighted in green, "Gnomes" and "Jimmy" were in red.

Did green mean bad and red was good?

Who was I kidding?

I would never get out of this town. I needed a different plan. Maybe I should let Dad and Adam take it over. They might have more success anyway.

I yanked down hard on my tie to loosen it, took off my suit jacket, and unbuttoned and rolled up my sleeves. First impressions be hanged.

I opened my laptop to sort through my emails, hoping for a sense of normalcy. Sort, flag, or delete. I went down my inbox methodically and in control. I hovered over a reply from the Raymond & Johnson Law, my fingers frozen. It had been painful to inform them to disregard the last email, because I was, in fact, not looking for employment with them at this time.

After my disastrous morning and feelings of melancholy about my future, this would be pouring lemon juice on the wound. I took a long, deep breath and clicked open the email.

Mr. Scott Elliot,

It was good to hear from you again, and I'm sorry to learn that you are no longer seeking employment at our firm.

Perhaps the decision to work for your father will work in your favor.

We're experiencing a hiring freeze. However, there is a particular property in Hillsdale, Idaho, that a client of ours has been trying to purchase for the last three years: 20505 Janice Lane.

We have received an ultimatum to either secure the property by end-of-year or risk the client taking his business elsewhere.

The owner of this property will only deal with a local attorney. We have sent offers to Mrs. Carol Andrews with no success. She refuses to discuss any terms with us.

If you, as a "local," can convince her to sell to our client by December 10th, a substantial bonus and a position in our firm is waiting for you at the beginning of the new year. This is a limited time offer.

Let us know if you accept these terms.

Clyde Johnson

I shot up from my chair, causing it to rock back loudly.

This was it.

This could solve everything. I reread the email. With the large bonus, I would dissolve my dad's loan, and someone else could take on this firm without the same risk attached. It wasn't like I knew what I was doing here anyway. This also might be my only chance with Raymond & Johnson Law. I paced back and forth in the small space, my emotions bouncing between excitement and fear.

I dodged around a pile of boxes stuffed with blue folders. It would take me forever to turn this place into a well-oiled machine. If the lack of internet speed didn't kill me, Marissa might. For a woman so small, she was packed full of fire.

I pulled out my phone and typed in the property address listed in the email. Hillsdale Bed and Breakfast. I pulled up the real estate estimate and scanned the results. The property had potential, with natural hot springs, a pond, and extensive acreage. There was skiing nearby, and it had a country charm. I assumed their client would want to turn the property into a resort or venue of some sort. The offer was well over the estimated asking price.

This could work.

It was my bright, shining light at the end of a long, dark tunnel. I had to take it. I sent my reply that I accepted the terms of the agreement and would keep them updated with my results.

I straightened my tie, put on my jacket, grabbed my keys, and locked up the office. *Some kid must have drawn a smiley face in the dust in my passenger window.* I needed to be professional. The owner of the bed-and-breakfast would hopefully take me seriously. I grabbed my set of microfiber towels I kept in the back ever since the dreaded pumpkin incident and wiped down my gray Mustang convertible. I babied my car a bit, but it was because it's the one thing I had splurged on—an outward expression of the life and job that would come my way.

Typing the address into my phone, I headed towards the bed-and-breakfast. It was a seven-minute drive. I drove past a few ancient buildings, through the only stoplight in sight, past the Hillsdale School grounds and into a residential neighborhood.

Janice was a quiet street, like every other street in this town. Maybe, if I could stay at the bed-and-breakfast, it would keep me from having to drive back and forth to Clifton or sleeping on the stiff couch in the office.

Also, it would give me time to convince the owner to sell in case I was unsuccessful on my first attempt.

Potholes and cracked cement roughly greeted my Mustang as I pulled into the empty parking lot.

At least that meant there should be vacancies.

I stepped out of the car, grabbed my leather briefcase, straightened my jacket, and walked up the sidewalk and past a wooden, faded sign for the bed-and-breakfast. The Victorian style house had two stories with a large wrap-around porch. There was light green paint chipping in several places, one of the windowpanes on the second story looked to be cracked, and there were several broken chairs on the porch. The grass needed mowing. A tree had fallen in the yard, and the house was decorated with dead flowers. It had potential, but it was also a big project.

I envisioned it as it could be. It could do so much for the town. The number of jobs and income alone would be a boon if this place was running at max capacity. I peeked around the porch and saw several barn-type outbuildings, a big pond with ducks, and a gazebo. It looked like I had stepped into a fairy tale. Albeit one that needed a good cleaning.

The door was wooden and sturdy, with frosted windows. The doorbell had a sign that read, "Broken, yell ding dong." I stiffened. There was no way I would be doing that. I knocked on the door.

Nothing.

I knocked again.

Recognizing the sound of a basketball thumping farther down the sidewalk, I turned and watched a group of boys, around eight to twelveish, roughhousing and passing the ball in the middle of the street.

I was glad I didn't park there. If they missed the ball and it hit my car, it would be as if someone had punched me right in the gut.

So much in my life was going wrong. My car was the one thing I had that was right.

I turned back to the door. This was a business. *Do I go inside?* I knocked again and looked at my watch. *Should I come back?* I reached for the knob. If it was unlocked, I would open it and holler. I turned the handle, but then the door opened and a woman with graying hair appeared behind it.

"Sorry about that, no one usually knocks. I didn't recognize the sound. Wondered if it was the heating acting up again." She was probably in her late fifties or early sixties, with soft edges. She had a warm smile, kind eyes, and a bright Halloween sweater. As she noticed my tie and briefcase, her eyes went from bright to angry.

She scowled. "Look, if you are another lawyer from that Raymond & Johnson Law I already told you. Stay off my property and leave me alone! I have no interest in selling to someone who is going to come in and ruin the place." She shoved the door in an attempt to close it, and I held out my hand to stop her.

Whoa. It took me a second to process her change in demeanor.

Okay, no offer for now.

"Hi, I'm Scott Elliot. I'm the new lawyer taking over for Harry." I brought my hand back as the woman glared at it. Maybe if I leaned into the Harry-replacement piece, she would let me stay? It would give us a chance to get to know each other and then address the offer.

The woman's mouth pinched, but she eased the door back open. "You're Harry's replacement?" Her eyes narrowed. "And you aren't here from the Raymond & Johnson firm?"

Yep. Not the time to mention that connection.

"I'm currently working at Hillsdale Law for my father, who is a friend of Harry's." I smiled and tightened my hold on my briefcase. "I was hoping to find a place to stay in town and cut down on gas money, so I don't need to drive back to Clifton as often." I wasn't lying. I loved my car, but it wasn't exactly fuel efficient. Even in Econ mode.

I heard some commotion to the right and looked over. The group of boys had moved to the parking lot with my car. They were shooting up at a makeshift hoop through the tree branches. My back stiffened as I watched them from the corner of my eye.

They were playing at the back of the lot. There was a good distance between them and my car. I pried my eyes away and focused on Carol. This was my priority. This was my ticket back to the life I wanted.

"I was curious if you have any rooms available."

She tipped her head back and forth, weighing her answer. "I've got a strict no-lawyer-policy. But none of them have been one of our own." She paused, resting her hands on her hips. "How long do you plan on staying?"

I recognized her question for the test that it was. If I said I was getting out of this town as soon as I could, she would send me packing.

"I need a place to stay until I can find something a little more permanent. The couch at the office has more springs than cushion." I shrugged my shoulder. *I would get further with her if I acted all neighborly.* "What's the cost per month?"

"Very well." She opened the door the rest of the way and the knot in my stomach eased.

"That would be wonderful—"

A loud metal thump, one that sounded like a ball hitting a car, brought my shoulders to my ears. I turned to see the boys examining my car door.

No! Not the car. Please.

"Hey!" I rushed over to them. A small dent in the passenger door was visible. I hadn't even paid it off, and it was already looking used.

Seriously. Can nothing go my way?

"You guys just hit my car." I pointed to the dent.

I turned to the group of them, who were now huddled together behind one of the bigger boys. The ones in the back looked scared, but the tall one stood with his arms folded in front of him, not even sorry for what had happened. I knew his type. They thought they owned the world and could do whatever they wanted. I was often the brunt of the basketball team's jokes throughout junior high and high school.

"What do you have to say? Anything?"

Someone stepped near my car from behind me. I turned to see Carol's guarded expression.

"Mr. Elliot. They're just kids, and I'm sure it was an accident. Boys, apologize."

The boys chimed in an apology.

Just boys. A lot of injustice can be excused by kids being *just boys.* My entire youth was proof. I turned to see Carol watching me cautiously. "I bet Randy down at the gas station would try to pop it back out for free. He invented this new tool—"

"Accident or not, this will need to be paid for, and it will be done by a professional."

Carol glared. "It's hardly even noticeable."

"I notice it. The people I hope to one day work for will notice it. I'm still paying it off and it already looks used."

Carol's eyes lowered. "I see. I'll take care of the damages then." She turned to the group of boys. "I've got some cookies that I just pulled out of the oven. How about you boys go help yourself?" She turned back toward me.

"That's it. No consequences?"

Her eyes filled with fire. "I assure you their lives are nothing but the awful consequences of other people's choices. They need a safe place to be, and I'll always provide that. I think it's time you left my property."

Her reply pulled me back and made me pause.

What did she mean? I looked at the boys as they rushed into the bed-and-breakfast. Skinny frames, dirty worn shoes, and unkempt hair.

My stomach dropped. I watched as the one bigger boy ushered the smaller ones inside in a protective way. She was right. I had no idea who these boys were or what their lives were like. They were not the ones who'd hurt me. I lashed out because of stress and because of my car. I made a hasty judgment.

"You're right. I have no idea what these boy's lives are like. I apologize." I ran my hand through my hair. "It's been a rough week and I let my temper get the better of me. But that is no excuse."

Carol's eyes didn't soften. "I think it's time for you to leave."

"Wait, I really would like a place to stay."

"No lawyers, and my answer is still no to Raymond & Johnson Law."

I felt myself reeling as my deal with the firm slipped through my fingers.

No, no, no. I have to save this!

"About before, it's not what I meant. I do plan on being here for a while and would like a place to stay. Please reconsider."

"Looks like we don't have any vacancies right now." She turned to head back to the house full of boys.

I flinched. "No, wait. Please, give me a chance."

Carol looked back at me; her eyes narrowed. It was obvious she didn't trust me and would not be letting me anywhere near the B&B tonight. She placed a hand on her well-rounded hips. "You just had your chance. You may work in Hillsdale, but you aren't one of us." She stormed back to the house and slammed the door, causing the hanging porch light to swing with the thud.

How had I made even more enemies in this small town? I headed back to my dented car.

Perfect.

Chapter Eight

MARISSA

I COULDN'T MAKE HEADS OR TAILS OF THE WHOLE SCOTT situation. Sometimes he seemed like the guy from the corn maze, fun, charming, and almost flirty. Then he would morph into this stuck-up businessman and become someone new. And by new, I meant rude.

I pulled my hair into a high ponytail and walked outside, then climbed into my old Honda Accord.

I had spent the last few days trying to set the office up the way he wanted it, sorting through files and uploading them into the new software. Scott's professional side was not a fan of the internet speed. *Wait 'til he sees what happens in a snowstorm.*

Sometimes he was sweet and patient as he leaned down over my shoulder, pointing at the screen on my ancient monitor, teaching me the software. He smelled like cinnamon; my heart would race, and my fingers would get all tingly as his hands brushed near mine. And when he smiled at me . . . I was a goner.

None of that mattered. I had no desire to become more than

friends with anyone, especially not with someone in Hillsdale. I shuddered as I imagined the amount of gossip that would generate and how fast it would spread if I dated Scott.

Not that it was an option, anyway.

I yanked hard on my car door, trying to convince it to open. I eventually won and turned the key in the ignition. The Beast didn't like to start up on the first try, but after a few times, she would turn over and get me where I needed to go. I headed down Main Street to Merritt's. I was a few minutes late, but it wasn't a long drive. Nowhere in Hillsdale was a long drive. You could get from one corner to the next in less than ten minutes, and that was with the twenty-five mph speed limit.

Faith and Rose had warned me in advance that tonight would involve lots of questions about Scott, and to be prepared. I would never be prepared to discuss the complexity of Scott. I put my car into park, grabbed my purse, and stepped out, slamming my door shut in one fluid motion. When it didn't latch, I tried again, throwing my hip into it this time. I didn't bother locking it. I would have to pay someone to take the Beast off my hands. I loved her though, in her broken, rustic way.

Merritt's was one of the few sit-down restaurants in town that wasn't connected to a gas station, and tables could fill up fast, even on a Thursday night. I pulled open the heavy wooden door and inhaled the smell of baked bread and greasy food; my mouth watered.

"Hey, Marissa," Merritt's granddaughter Jesse smiled. She was a high school senior now but had worked here since she was about fourteen. She stood behind the entry table and was pinching her shoulder to her ear, holding a phone in place. "Faith and Rose are in the left back corner," she mouthed as she continued taking an order on the phone.

"Awesome, thanks Jesse." I whispered and headed to the back.

She nodded and gestured to the stack of menus on the edge of the table. Her eyebrows pulled up in question.

"No need, but thanks." I wouldn't need the menu. It hadn't changed since I started coming here in high school.

I wound around the booths and headed to the left. The buzz of conversation and the smell of pumpkin circled me. Angie Merritt must have added the pumpkin pies to the menu this week.

Rose sat on one side of the table in her gold hoop earrings, red high heels, and dark eyeliner. Faith's back was to me with her hair in a wispy bun, wearing a button-up shirt and slacks from work. She rubbed her temples. I wondered if some parent was giving her trouble again.

"Hey, have you ordered?" I asked as I sat down next to Faith.

Rose nodded. "I got you hot chocolate. Jesse will get the rest when she brings the drinks."

I nodded. "Did you remember to add—"

"Yep, cinnamon and whipped cream," Rose finished.

I blushed a little. I always added cinnamon in my hot cocoa, but now it reminded me of Scott, and that felt different.

"Alright Mar, spill it." Rose grinned. "Essentials first. Is he dating anyone?"

I rolled my eyes. "Crazy, but somehow, his dating life hasn't come up this week."

"It would've come up if I was talking to him." She fiddled with one of her earrings.

Rose wasn't wrong, nor was she boasting. It was just a fact, when Rose was around it was easy to tell who was single and who wasn't.

"I stalked him online." Rose continued. "Couldn't find any pictures of women, just boring law stuff. He graduated top of his class though, Eagle Scout, awards, blah blah blah."

Not the scandal she was hoping for. I chuckled.

"Yeah, that doesn't surprise me." I grabbed a sugar packet and started trying to balance it on its edge. "He seems like the type of person where coming in second isn't an option, especially with his career." I thought back to his growing list of rules for the office and his expectations.

"And yet he is in Hillsdale?" Rose's acrylic nails tapped the table. "Helping his daddy doesn't really give me the cutthroat business vibe . . ."

"True." For someone who was so driven, it seemed odd for him to be here. "Haven't figured that out yet."

"Hey, are you okay?" Faith leaned against me with her shoulder. "I still can't believe you are working with him."

"Not with him. For him," I sighed. "It's emotional whiplash all day. He has these rules and likes things to be just so." I had felt the urge more than once to reach up and mess up his gelled hair. It was too perfect, too contained in place. It bothered me. "But, then he would relax and be sweet and flirty, like on our date." I flicked the sugar packet over and watched it flop onto the table. I reached up and rubbed my forehead.

"It's like Dr. Jekyll and Mr. Hyde, business edition. I can't tell if I should be offended by him saying I needed to not sit on his desk, or when he said my ripped jeans were not professional office attire. He is so focused on establishing clear rules and expectations. Which I get, but he is going about it in the wrong way. He even made Mrs. Bates cry." I sank back onto the bench. "But then he drops that stiff exterior and is all sweet, and I'm even more uncomfortable."

"Why?" Faith asked. "I would say that's a good thing." She looked at Rose for confirmation.

Rose studied me with her knowing eyes, and I went back to studying sugar packets.

"Are you going to go out with him when he asks?" Rose challenged.

"What? No." I sat back in the fake red leather booth. "He isn't going to ask me out."

Why would she think that? Did I look like I wanted him to? I didn't.

"And even if he did, the answer would still be no. I'm not looking for a relationship, and especially not in Hillsdale." I thought back to Ashley and the remarks the other morning. "People meddle too much, and dating for me is complicated enough as it is."

"Oh, please." Rose leveled me with a glare. "Not this again. Mar, you are more than some stupid ovaries."

I cringed. "Keep it down." I glanced around at the tables next to us. Everyone seemed occupied in their own conversations for the moment. "I know that—I do. But you've got to admit it complicates things a bit."

"Is this about Tyler's mom again?" Rose frowned. "I've told you, one word and I'll burn her house down."

I had dated Tyler during our senior year in high school. And his mother had always been nice, until we talked about going to college together. A high school relationship was fine, but after that, he needed to grow up and start looking to the future. One that included grandbabies.

It worked.

She showed pictures of her grandbabies to anyone she could trick into looking. When he came to the Easter egg hunt last year, Tyler attended with his wife and little twins. It looked like he was a great dad.

"I don't want anything to do with her or her son anymore. It's more than that. Before the accident, people asked me what I wanted to do when I grew up. I used to know my answer, to be a mother. The mom thing won't be a thing." The sugar packet flopped onto the table. "I just want to live for me for a bit. Find my place without everyone focusing on what it won't be. I don't think I can do that here."

Rose sat back in her chair. "My sister made me watch her give birth." She shuddered. "Nasty. Maybe you're lucky."

Faith pivoted away from Rose and faced me full on, pulling me into a shoulder hug. "It's okay for both. It's okay to want kids. It's also okay to find your place without them. You need to find what you want now."

I nodded, looking away, no longer wanting this conversation. Faith kept pushing therapy, but I think some things were best left in the past. I wanted to move forward.

Jesse came over with a tray balanced in front of her and set out the drinks for everyone. I thought of Scott when I saw the cinnamon sprinkled on top of my hot cocoa.

"You ladies ready to order?" Jesse asked.

I ordered fries and a piece of pie. Rose raised her eyebrow at my dinner choice of straight carbs. I glared at her in challenge, and she didn't push as she ordered a salad with dressing on the side. Faith ordered a large slice of chocolate cake. Something was up with Faith. Sugar was always her therapy of choice.

"How's work, Faith?" I asked.

She let out a long sigh. "I'm not ready to go into it. I might say something I regret."

Rose snickered. "Yeah, she might even say she doesn't like someone." She faked a gasp.

"Is it a past, parent, PTO, or student?" I asked. Faith didn't enjoy talking about her past either, but she seemed extra tired and worn out.

Faith sighed. "Tonight is about you. We can go over my drama another time." She waved off my question. "What if we make London happen? Give you something to focus on. With Nan dating and Harry gone, it's like Fate is answering you."

"Here she goes again. Or you could go out with Scott?" Rose pushed. "It's going to happen. It's only a matter of time."

I shook my head. I wasn't sure I believed in Fate getting me to London, but if it would get Rose off my back about Scott and burning houses, then— "London it is."

Faith gasped and started clapping. "Really?"

I chuckled at her excitement. "Sure. Let's make a plan."

Rose leaned back from the table. "Did I hear you say the P word?"

I sighed. "Just this once."

Gross.

Chapter Nine

MARISSA

Nan giggled at the breakfast table as Bert brought her some coffee, then she swatted his backside. He sat beside her, and they started kissing. When he knocked her dentures loose, I was out. Like running-for-the-door out. I didn't need that visual . . . ever again. I shuddered.

I realized that I'd forgotten my jacket and keys, but there was no way I was going back in the house for them. I rubbed my arms as I hustled down the sidewalk. The chilly October day was beautiful, but much too cold.

A bright orange leaf danced through the air as it fell to the ground. Fall, the season of change. I wondered if that was why it had always been my favorite. If the change was waking up each morning to a scene of Bert and Nan making out . . . no thank you.

It was time for a change of my own, and now, before I lost my nerve. Nan had Bert. Obviously. Which meant she no longer needed me. I felt anxiety squeeze my stomach. That happened sooner than I expected. I knew I would most likely end up in a house full of cats, but I thought I would have Nan for a while.

Harry was gone. He didn't need me at the law office either. Scott would adjust to Hillsdale; it would take time. He would figure it out.

It was time to leap and see if this dream I had reached for could happen. I didn't want to sit around and be in the way. If I didn't jump at the chance now, I might chicken out again. I had about five thousand dollars saved. I bet I could make it work. I no longer had time for a well-thought-out plan. I could figure it out as I went. I was ready to leap. I was ready for a change. I took out my phone and texted the girls.

Marissa: I'm buying a ticket for London . . . today. I want to go soon.

Adrenaline rushed through me.

Faith: Dancing Gif. What about forming a plan?

Marissa: Plan Schumann. It will work out. Fate and all that.

Rose: Sexy accents. Yes, PLEASE! Take me with you. Are you sure this is what you want?

Faith: Are you going to give two weeks notice? Like, how soon are we talking?

My shoulder slammed into the mailbox along the sidewalk. Ouch. Ashley's cat hissed and scampered away. Whoops. I needed to pay attention to where I was walking.

Would Scott need two weeks?

Marissa: Not sure yet. Will see.

I put my phone away and speed-walked the rest of the way. Opening the door to the Hillsdale Law, warm air surrounded me as I made my way to my desk. I was thirty-five minutes early and still didn't beat Scott to the office; a light glowed from under his door.

In the last week, every time I passed the law office after hours, I saw his car in the parking lot. Did he ever sleep? How many hours a week did he work? If I had said yes to going on a second date, would he have even found the time?

I wondered what a date with Scott would be like. Not a rush

through the corn maze, but something else. Would we have held hands again? Would he have a ridiculous thought-out plan by the minute?

I turned on my computer. Nope . . . No thoughts of dating, Scott or otherwise. I blamed Rose. She was pushing me to date him. If she liked him, why didn't she just date him? My stomach tightened. Weird, not sure I liked that idea either.

I needed to keep my thoughts pointed to London and only London.

I needed a distraction.

Plane ticket. I should start looking. Like right now, but I needed a departure date.

I heard some rustling within Scott's office and decided to see if he needed two weeks notice before I chickened out.

I stood up, went to his door, and threw it open. It slammed into the wall. "I'm leaving for London!"

Scott jumped in his chair, hit his knee on the desk in front of him, and cursed. He must have been asleep based on the red hand-print on his face and rapidly blinking eyes.

Whoops.

His hair was sticking up on one side, his shirt sleeves rolled up, and his top three buttons were undone. He looked very un-put together, and I wanted a closer look.

"Wait, you're what?" He shook his head. Still in a daze, he reached down and rubbed his knee, his forearm flexing.

Right.

Leaving.

"I'm headed to London. Thought you should know, since you'll need a new office manager. I was wondering, do you think you need two weeks, or can we expedite this? I'm hoping to leave ASAP. Maybe this weekend? Maybe tomorrow?" I couldn't stop moving my hands. I clapped them in front of me. "There's this thing with Nan and Bert and I was thinking about buying a ticket, like now." I smiled as he stared at me, trying to put together the dots I threw at him.

I took a deep breath to stop my rambling. Maybe he needed a minute. Nan always said I needed to give people a minute to process in the morning before I started rattling things off. "Anyway, I'm going to go look at plane tickets since I don't start work for another thirty minutes. I'll let you wake up. Then we can chat."

"Wait, trust me," he stood, holding up his hand to stop me from leaving. "I'm plenty awake now." He frowned and rubbed his left eye. "You're going to London? Like Europe, London? This weekend? How long are you staying? Who's Nan?" He ran a hand through his unkempt hair, the soft blond curls falling over his forehead. He always had his hair gelled and stiff. I liked this version better. I wondered if his hair felt soft.

Leaving.

Leaving this office right now and leaving for London.

"Yep. Isn't it exciting? Nan is my grandmother. I live with her. She has a boyfriend now." I gave him a cheerful grin and looked away from his hair as I rocked back on my heels. "I've always wanted to go to London. Why not now?"

Scott stood. "Okaayyy." He drew the word out, unsure of what to say next. "What are you planning on doing there? Is it just travel? How long are you staying?"

My lips pulled down in a frown. "I've a few thousand saved up. I kinda want to go for it and see where it leads. Not sure when I will come back. I don't have a plan."

Scott's eyes widened in shock, no longer sleepy. "You want to go to London without a plan and see where it leads? Please tell me I'm still dreaming . . ."

"It's been a dream of mine for a bit, just not a detailed dream. I'm sure it'll work out. Sorry, I can be a lot in the mornings." I looked around the office. "Are you sleeping here?"

"Why didn't you tell me sooner?"

I shrugged. "I just decided for sure this morning, and I kinda told you in the corn maze. I told you I was thinking of leaving the country."

Scott pinched the bridge of his nose. "I thought you made that up, so you didn't have to go on a date with me."

"No. I mean, a little maybe." I winced. I needed to stop rambling. "But my friend Faith asked Fate and London, and long story short, I need to go now."

Scott's eyes widened further. Yep. I was, for sure, coming off as a crazy. I wondered if he was glad that I said no to that date now. "The timing is right. So, I'm going." I rubbed the ends of my sleeves in my palms. "ASAP, do you need two weeks notice, you think?"

Scott stared at me, clearly in shock.

"You want to go to London . . . next week . . . because of Fate?" His eyebrows scrunched down, forming a deep crease between his eyes. "With no plan. Do you know where you are staying? What areas are safe?" Scott turned a little pale. "You cannot go to another country and wing it! What if you run out of money? Can't get home? Get mugged?"

"Ugh. Plans aren't my thing, remember?" I would not let him ruin my mood. "I'll get a job."

"Marissa, you can't just get a job. You would need a work visa."

I sighed. "Oh . . . I'll sell seashells or something on the side. I can stay in hostels and figure it out as I go." The seashell thing was maybe a bit much, but if he thought I was crazy, I might as well sell it. Plus, I was kinda hoping I would give him non-planning nightmares.

He rubbed his forehead. "Seashells . . . in London?"

Nope, not having this conversation.

He shook his head. "Marissa, this isn't safe! The plane ticket could eat a few thousand dollars up alone." Scott paced back and forth, rambling off questions that tore through my excitement.

"More money would always be nice, but I need this. I'm not your responsibility to worry about." I fled his office before he could ask more questions. Questions would stop my momentum, and that's not what I needed right now. "I'm going to look at flights," I called over my shoulder. I needed to channel Faith's energy and belief in Fate and romance. *Well, maybe not the romance part. Just Fate.* I needed to work on finding myself first.

I ran toward my desk, but Scott and his long legs were faster.

"Whoa, wait." Scott grabbed my arm, bringing me back around to face him. His eyes were gentle, but he was going to ruin this with his logic. I could feel it. "Please, don't rush into it. I would hate for something to happen to you. What's so important that it can't be planned? What about your grandmother? Surely she would feel better if you had some sort of itinerary."

I stepped away from his closeness. The concern in his eyes was making my head swim. "I don't want it thought out and planned. I'm hoping this whole Fate thing will take over." I shrugged. He was right. Nan would need some of these answers too.

"Last time you referenced Fate, I got hit with a pumpkin and got a black eye."

I felt my spontaneous adventure fall and my excitement drop through the holes he had torn through my sails. Maybe I would need to plan this out . . . a little.

"Okay, I'll think about it."

I could at least look at tickets for planning. Ugh. I walked toward my desk and felt Scott cautiously following each one of my retreating steps. I sat at my desk and opened the web browser.

My phone rang. It was Carol Andrews. I felt another squeeze of anxiety. I answered it and put the phone to my ear as I scrolled through flights.

"Morning Carol, how's the B&B going? Did Letty lose her cat again?" I knew she would be asking me to help her with something. She was always hoping I would come by and chat or help her run this event or another. My history with the B&B was complicated.

Scott's eyes flew open wide. I looked at him with a questioning glance. What did he look excited about?

"Hey Mar, everything is fine. Letty always has a lost cat, but that's not why I called. I was wondering if you'd head the committee for the trunk-or-treat this year." Carol must've been baking again because pans rustled and clanked in the background. Something clattered to the ground, and she swore.

"Wow, umm, that's sweet, and I appreciate your untested faith in my abilities, but I don't think it's a good idea." I shoulder pinched the phone and continued to scroll.

"Come on, you'd do great, and this time I'm desperate." She sighed into the phone. "I ended up rolling my ankle pretty bad last night trying to reach the bins above the barn. Darn thing is all swollen." Everything was held at the B&B: weddings, community events, birthday parties, and concerts. She was the community mom of sorts, and everyone relied on her.

My mom and dad's joint funeral was beautiful there. Even in the haze of grief, I could tell the time and effort it must have taken to host it. She and Mom were best friends in high school. It couldn't have been easy.

I leaned back in my chair and scrunched my nose. Someone else could step in, right?

She needed help, long-term help, with the place. Her book group ladies could only do so much. The last time I talked to Randy, he said he kept catching her asleep out in the pavilion, broom in hand.

I wasn't the answer, though. I couldn't be the answer. The place had too many memories tied to it. And if I agreed to help her, she would want to make it permanent.

"I know you don't want roots here Mar, but this can be a one-time thing. I really need some help. I can pay some, use it for your Europe fund."

I hated the thought of letting Carol down. She was always there for me, in any way I let her be. She had given me my car when she saw me walking to work in the winter four years ago, and a check for five hundred dollars with a card at graduation that mentioned it was for Europe.

I sighed. If her ankle was hurt, she would need help. I felt my throat tighten at the thought.

Could I help her?

I was going to have to plan anyway, and the trunk-or-treat would be in less than a month. That wasn't bad. I tipped my head back and forth. "I don't know." Even a one-time thing felt risky. I would need to spend time at the B&B, which made my stomach churn.

"I already have a committee lined up to help, and I'll be there too."

Being part of the committee was more my speed. I was more of a sideline girl. "Can one of them run it?"

"No, I already asked. You're my last hope. Please, Mar."

My mom would not like the thought of me not helping Carol if I could, but I wasn't sure I could. I'd avoided the place for so long now. "Can I think about it and get back to you?"

"Yes," I heard the relief in her voice. "Thank you for at least considering."

"Okay, I'll call you tomorrow. Bye."

I hung up and went back to scrolling plane flights to London.

"Was that Carol Andrews from the bed-and-breakfast?" Scott was peering over my shoulder at the flights.

"Yep." I looked over at his expression. It looked almost hopeful. "Have you met her?"

"Yeah, I was hoping to stay there." He gestured to the blanket on the office couch. "It didn't go over well."

I cringed. "Yeah, lawyers aren't her favorite."

"So I gathered."

"Not your fault. It's all from some persistent investor guy. They won't leave her alone."

He motioned to my phone. "What did she want?"

My eyebrows lowered. "Why?"

Scott rubbed his palms together. "I was wondering if she sounded angry. I need to try again, and I'm not sure how to go about it. I made a complete mess of it last time."

That made sense. "She seemed fine, needs some help with the trunk-or-treat this year and was wondering if I'd head that up." I clicked to the next page. "Wow, there are some cheap red eyes if I leave next week . . ." I saw Scott flinch.

"If you want to get on Carol's good side, you need to become a community man. That'll always win her over. Maybe you should run the trunk-or-treat." I laughed and shrugged.

"Wait." Scott held out both of his hands as if calming a wild animal. "That's it. Let's talk about this London thing. I may have an idea." A wide grin formed on his face, and he snapped his fingers. "I think I found a solution to both our problems."

"I'm all ears." I turned my chair toward him. He braced his arm on the desk and was towering over me. His eyes were bright, and my throat went tight.

"Marissa, this is perfect!" He wrapped me in an awkward hug. I was enveloped in cinnamon and strong arms.

Nope. Not perfect. This was not where I wanted things to go.

Scott stepped back and rubbed his hands. "I need a place to stay, and you need a plan . . ."

I grimaced. "I don't like—"

"I know you don't like plans, but they are my thing." He paced back and forth. "What if I plan your trip to London and you can help me get on Carol's good side with the trunk-or-treat thing? We could run it together."

"I don't know . . ."

"Let's talk about it over lunch." He looked at his watch. "Or breakfast." He smiled. "You're an angel. Let's walk to the Merc together. We could have breakfast. Betty Ann told me they have the best maple bars, but they sell out by eleven. I'm never there that early."

I'm always game for donuts but walking together to the Merc and sitting there for breakfast sounded too much like a date. As the town rushes in and out, it might spread the wrong idea. And wrong ideas spread fast in Hillsdale.

Chapter Ten

SCOTT

This was going to work.

Marissa could help me get on Carol's good side, and then I could still take the Raymond & Johnson Law offer. The bonus of it all? I wouldn't have nightmares about Marissa being murdered in London by helping her plan her trip.

"How about I grab us breakfast? You can finish up whatever you were working on." Marissa nodded at my office door.

"I don't mind going together." I didn't want her to get scared and rush a ticket to London.

"Yeah, but it might look like a date." She looked down at her shoes. "I'm sure it's not, but the people in this town like to talk."

I tipped my head to the side. She was adamant about this no-dating thing. Was it because she didn't want to date me, or was she worried about Hillsdale? Although I was learning the hard way to take her lead where Hillsdale was concerned.

"It's the least I can do after waking you up like I did." Her cheeks turned red.

"Deal." I held out my hand to shake hers. I wanted to show it was a business deal.

She raised an eyebrow but fit her hand into mine. It might have gone on too long for a business handshake, but I wasn't sorry. She stood up out of her office chair.

"Are you sure you don't want me to come with you?" I helped her arm through her jacket, and her hair brushed my arm. I caught the smell of apples. She looked up at me over her shoulder and smiled.

If she hadn't already turned me down for a second date once, I might have asked her again right there. I had to admit I was drawn to her, and not only as a puzzle to figure out. She was beautiful. I shook the thought away. No mixing business with pleasure. Things were precarious enough as it was. Reaching into my back pocket, I grabbed my wallet and handed her some cash. "I'll pay, though. This is a business expense for sure."

She grinned and shrugged. "Okay, if you say so."

My phone started ringing. I grabbed my phone from my pocket and saw the caller ID: Clyde Johnson.

Just in time . . .

"I need to take this."

She nodded and headed for the door. "I'll be back soon." She went through the front door as I headed back to my office and closed the door.

"This is Scott Elliot." I sat in my chair, wincing as it squeaked. I should get a new chair, but I wouldn't be here long enough to need one.

"Morning Scott, this is Clyde. I was wondering what you thought of my offer." His voice carried a no-nonsense tone. "I need to know if you are serious."

"Yes, I couldn't be more serious. I'll make this work." A weight lifted off my chest. It was good to have another plan in motion.

"Perfect. Have you contacted Carol?"

Do I tell him about my disastrous attempt?

Maybe he wouldn't trust me if I did.

"Scott. Did you hear me?"

The man wasn't patient. I cleared my throat. "Yes, I met with her. I didn't talk about the offer. I want to befriend her first." That wasn't a lie but wasn't the full truth of how disastrous it went.

"And are you . . . befriending her?" I could hear the skepticism in his voice.

"I have a plan in the works."

He grunted through the phone. "Perfect. Keep me updated. And Scott, if we don't have the paperwork signed by the tenth of December, the offer is off. Understood?"

"Yes, sir."

"Great. How soon can you come in? I'd like to show you around the office and get a few things signed."

I was going home for dinner on Sunday, but I should be able to do both. Besides, this took precedence over fixing anything at the Hillsdale Law. This was my second, second chance.

"I can come in Saturday afternoon if the office isn't closed for the weekend."

I heard a chuckle. "The office is never closed. Saturday, three in the afternoon."

I nodded. "Thank you for the opportunity."

"And Scott, this is the last chance if you want to make this work."

The phone clicked as Clyde hung up.

This would work. This had to work. I needed to convince Marissa to help me get on Carol's good side. I leaned back in my chair, and it groaned in protest. The chair cracked, snapped, and gave way. My arms floundered as I fell backward. I grabbed for the desk but got folders and papers and took them with me. My back screamed in pain as I lay on the floor with the chair back angled into my back, the papers raining down all around me.

Great.

I cursed Harry, his stupid folders, this stupid chair, and all that had me stuck in Hillsdale.

Hearing the front door ding, I felt the urge to rush and stand, but if I moved too fast, the folders would be in a bigger heap to sort later. Besides, Marissa must be used to seeing me flustered.

"Lawyer, where you at?" I heard a woman's voice and heavy footsteps heading right toward my office door.

Not Marissa. *Crap!*

I scrambled to stand and my back spasmed in protest. A woman flung open the office door, followed by a man, maybe her husband, who looked like he would rather be anywhere but here. They searched around the room, to the toppled chair, floor covered in papers, and me standing in the middle, holding my back in pain.

Ugh, why can't I make a good impression in this town?

"Oh yeah, Ann, this is a great idea." The man gestured to me. "This guy is obviously the answer to all our problems." The man folded his large forearms and glowered.

The woman huffed but continued to press into the room. "Are you a real lawyer?" She put her hands on her hips.

I pulled my tie straight and scooted the papers under the desk with my foot. "Yes, I attended law school at—"

"See," Ann turned to the man, hands still on hips. "Now tell him what happened, Frank."

The man rolled his eyes. "Let's go."

"Fine, I'll tell him." Ann looked back at me. I gestured to the two chairs in front of my desk.

She shook her head. "I'm too mad to sit right now. Frank here has been cheated. Tony was trespassing on our land again."

"Someone was trespassing?"

"Yes, and he took some of our new fertilizer blend and smashed several of our biggest pumpkins."

Okay. "What legal repercussions are you hoping for? To sue?"

Frank harrumphed and scowled. "Nonsense. I ain't got time for any of that."

Okay, not sue . . . then what? I straightened my sleeves.

"Have you filed a police report? If someone was trespassing, you should start with the police." The first time, I told a client to get mental health help, and now I was sending clients to the police.

What did they think I did?

Ann sighed and looked exasperated at Frank, who turned and headed into the foyer. "See, I told you, it would lead to nothing. Now let's go." I had flashbacks of Mrs. Bates storming out in tears and Marissa upset. Would Marissa be mad at me for sending them to the police? I followed them to the foyer. I needed Marissa to not be upset with me. "Is there a reason the police wouldn't work?"

"Max." Frank gestured like it was obvious. "His cousin, the police chief." He folded his arms over his brawny chest.

"Surely, he'll still be able to perform his job regardless of his relation."

"What are we going to do?" Ann broke into tears, causing a look of panic in Frank's eyes.

"Now Ann, no need for waterworks. We'll still beat him." He nodded towards the door. "Let's go."

"Ugh, where is Harry? He'd know what to do." Ann crumpled into Frank's arms, who patted her awkwardly on the back.

What did I do this time?

The front door dinged, and Marissa walked in, holding a drink carrier and a paper plate with maple bars.

"Oh, thank heavens. Marissa, you're just who we needed." Ann smiled.

Ouch.

I deflated. So far, everyone wanted Marissa's help over mine. No one wanted a lawyer, anyway.

"Hey Frank, morning Ann. How're the pumpkins coming this year?" Marissa crossed to her desk and set down the food.

Ann pulled her into a hug. "That's what I was trying to talk to him about." She glared at me, and I raised my hands in confusion. "Tony's up to it again. He stole our new fertilizer, and he even smashed several of our biggest pumpkins."

Marissa's hand flew to her mouth. "Oh, no!"

What was the big deal with these pumpkins? I waited, betting Marissa would send them to the police too.

"Please tell me you have the biggest pumpkins still hiding." Marissa nodded to Frank.

Frank smiled. "Oh, you know I do. The whole town keeps guessing where my pumpkin stash is. No one has found it yet."

"That's a relief." Marissa tapped her finger on her leg. "He's getting bolder this year."

"Yes, and the man should be punished. He keeps coming and doing more and more. If someone doesn't stop him, he'll keep coming." Ann put her hands on her hips, the fire back in her eyes.

"You should go to the police." I said, unable to keep the opinion to myself any longer.

Marissa shook her head no. "Um, I doubt that will do it with Max—nothing will come of it. Plus, no proof I'm guessing, other than history." She tipped her head back and forth in thought.

Ann and Frank both nodded in agreement.

"You know what? I would go to the president of produce. Who is it this year?" Marissa asked.

"Tara Hansen," Frank nodded.

President of what? In what world was a produce person better than the police?

"If you can prove Tony has tampered with your pumpkins, that should get him disqualified," Ann said.

Frank bristled. "No way. I want to beat that man in front of the whole town. Fair and square. I don't need him acting like he could've won for an entire year."

Marissa waved him off. "Right, tell Tara you suspect something and that you are setting up cameras. The fear of being caught and disqualified should hold Tony back, at least a bit. You only have a month and a half left." Marissa snapped her fingers. "Oh, and you could tell Ashley about where your pumpkins are."

"What!" Frank growled. "Might as well yell from the pulpit, that woman can't—"

"No, hear me out." Marissa held her hands in front of her. "Tell her a decoy spot, but not to tell anyone. The location will spread like wildfire and will send Tony looking in the wrong direction. Between that and the threat of being disqualified, you should be good till weigh-in."

"Genius." Ann relaxed. "Oh bless you Marissa, I'm glad you are at least still here."

Ouch. Again.

Marissa gestured to me. "Oh, Scott is not bad, just new. It took me a while to fit in here too."

With that, the woman gave her another quick hug. "I still want to see Tony get some comeuppance."

"Oh, he will, when I beat him." Frank grinned. "Again."

"Alright Frank, let's go talk to Tara." Ann turned and headed toward the front door.

I sighed and leaned against my office door. "Ok, so am I mistaken, or was that whole thing about a pumpkin?"

Marissa smiled, looking at the door as she watched the couple leave. "Not just any pumpkin." She turned to her desk. "*The* pumpkin. There's a pumpkin growing contest every year. The whole county gets in on it. Frank wins every year and Tony is always trying to take his title." Marissa grabbed a cup from her desk and held it out to me.

She looked at my open office door and the papers scattered on the floor. She raised an eyebrow. "Did you have a party without me?"

I rubbed the back of my neck. "Nah, leaned back too far in that chair and it broke. The papers were a casualty of proximity." I rubbed my back. "You might have been right about the desk being safer."

Marissa sat on the floor near the papers. She began sorting them into piles and putting things back in various colored folders.

"How do you know all this?" I motioned to the mess of papers. "Some were from five or six years ago."

"Well, I did work here then. Plus, nothing is ever resolved, just buried and brought back up later." She started picking up a blue folder. "This one is about all the disputes against Coach Peters. Instead of starting a new file for each complaint, Harry put them all in one folder."

I grabbed some papers. "These are all against Coach Peters? What did he do?"

"Nothing," Marissa grabbed a paper. "Played one kid too much, and played one not enough. Won by too much, lost when he should've won." Marissa grabbed the folder. "He is the best coach we've had in ages. Not a bad guy, caught in a hard spot sometimes. Can't please everyone, you know."

I stared at the enormous stack of papers piling up. "Did Harry charge everyone when they opened a file or complaint?"

"Nah. He would just listen to them for a few minutes, show them he wrote it down, and then they were on their way."

"It's no wonder this place is a mess, with no profit. It's more free counseling services than law."

Marissa smiled. "Yeah. Harry was focused more on people than profit."

"You can't run a business like that," I added, not wanting to upset her, but even if I didn't save this firm, someone would need to and that person would need to make some changes.

"You're not wrong." She picked up a blue folder and put a pile of papers in it.

I sat on the floor and started handing Marissa papers. She could sort them far faster than me, anyway.

"So, why are you still working here?" I hoped I didn't sound rude, but she always talked about it being a means to an end.

"Partly money."

I should offer to help her achieve her goals, so she would be more willing to help me with mine. "I also think it's time for a bonus, that should help you achieve your goals." When I joined Raymond & Johnson Law my bonus could help pay up my depleting savings, this would be a necessary step in the process.

She smiled. "That would be awesome."

"You said partly money," I prodded.

"Hillsdale isn't the easiest place to fit in sometimes. When I came here . . ." She paused and I didn't press. "It was rough. Harry offered me this job, and it gave me a distraction when I needed it. He was kind to me, but also didn't look at me like I was broken. After a while, his wife became sick, and I couldn't leave him when he needed me. Plus, there is Nan I need to look after."

"That's your grandma."

"Yeah." She grabbed more papers and stuck them in various folders.

"But you're leaving now?" My eyebrows pulled down. "What changed?"

"Harry's gone and Nan is dating Bert." She stacked all the folders.

Where does Carol fit in all this? I stood and offered a hand to help Marissa up. She eyed me but set her soft hand on mine. I squeezed it as I pulled her up beside me.

Time for donuts. "Let's eat." I walked beside her as we grabbed the food and headed to the foyer couch. "How do you know Carol?"

She sat beside me. Our legs brushed against each other. "Carol is complicated." She took a big bite into her maple bar and then licked some frosting off her finger. "I hate thinking of her overextending herself while she's hurt." She leaned back into the couch and sipped her drink. "Thanks for breakfast." Her cheeks turned red. "I left in a bit of a hurry this morning. What's your plan exactly?"

"I would love to not sleep on this couch. Maybe if you help

Carol with the trunk-or-treat, you could help persuade her to let me stay there?" I took a slow breath. "I would help you plan the trunk-or-treat, Europe, and any other planning needs you require." I bumped her leg with mine.

Marissa's pink lips took a bite of the maple bar and sighed.

"What do you think?" I leaned toward her and bumped her with my shoulder.

"Carol has done a lot for me, for everyone really." She looked up at me. "Only if you promise to help with the whole planning thing. Deal?"

"Deal." I tried to keep my voice neutral. If she knew how much I had riding on this, she may change her mind.

"Any list of plans for Europe?" I picked up a maple bar and bit down on the warm maple frosting.

Marissa pulled out her phone with its sunny case. It fit her. She was like a magnet of sunshine, radiating warmth and smiles. "I have a Pinterest board with some ideas, but not much."

I held back my screams of terror as I glanced at the home screen of her phone. It was covered in icons, not in folders, and had a bubble that said she had over two hundred unread emails and fourteen voicemails. And that's what I saw at a glance.

Not my circus, not my monkey . . . I kept my mouth shut. Or I guess not my messages, not my business. Did she know there was a folder option that could organize it all?

Chapter Eleven

SCOTT

I FLEXED MY FINGERS TO CALM MY JITTERS AND PULLED into the visitor parking spot. The tall building screamed its importance to all the surrounding smaller buildings. The Raymond & Johnson Law sign was bright for all to see. Even on a Saturday afternoon, the parking lot was full of shiny cars, tailored suits, and stiff ties.

For once, my car fit in versus standing out. *For once, I would fit in too.*

I stepped out of my Mustang and took a deep breath, reminding myself that, according to this last months magazine, a good part of landing a job was believing in yourself. I straightened my lucky blue stripe tie, which was tied to perfection in a Windsor knot. My shirt was wrinkled under my gray suit jacket, but after driving all morning, it couldn't be helped. Thankfully, the dry cleaning had gotten out the pumpkin stains.

Confidence shines bright. I envisioned my success. My life. The penthouse, big office, winning a prestigious case, my name in the paper as a top lawyer of the Raymond & Johnson Law firm. This was the life I wanted. This was the life I would receive. I merged into the other suits like a chameleon heading for the front doors.

Inside, the foyer was large, with expensive leather couches, polished floors, and industrial lighting. I walked over to the reception desk with purpose. *I belong.* Three women with dress suits, tight buns, and scowled lips eyed me with suspicion. Marissa with her faded jeans and a bright smile flashed into my mind. She greeted everyone like a long-lost friend.

This office was different, but different was what I wanted.

"Hello, my name is Scott Elliot. I have an appointment with Clyde Johnson."

The blonde frowned and scanned me from head to toe. I knew she could sense my shirt's wrinkles under my coat. She looked down without saying a word and began clicking on her keyboard. I clenched my hand tight on my briefcase. Do I ask her again? Was she looking it up?

Don't squirm. She can smell fear.

Confidence.

I belong here.

She glanced up and nodded at the elevators down the left hall. "Fifth floor. Conference room 532. I'll let Mr. Johnson know you are here." She looked back at her screen in dismissal.

Her stand-offish, rude behavior wasn't helping me feel confident at all. Mom always said you catch more flies with honey than vinegar, not that I even wanted flies.

"Thanks." I tried to imitate my twin brother Michael's charming smile.

She went back to ignoring me. I walked toward the elevators and joined a group of suits and briefcases. They were confident, oozing professionalism, and ignoring me.

Was their firm big enough that they didn't recognize new faces, or did they not care?

A man with stiff hair and shoulders began looking around the elevator. "Does it smell like pumpkin in here?"

A woman with short black hair scoffed. "Becky probably spilled lattes again. The girl is a wreck."

I eased to the back of the elevator and tried a subtle sniff. I couldn't smell pumpkin. Could it be my suit?

"Why don't they just fire her? Office assistants are a dime a dozen. I heard her complaining to Dianne about sixty hours last week . . . please. That's child's play." The conversation continued as they stepped off the elevator on the third floor.

The doors closed and I reminded myself, confidence. The life I want. I stood tall as I continued up to the fifth floor. I double checked my suit for stray pumpkin.

The doors opened as I was sniffing my sleeve. Perfect.

A woman in black high heels, a warm smile, and kind eyes met me. "Scott Elliot?" Hers was the first smile I had seen in the entire building. It was a source of calm and kindness that I needed.

I dropped my arm. "Guilty."

"Perfect. Follow me. We better get moving because Mr. Johnson only has a few minutes to meet with you."

I followed her through the office toward the conference room. There were floor-to-ceiling windows looking down on the city. The wall to the left was covered with head shots and plaques. Top lawyer of the year, and I visualized my picture among them.

She opened the door to the large conference room, oversized chairs, and more floor-to-ceiling windows. "Please have a seat. I will let Mr. Johnson know you are here." She smiled at me.

"Thank you for your help and your kindness." I held out my hand to shake hers. "I'm Scott, as you already know."

Her head tipped back in surprise, and she put a hand to her heart. "You are so sweet. That just made my day." She blushed, and I thought I saw tears forming in her eyes. "My name's Becky. Ignore the waterworks. It's been a rough morning . . . several, actually."

She reached out her hand, and I shook it. Becky, the intern, the one they were complaining about on the elevator. This place would crush her. She turned and rushed away.

I looked at the large table with over twenty chairs. Which one was I supposed to sit in? If I picked the wrong one, could it give the wrong impression? I wiped my sweaty palms on my suit pants.

Don't blow it. Don't blow it.

Confidence.

Hearing the door behind me, I turned and saw Clyde Johnson. He was tall with gray hair and lines formed around his mouth in a permanent scowl. He exuded prestige and power in his stance. He completely dominated the room.

"I don't have much time, but I'm glad you came on short notice." He gestured to a chair on my left. "Sit." He sat across from me. "I wondered if Ron would keep you on his leash forever." Clyde frowned. "Wow, you look just like your dad used to."

How did he know Dad? Maybe it was from my father's picture on the new website. I insisted he used his headshot from several years after college. The one where he looked professional versus the one Mom sent me, where he had a goofy grin and his typical Hawaiian shirt. People want to know they're taken seriously.

"Alright, let's get down to business." Clyde slid a folded paper over to me on the wooden table. I opened it. I saw a number with more zeros than had ever been anywhere near my name. Clyde Johnson's satisfied grin spread. "That includes your sign-on bonus, stock, and guaranteed three-year employment." He smirked.

I tried to return my eyes to their normal size and nodded nonchalantly.

"Should be enough to cover whatever your dad has gotten himself into. We're excited to have you here." He nodded, gesturing around the office.

I cleared my throat. "That is a very generous offer." I wasn't sure how I felt about the way he was talking about my dad. Sure, I had similar thoughts, but it's one thing for me to think it versus someone else to say it. My dad was nothing like Clyde, but he was still my dad.

"An assistant is printing off papers now that I'll need you to sign before you leave the office." He gave a wolfish grin. "I would hate to think you can go behind my back and sell to someone directly to get more money. I'm afraid I'm quite lethal when crossed. Understood?"

I nodded. "Understood. This is a wonderful opportunity. I have no intention of doing anything other than joining you."

"Perfect. Now, this is all contingent on you getting Mrs. Andrews to sign over the property by December tenth," Clyde continued. "Which is less than two months. I'm in a tight spot. I need this property and fast, which is why I will pay accordingly." Clyde nodded to the paper.

"I understand. I'll do my best." I straightened my shoulders.

"I will need better than your best. Do not disappoint me." He nodded, stood, and left the room.

Clyde was a bit rough around the edges, sure. I'm sure you don't get where he was in life without a no-nonsense attitude. I would need to do the same for the life I wanted.

I reopened the paper to make sure the number hadn't changed. Not only was this a chance to get my dream job, I could set myself up for the future, pay down my debt, and help Dad get out of the Hillsdale situation. Becky came back, hustling in with a non-compete paper, which I signed. I walked back to my car in a trance, noticing the dent in the passenger-side door, a glaring imperfection against the other perfect cars. I needed to call and make an appointment to have it fixed. I had to make this work. After the six-hour drive to Haven Falls and all the emotions that came with it, plus a week of sleeping on a couch, I was exhausted. I would drive to Clifton in the morning. Tonight, I was getting a hotel room.

ON SUNDAY MORNING, I DROVE TO CLIFTON AND PULLED into my forgotten studio apartment. I missed it this week. Even though it was small and dark, everything had a place. I minimally furnished it with used furniture and clean lines. Except for the kitchen. It had bright yellow dishes, courtesy of Mom when she visited. She insisted sunshine was good for the soul, even just in color form. I had thought about changing the dishes, since they didn't fit in with everything else, but every time I looked at them, I felt warmer. Maybe Mom was right? Plus, I didn't have extra money.

I had a few hours before I needed to go to my parents house for Sunday dinner and I needed to decompress before Mom and my sister Jessica bombarded me with questions.

Changing out of my suit, I checked again for pumpkin smells. Nothing. I packed a bag of clothes for another week in Hillsdale. The time and money it took to drive the hour back and forth between Hillsdale and Clifton wasn't worth it.

Plopping down on my bed, I grabbed the extra blanket. It was cold in here, but no use paying for more heat than necessary. Every penny counts. I bet Dad had an air mattress in his camping stuff. Maybe I could borrow it for Hillsdale. The couch was too short and either my legs were lifted high off the end, or my neck was crooked. I should check my lease for loopholes in the contract for this apartment. I would need a new place if I moved to Raymond & Johnson Law.

My phone vibrated in my pocket.

James: Well, I knew it. I must have done something wrong.

Great. What this time . . .

Scott: Hey—what's up man?

James: I've no idea what I did wrong this time. I followed the rules. No costumes, no rings, no social media posts . . .

Scott: Okay. So, what's going on?

James: Anna isn't answering calls or texts. When I went to her apartment, her roommate said she wasn't home . . . but I see her car in the parking lot.

Wait. I sat up.

Scott: Saw or see?

James: See. I'm right next to it. And looking in the backseat, I know it's hers cause she left her jacket in it. If she was kidnapped, she doesn't even have her coat.

Scott: James. Just because she didn't answer a text doesn't mean she is kidnapped. Get away from her car and drive out of the parking lot. You look like a creeper.

James: Ugh. Fine. I will text when I park.

I waited a few minutes, praying James left the parking lot. I picked up one of the financial journal magazines on the bedside table but couldn't focus on it. I picked up the phone.

Scott: Did you leave?

James: Yes. I'm thinking it must have been the gift.

Scott: What gift?

James: A pig.

Scott: You got her a pig?

I don't know where to start.

James: It was a cute little piglet with a note. Not a big gross one.

Scott: WHY did you get her a pig? Please tell me you mean a stuffed animal . . .

I set the magazine aside and laid back on my bed. Yikes. Please be stuffed.

James: Nah, it was a real one.

Scott: Where did you even find a pig? What is she supposed to do with it?

I read his text again. A piglet with a note . . . oh no.

Scott: What did the note say?

James: Just that it reminded me of her.

I closed my eyes and chuckled. Oh James, the ultimate man at failed grand gestures.

Scott: So . . . You bought her a pig with a note that said it reminded you of her. And you don't see that as a bad thing.

James: Yeah, because on our last date she laughed so hard she snorted. Plus, she loves animals. It's perfect, right?

Scott: James . . . you told her she reminds you of a pig.

James: She does. It was a cute pig, plus she snorts when she laughs.

Wow. I rolled over on my bed.

Scott: Yeah . . . I'm not surprised she isn't talking to you. She won't like being compared to a pig, even a cute one. How about you don't get ANY woman a gift without running the thought by someone?

James: He's cute. Here, let me find pictures. I'll show you.

I chuckled. My mind was blank. I could think of no solution where he could fix this.

Scott: It doesn't matter how cute it was. I don't think we can save this one. What have you been texting her?

James: Pictures of the pig that I took and asking if we could get together.

Nope. Not even going to try.

Scott: I'm in town and headed to the parents for dinner. Meet me there?

James: Yes! I love your mom's cooking.

Scott: Me too. Excited for something other than tuna and crackers or peanut butter and jelly sandwiches.

Bag packed for the week, I headed back to my car, which had become more of my apartment. A box with organized food, a bag of clothes for the week, and toiletries. Thankfully, the bathroom at the office had a shower. I drove to my parents' house in the historical district.

The red brick exterior complemented the white shutters on the windows. The flower boxes at the front were meticulously cared for. Everything about the house screamed love and stories, from the white picket fence to the porch swing. My mom loved this house. It was where she raised us, but before then, she even saved the entire area from being demolished into a parking lot, having Dad help her turn it into a historical district. It was how my parents met. And yet, my parents risked losing it all. For a random friend's business. I shook my head. Why would they do that?

As I walked up the sidewalk, each stiff layer I had built around myself began melting away. Everywhere else was a stage. I had to dress and act a certain way to prove I was capable. But here among my family, I was just Scott, for better or for worse. I loved being a lawyer, but the person I was trying to become sometimes drifted away when I was here. Mother wouldn't settle for anything less. I showed up in a suit and a stiff attitude once. She held dinner so I could go change and come back as her son. She just wanted me.

Opening the front door, the original hardwoods showed the age of matchbox cars, roller skates, and roughhousing covered with a soft rug. I smelled Mom's rolls baking, and my stomach jumped with excitement.

"Scotty!" I heard three-year-old Ellie Jean call and soft, quick steps came rushing down toward me, her hands outstretched.

I reached down and lifted her up in a hug.

"Hey, Jelly Bean. How's the dragon today?" I chuckled and pulled her in for a hug.

She covered her mouth with pudgy fingers and laughed. "Mama said I could only call her a dragon at bedtime."

"And why is that?" My older sister Jessica walked into the room from the kitchen with a smile and an apron tied around her bulging belly.

Ellie giggled, "Cause you turn into a dragon when I don't go to bed."

Jessica bopped Ellie's nose. "That's right." Jessica reached me and gave me a hug. "It's great to see you."

"Hey, Scott." Mom came into the room and gave me a tight hug. "How's everything going, hun?" She looked me over, inspecting for loose-fitting clothes or bags under my eyes.

"I'm good, Mom—promise." Her lips pinched but she nodded.

"I hope so. About last time . . ."

"You mean when you invited everyone single you knew?"

She laughed and looped her arm through mine and pulled me to the kitchen. "Sarah has been asking about you. I think you should go on a date."

"Did someone say date?" My twin brother Michael busted through the front door with a huge smile and carefree attitude. Ellie giggled. Her eyes lit up, and she squirmed in my arms. I sat her down and watched as she rushed over to Michael. He swept her up in his arms and tossed her in the air.

"I don't want to hear about your dating life." Mom rolled her eyes. "I meant Scott."

"What dating life? Scott has a dating life?" Michael laughed and shoved me.

I knew he was teasing, and it was his way, but whenever Michael was around, I immediately felt like I needed to stand a little taller and prove my worth a little louder.

"I choose not to date, Michael. I don't have the time right now. Just because I choose not to lead a hundred different women on, doesn't mean I can't date." I folded my arms.

Michael chuckled. "One hundred, huh? Wow, rumors are going up."

"Now, don't you two start." Mom eyed us both in a way that made me feel ten years old. "Oh, my rolls." She dropped my arm and rushed to the kitchen, and we all followed her.

I saw my dad in the kitchen, leaning into the oven, pulling out the rolls. Mom smiled at him. "I figured you might forget, and I wouldn't let these rolls go to waste. You already gave the other batch away to the neighbors. I'm a charitable man, but it only goes so far . . ."

Mom blushed and swatted his arm. "Oh, you tease."

"No, I would gladly sell my soul to the devil for these." He set the rolls on top of the old electric stove and put the hot pads away. "Scott, glad you could come. How's things in Hillsdale?" Dad strolled over and pulled me into a hug. "I want to hear all about it."

Michael, Dad, and I all hovered around the rolls, watching them, hoping they would cool down faster.

"Terrible." I decided not to sugarcoat. "I thought your firm was bad . . . but this."

Dad flinched. "That bad, eh?"

"It's everything. The system is a mess. He used stickers and random papers stuffed in folders. The people there think I can help with all their petty squabbles and pranks. No one pays for anything." I rubbed my forehead. "I want to get your house out of debt fast, but I'm not seeing very many options."

"It's just a house," Mom responded, but I knew her well enough.

"A house which you love."

"True," Mom sighed as she looked around. "I love it. But, at the end of the day, it's just a house."

"A house that I won't let you lose."

Mom gave me another little hug. "You're too good to me. And I appreciate all you do for us. I do hope you are taking some time for yourself, though. It's not healthy—"

Dad nodded. "I have some extra time. Maybe I could come help this week. Harry mentioned his office assistant would help the transition . . ."

"Oh, she's trying."

Mom's eyes lit up. "She . . ."

I didn't want her getting any ideas. "It's just business, honest. But she might be my only chance to help resolve your house debt, if I can convince her."

Mom's eyebrows lowered. "What do you mean?"

I shrugged. "It's complicated, but I have a plan."

Michael teased, "If it's complicated, there's always a woman involved." Ellie Jean leaned out of his arms to come back to me, and I greedily took her back.

Mom clapped her hands.

"Not like that, Mom. We're not dating." I didn't want her to get her hopes up for romance. "I'm kind of tricking her." I flinched and looked away from Mom.

"Are you taking advantage of someone, Scott?" Her hands went to her hips.

"No, honestly, she is gonna help me with something and I'm going to help her. It's fine. I need her to help me get a deal with Raymond & Johnson Law in Haven Falls. It will fix everything." I reached over and grabbed a roll. "Win-win. You don't need to worry."

Dad's lips pulled down and my mom bounced between excitement at me working with a woman and chastisement. I could tell she wasn't sure which to express first. "What do you mean by tricking her? And what's this about Raymond & Johnson Law?" She looked at dad, who shook his head no.

"Let him find his path, Emily."

"Don't worry, Mom, I got it figured out, promise." I wasn't sure if I said that for my benefit or theirs. "Really, it's not a big deal."

James threw open the door and saved me from continuing the conversation.

"I'm so hungry, Mama Elliot!" He smiled widely.

Mom grinned and gave him a hug. "Well then, let's eat."

Chapter Twelve

MARISSA

I MET CAROL AT HER HOUSE FOR BREAKFAST. SHE always made the best chocolate chip pancakes, which I had more than a few times with my parents before the accident. I had come to the B&B very rarely since. I asked Carol to meet at Merritt's, but she insisted it be here. If I was going to help with the trunk-or-treat, I would need to stop avoiding it sometime.

A lot of it looked the same from my memories. Broken cabinets and mismatched dishes. Then there was the wall full of pictures from community events. I picked a chair with my back to the wall and eased into the old wooden furniture. "You didn't need to make me breakfast with your ankle hurt." I frowned. I had come over to talk about the trunk-or-treat, but she had already finished making them. "If I knew you were going to do that, I would've shown up earlier and made them for you."

Carol grimaced. "My ankle already hurts. I don't need a trip to the dentist too." The memory of us playing frisbee with my burnt pancakes when I was seven resurfaced.

I rolled my eyes and grabbed two pancakes from the plate and drizzled them with her homemade vanilla maple syrup. They melted in my mouth and left my tongue coated in butter and sugar.

"I know you are trying to butter me up." I grinned at my joke. "Literally with this trunk-or-treat thing . . ." I took a bite and closed my eyes, enjoying the soft fluffy goodness.

"Yes, I could really use your help." Carol was a spitfire; I would give her that. The last few years had taken a toll on her. But no one matched her energy at being loyal or stubborn.

"I know this place has a few hard memories for you, but it had good ones too. I wanted to start off as happy as possible."

The sweet, sticky syrup must be coating my throat because I couldn't swallow. I coughed and reached for a glass of water.

"So . . . about the trunk-or-treat."

I was avoiding the subject and Carol knew it but didn't press.

"Are you sure you can't get someone else to run it?" I took another bite. "Plans aren't my thing. Besides, I was hoping to go to London soon." I know Scott said he would help me, but I would still feel better on the sidelines. Or not here at all. My stomach felt all queasy and my hands were clammy. I didn't like being in this kitchen. I could still picture my mom gossiping and laughing with Carol at this table.

"Run to London, you mean?" Her mouth pulled down into a frown.

I set my fork down on the plate with the chipped light purple edge. "What's that supposed to mean?"

"Oh, I know you, girl. You talk about leaving anytime anyone brings up the accident or commitment, but no." She folded her arms in a challenge. "There is no one else. I need your help this year."

I stabbed another piece of pancake and dragged it around in the syrup. Wanting a new start wasn't the same as running. Right?

"What if I helped on the committee?" I had no interest in heading up the whole thing. Way too much pressure.

Carol shook her head no. "Mar, you can do this. I know you can." She leaned forward and patted my hand. "Besides, I have several committee members already lined up. Granted, I need a few more. Please Mar, I need your help, just this once. Then if London is what you want, by all means, go for it. I won't ask you to stay again."

I eyed her ankle. She had tried to get me to run the B&B for the last three years. Did she actually roll it?

Carol sighed exasperatedly and pulled up her khakis to show me her bruised ankle. It was swollen and slightly purple.

"Yikes. Did you get it checked out?" I licked the syrup off my thumb.

"Yeah, just sprained. Doug said ice and elevate."

I nodded and took another bite. What could it hurt? Even if it went bad, I would leave soon, so no one could stay mad about it for very long. I would need his help, but he seemed more than willing as long as . . .

"Speaking of extra volunteers, I'm working with—"

"No." Carol scowled as she leaned back in her chair.

"Oh, come on, Carol, Scott isn't bad. Plus, he does need a place to stay." And I need him to help me plan my Europe trip.

"He yelled at the boys."

I flinched. Hopefully, there was a good excuse, because that was one of the fastest ways to burn bridges with Carol. She took in any child that needed a snack and a place to be.

"Look. I know lawyers aren't your thing."

Carol shrugged in acceptance.

"But I think Scott is here to stay. He is helping at the firm and trying to learn to get along with the people here. Your support would go a long way . . ."

She pinched her lips.

"And he is sleeping in the office a lot of nights, on that crappy couch." Then I gestured to her swollen ankle. "He could help at the B&B too, if you let him stay."

"I'm not some invalid that needs to be taken care of," she growled.

I raised my eyebrows in question. "Oh, then you don't need my help with the trunk-or-treat."

Carol huffed. "Alright, fine. Here is the deal. If you promise to run the trunk-or-treat, not just help . . . I will let him stay here. But if he yells at those boys one time or tries to talk me into selling my place, he is gone."

I nodded. "Deal." Yes! I refrained from fist-pumping. First step trunk-or-treat, next step London.

Carol grinned. "You are just like your mother, you know."

I stilled, unsure if I wanted the conversation to continue or stop. Carol's smile turned sad. "Your mother could always talk her way into getting anything she wanted." Carol chuckled. "I miss her." She looked at the picture wall behind me. I stared at my red shoes, forcing my eyes to stay clear. I missed her. Her smile. Her laugh . . . Carol searched my face. She had a resolved look in her eyes, the kind that meant she was going to ask questions. The ones everyone wants answers to.

'How are you holding up? Do you want to talk about it? Did you ever talk to anyone about it?

I wanted everyone to leave things be.

Time to go.

"Okay, I better go." I grabbed my jacket and pushed my arms through the sleeves. "Text me when you want to meet up next." I stood and took my plate to the sink, rinsing off the syrup, and headed past Carol. Her knowing eyes watched every step I took. *I wasn't running. I just needed to get to work.*

"We're meeting tonight at six. You can tell your lawyer friend to come back then."

I nodded and hurried out the door.

I had thirty minutes but didn't want to go back home and sit in my room. Sitting around, surrounded by thoughts and memories, sounded like a very unproductive morning. I decided I would head to the office and tell Scott the good news. I couldn't wait to see the look on Scott's face. Maybe he would pull me into a quick hug again, like on Friday. Not that I wanted him to, but he smelled delicious. Besides, I was leaving soon. That made hugs safer, right?

My increased heart rate was only excitement because Carol agreed to let him stay. It had nothing to do with seeing him. I straightened my shirt and took a deep breath. Why was I feeling nervous? It was just Scott, and nothing was different. *We were helping each other get what we wanted.*

Friends.

Teamwork.

I opened the front door to Hillsdale Law.

No beating around the bush about it. If we were going to be partners and friends, I needed to get comfortable being with him. Friends were excited to give each other good news. It was fine. I rushed to his office and pulled the door open.

My foot became rooted to the spot, and the air whooshed out of my lungs.

Wow.

Scott was in shorts and no shirt. His hair was wet, and the water droplets that were running down the back of his neck captivated my attention and continued down his toned back. He had earbuds in, and he knelt on the ground, pushing air out of the mattress on the floor. My mouth went dry. Wow . . . just wow.

He was relaxed and rocked his head to his headphones. This man was no joke in a suit, but this was even better. I felt my cheeks flush with heat.

I wondered if he was listening to music or a financial podcast? The thought made me chuckle. I should let him know I was here and stop watching him like a creeper.

Or . . . instead . . .

I tiptoed toward him.

"Morning Sunshine!" I yelled as I leaned down and grabbed his shoulders.

Scott yelled and jumped. The back of his head collided with my nose, hard.

My eyes watered, and I grabbed my nose.

"Geez, Marissa! You're going to kill me." Scott held one hand to his heart as he ripped out his ear buds and turned to face me. He stepped over and picked up a t-shirt and threw it on.

My nose throbbed with pain, but I couldn't help but laugh at how badly I had gotten him.

"Oh my gosh! Your nose!" Scott stood and ran to his desk, grabbing some tissues.

That's when I felt the warm moisture drip. Bloody nose. I grabbed the offered tissues. I felt Scott's hands on my shoulders as he led me to his office chair. I looked at the duct tape head rest and shook my head.

"I'm not sure I trust it enough to lean back on that."

"Good point." He turned and led me to the couch in the foyer and kneeled in front of me. "I'm so sorry, Marissa. I can't believe I hit your face."

Seven-thirty and I already had a man on his knees. Not bad. I shook off the thought. "I'm not exactly faultless." I tipped my head back as the tissue became soaked. "Might need some more tissues or ice."

Scott rushed to the mini office fridge and grabbed some ice in his hands. He started walking around, trying to find a bag or something. He grabbed several tissues and began wrapping the ice cubes. The paper tore and stuck to his wet hands in pieces.

"Ugh. Seriously." He shook his hands.

He looked adorable. He was frazzled, and all for me. I felt butterflies in my stomach stir before I slayed them with common sense. Friends. Teammates. Nothing more.

"Maybe try paper towels instead." I nodded at the small bathroom.

He nodded and rushed for the paper towels, swearing under his breath.

"Scott, I'm fine. Promise. Maybe it's karma for the pumpkin."

Scott came out of the bathroom with several paper towels. He handed me the ice bundle, wet tissues still clinging to his hands.

"Are you early or am I running late?" Scott checked his watch.

"I'm early." I grinned. My nose had slowed down, although I wondered if I was going to end up with a nasty bruise. "I have some good news."

"I hope it was worth all that." He gestured at my nose, and I saw him stiffen out of the corner of my eye. He was unmoving and staring at me, well, not me, but my stomach. I felt my body go rigid as I looked down at my exposed stomach with its ridges and scars. My shirt must have come up during the whole nosebleed fiasco.

Questions registered all over his face. Nope, I did not want this conversation. I yanked my shirt down, stood and headed towards my desk. I would get to work. I took a few steps to my computer, realizing too late that I stood too quickly. My vision blurred around the edges, and I swayed.

Crap!

Scott rushed to my side and put an arm around my waist.

"Whoa, slow down. Are you okay—"

"I don't want to talk about them. The scars. They're from a long time ago." I felt the anxiety crawl up from my stomach to the bottom of my throat. I didn't want to see the pity; I didn't want the questions.

Please, let this go, Scott.

"Marissa, I meant the nosebleed and then almost passing out." His gray eyes felt calm and safe.

He ignored my scars. He wasn't going to push and prod. The thought made my eyes prick with tears. Ugh. What was with me today?

"Here, I think you should sit a few more minutes."

I took a deep breath as Scott led me back to the couch.

"What's your good news?" He sat down next to me, not close

enough to smell his cinnamon scent, and I wanted to lean in closer. Would that be weird? Yes. I closed my eyes and leaned back.

Boundaries, woman. You are in no state to decide right now.

"I got Carol to agree to let you stay at her place."

"What?" He leaned back. "No way! How?"

My eyes peeked open, and I looked at him. "I told her I would do the trunk-or-treat." I pointed at him. "But you'd better help me."

Scott sighed in relief. "Yes. A thousand times, yes." He sank back into the couch, but this time he was close enough to surround me in a cinnamon scent. "Must be an early Christmas miracle. I don't know how you do it, but you have a way with people in this town."

His comment reminded me of what Carol said about my mom. But I didn't want to think about Mom, or scars, or the past. I didn't want to think about anything. Except maybe London.

"Have you ever planned a trip to London?" I raised an eyebrow. "Or a trunk-or-treat?"

"Nope." Scott shrugged. "How hard can it be? We're a great team, after all."

I leaned toward him, not romantically, but a side-hug lean. I was saying thanks for being my friend and not pushing about the scars. Plus, after my morning, I was exhausted. He stiffened for a second, but then I felt him soften and lean into my side.

"We should come up with a good team name. All the greats have them."

He chuckled. "Any ideas?" I felt him nudge me with his shoulder. "And don't you dare say Smashing Pumpkins."

I laughed and all the stress of the morning melted away. It left me with Scott, bloody tissues, and hope for the future.

Chapter Thirteen

SCOTT

BETWEEN THE ANGRY SCARS ACROSS MARISSA'S stomach and the realization she had gotten me a place to stay at Carol's, I couldn't decide if I wanted to kiss her or ask her a million questions. It was obvious her scars were not new, and she didn't want to talk about them. Did they hurt her still?

She leaned into my side. With her ponytail close to my nose, I was reminded of green apples and sunshine. She shifted and pulled her shirt down to cover her scars.

That's why she does that.

What had happened to her? Something stirred in my chest that made me want to protect her from further harm.

If I put my arm around her, would she like it? Would she run?

"Well, that was quite the morning." Marissa put her hands on her knees and stood, walking to her desk.

I immediately missed her warmth.

"Carol said to come by after work. Meeting is tonight at six. Maybe we could both show up early. She can go over the trunk-or-treat stuff and get you a place to stay."

"Sounds like a plan." I stood and ran a hand through my hair.

She rolled her eyes at my word choice and went back to her computer.

"Speaking of a plan . . . this means you're on for planning London."

"Yep. And I will plan a trip that will get you safely back home."

She scrunched her nose. "Let's focus on leaving and not too much on coming back for now."

"Will you be coming back?"

"I mean yes, probably, but that is a depressing thought. Let's just focus on the fun."

I could do fun, right?

I DROVE TO THE BED-AND-BREAKFAST AND PARKED ON the street. No need for any reminders of why Carol sent me away the first time. They held the meeting in the community center, a barn-like building that was down a dirt path to the left of the parking lot. I didn't know how you could tell. There weren't any signs anywhere.

As I walked down the pathway, I marveled at this property. It was amazing. According to the listing, it had ten acres of grassy hills, colorful maple trees, natural hot springs, proximity to skiing in the winter, and was full of peace and tranquility. It would be in Carol's best interests to sell. She could do a lot with that type of money. Plus, the new resort would add needed growth to Hillsdale.

Win-win.

Why did she always refuse?

I pulled open the door to the barn. It had cement floors, a small kitchen, a stage of sorts, and folded tables and chairs stacked along the wall. Two folding tables were in the center, lined with chairs on each side, and a stack of papers in the middle. Marissa sat near Carol, and they leaned over a few notebooks and clipboards. The meeting didn't start for another fifteen minutes, but I believed fifteen minutes early was on time, or else you might as well be late.

Carol looked up at me and frowned. Yep, still not friends, but I would do my best to change that.

Marissa sagged in relief. "I'm so glad you're here." She waved me over to the seat next to hers with a smile.

"Marissa, I want you to run this." Carol eyed me up and down before adding, "Not him."

"Oh, I will, but he is my community co-captain thingy." She leaned over and whispered to me, "Is that a word?"

Her mischievous mouth pulled up in a grin, and her lips were dangerously close to mine. I felt a pull in my chest. Protectiveness? I tried and failed to hide my grin. "If not, it should be."

She tipped her head back and snorted. "Works for me." Manly pride that I was the one who made her laugh inflated my ego.

Carol still glared but said nothing.

"Okay," Marissa sighed. "Let's start by dividing the groups. I can wrap my head around that."

Marissa turned a page in her notebook and started writing. "We will want a trunk section. We'll need judges for the best display, a game section, and a food section." She tapped the pen on the table and pursed her lips. "Can I get the volunteer list again?"

Carol leafed through some papers and slid a sheet of names over. She pointed to the top. "These are the ones that said they will help, *and* I know I can count on." She pointed to the lower half. "These few either didn't confirm or I doubt their consistency. They're not to be put in charge of anything."

Marissa nodded. "We can't put Ashley with Jessica. They would gossip and get nothing done." She began making different lists. "I heard Jacob was getting a divorce . . . better not put him with Ashley either. Too much drama." She continued through the list, mentioning different relationships and options.

I raised my eyebrow in surprise. For someone who hated planning, she was taking to it like a natural. Marissa continued to look to Carol for confirmation, who nodded. When Marissa wasn't looking, there was a proud parent look in Carol's eyes.

Marissa wrote my name on her list of volunteers.

Carol's eyes shot to me. "I have an idea for Mr. Elliot's committee. Unless Mr. Captain co-chair has any objections."

It was a test, and I knew it. I nodded confirmation. "I would happily work with anyone on any project you choose."

"Perfect." Carol grinned. "That group of teenage boys you met the other day. They have agreed to help prep some of the game booths." She set down her clipboard. "I would like you to assist them." Carol stared, daring me to back down.

Nothing like trial by fire. "I'd be happy to." I had often thought of those boys and my angered outburst at them. I was glad for a chance to apologize and make it right.

Carol scowled. "I would hate for any more miscommunication to take place and will keep an eye on you." She sat tall in her seat. At that moment, I knew I was placing myself between a mama lion and her cubs.

"That would be wonderful." This was a high risk, but it could have high rewards. If I could get on the boys good side, that would help tremendously with Carol's opinion of me, which would go a long way with becoming a part of this town.

Carol nodded. "You can take your stuff up to your room. It's the third door on the right upstairs."

I was clearly dismissed, but I nodded in gratitude. "I'll happily pay for the room. Let me know what it costs."

Carol leaned back in her seat. "Oh, for you, I'm sure we can come up with a special deal. How about eight hundred a month?"

Marissa flinched but said nothing. That was high for a room.

I blanched. I couldn't afford that for long, but this was my chance. I nodded. I only needed to stay a few months.

"See you tomorrow."

I then leaned over to Marissa. She looked up at me, her green eyes panicked. "We've got this," I winked. "Team . . ." I waited for her to fill in the blank.

"Sprinkles?" She smiled.

"How about sprinkles and raisins?"

"Gross." Her nose scrunched.

"Alright, we'll workshop it in the morning." I nodded to Carol. Her eyes flashed between Marissa and I. "Thanks again, Mrs. Andrews. I can see myself to my room."

I made my way back to the house and stepped through the front door of the bed-and-breakfast. The place smelled like baked bread and lemons. The floors were scratched and dinged. They would need a good refinishing. Several light bulbs needed replacing, and some sort of wiring was stapled along the wall. That would need to be addressed. The peeling wallpaper showcased an unfortunate array of previous patterns beneath it.

The wall hugging the stairs had several spots where the sheetrock needed patching, and the creaking boards of the staircase announced my presence. The carpet was threadbare on the edges of the stairs and you could see the strings underneath. At the top of the stairs, I turned and headed to my room. I passed two rooms on the right with updated windows and furnishings and wondered what my room would look like.

The knob on the door was bulky and metal and ancient, the type that would require a large metal key to lock. I pushed the door open, and it didn't budge. I was positive this was the room. I leaned into it with my shoulder and pushed. The door gave way and scraped along the floor in an arc.

Might need to work on rehanging that.

There was one bed in the middle of the room with a pink flower comforter and an iron bed frame. A small used-to-be white dresser stood in the corner, and the drawers stuck as I tugged on them. An old particle board nightstand to the left of the bed held a small lamp and a notebook.

I sat and the bed squeaked in protest, dust fluffing up from the mattress. Were all the rooms this rough, or was this a special present just for me? It was obvious Carol did not want me here—or to feel welcome.

This would not be easy.

I was no stranger to hard work or the complications that came with older houses. My parents home was full of problems, and often weekends were spent working on the house. I could start with this room. If I fixed it up, it would ease my guilty conscience, and I was sure the future client would appreciate it as well.

I set my small suitcase on the bed and changed into basketball shorts and a t-shirt before heading back for the stairs. There was a small shop-type building I passed on my way to the house. Maybe I would find some tools there.

I stepped out the front door and heard voices and a basketball bouncing. Sounded like the group of boys were back. I could take this chance to apologize. I walked over to the parking lot and watched from a distance as five boys passed, dribbled, and shot the ball through a makeshift hoop with maple tree branches. The oldest picked up the ball. He was the protector from earlier, and the leader, as the others followed him everywhere he went and mimicked his every move.

"I bet once you show them this trick, they'll for sure let you play at recess." The older boy tried to bounce the ball between his legs, but it hit his shoe and rolled off in the opposite direction.

"Oh yeah, they'll definitely start picking me first now." The blond boy with a skinny frame and glasses folded his arms.

"Shut up. I watched a video on YouTube; I can get it. Let me try again." The oldest boy jogged after the ball.

The smallest boy, who looked to be around seven, sat on the sidewalk and put his chin on his fist. "At least they picked you. They pretended like I wasn't even standing there last time. I have the worst luck."

It was like watching flashbacks of elementary school. Being picked last, or not at all. Hiding by a tree alone, pretending it was by choice. My tall awkward frame, glasses, and too big shoes didn't help either. Especially when I stood beside Michael. My twin had the confidence I lacked in social settings. The oldest boy tried bouncing the ball between his legs again and it hit his shoe.

These weren't the jerks who made fun of me in school, they were me. I was ashamed of how I treated them before and was full of determination to help them succeed and be on their team. I was excited to work with them for the trunk-or-treat. It would be the perfect way to get to know them.

The blond with holes in his striped shirt picked up a rock and chucked it. "I don't even care. Basketball is stupid anyway."

The older boy tried to bounce the ball between his legs, bouncing it off his foot again, rolling in my direction.

I stepped out from the trees. No time like the present.

"Hey, boys." I grabbed the basketball.

They grouped together, and the taller one stepped forward and stood in front of them. He squared his shoulders proud and defiant, despite the way his hand shook.

"Look, I'm sorry about your car," the older boy started, his hands placed in front of him in case of an attack. "It was an accident and won't happen again."

Geez. What did these boys think I was going to do?

I stepped toward them in the parking lot and bounced the ball between my legs, going back and forth several times.

"I know it was an accident, and I'm the one who needs to apologize." I grabbed the ball and looked them in the eyes. "I'm sorry. The way I acted was wrong."

Their eyes widened at the apology, unsure how to react. After a moment, the younger three grinned and seemed to accept my words. The older one seemed more cautious.

I nodded to the older boy. "You were really close. It helps if you place one foot a little further in front like this." I showed them again, switching between legs.

"Nice!" The short one with big eyes and glasses stood from the ground. "You're super good! I bet you were a basketball star in your school, and everyone liked you."

Hardly.

It broke my heart to hear. That's all they wanted. To be accepted and liked.

"Not even close." I passed the ball back to the older boy. "Try again." I looked at the youngest. "They picked me last or not at all."

"Then how did you learn those moves?" The younger one with big brown eyes scrunched his nose.

"My brother was the basketball star. He made me help him practice for hours." I confessed. "If you guys want, I might teach you a few skills."

All the younger boys looked at the older one. Eager, but wanting to follow his lead.

"Why?" He held his head high.

"Why what?"

"Why would you want to help us?" His eyes were guarded. No hope waiting there. He didn't want a handout, and he didn't trust me. He passed the ball back to me. "What do you get out of it?"

I shrugged. "Carol agreed I could stay here, so we'll be seeing a lot of each other and I'm going to be helping you guys with the trunk-or-treat booths. It might be nice to be friends."

He stood tall and unmoving.

"Plus, maybe if I teach you scalawags to control the ball, it will keep my car safe." I grinned, hoping that he knew I was joking and would take to the banter. "How else am I going to pick up chicks in this town?"

The oldest let a quick smile escape before it went back to neutral.

The blond boy looked at him. "Come on. I need the help, and let's face it, you have no idea what you are doing."

He sighed but took the bait. "No way you'll get any chicks in that shiny thing," he said with a small spark in his eyes.

I chuckled and bounce-passed him the ball. "Maybe not, but I need all the help I can get."

His eyes lit up as he caught the ball. "Now that's something we can agree on."

The rest of the group spaced out, and we began passing back and forth between us all. I gave little tips here and there, but mostly I just watched them. They were a ragtag bunch with little talent, lots of talk, and love for the older boy who protected them.

What was their story?

"What time do you guys play? I can try to come as often as I can."

"We're here every day." The one with glasses pushed them up his nose. "Until it gets too cold." He frowned. "I guess it's going to get cold soon."

Where do they go when it's cold?

"My name is Scott." I passed to the blond boy with glasses.

"I'm Josh."

I nodded at the rest. The smallest of the group stuttered through his name. It was something with a T or D, but I didn't catch it.

"What was that?" I leaned closer, and the boy blanched and turned away. The older boy stepped up. "His name is Todd. My name is Ethan." He pointed to the last of the group. "This is Jace and Brian."

We continued to practice for another thirty minutes, but it was getting dark and cold. I worried they needed to start home, but it wasn't my place to say that.

I glanced at my watch. "Nice to meet you boys. I need to go grab some tools, but I'm sure I'll see you around."

I passed the ball to Ethan, who caught it and nodded. I got the feeling he was still cautious of me, but he was at least smiling at me and not scowling now.

Chapter Fourteen

SCOTT

After a week and a half of planning and constant talk of the trunk-or-treat, I figured it was time for me to work on my end of the deal with Marissa. I waited outside the partially-abandoned strip mall, rocking back on my heels, my breath visible in the air. I checked my watch again. Apparently, Marissa did not know about the fifteen minutes early or you're late rule.

I stepped away from the door, allowing some high schoolers to pass in pairs. Wednesday date night for the win, except mine wasn't a date. Marissa double-checked twice when I asked her about an impromptu London planning activity tonight.

The art vision board night was the perfect way to get to know Marissa better, which would help me plan her London trip. It frustrated me that she would change the subject any time I asked her what she wanted her future to look like. Maybe this class would help her figure that out. The stubborn woman refused to carpool even though it was forty-five minutes away, and now we were late for class. Hopefully, her car would make it.

I heard Marissa's vehicle before I saw it. Four minutes later, she pulled into a spot. She hopped out, swung her door shut with a loud slam, and grinned at me as she rushed to my side.

"Hey." Her voice was soft. "Now, do I get to know what we're doing?"

"What happened to living in the moment?" I winked.

She chuckled and walked past me as I held the door open for her. I scanned our Groupon tickets, and we made our way to the back of the class, avoiding stray easel legs and piles of art supplies. We sat on paint-splattered wooden stools and faced our canvas boards.

"Now, as I was saying," the art teacher waved in our direction, "tonight is about creating a vision for your future, and I want you to use whatever medium you want." She pushed her black-rimmed glasses up her nose. She tucked back her curly hair, which matched the disarray of her art studio.

I looked at Marissa, hoping to see a grin. She was scowling.

"What do you think?" I whispered in her direction.

"Not what I was expecting," she whispered back.

"I think it'll be fun and it might help you figure out your future goals and what you want to do in London. Then I can use it to plan your trip."

She nodded. "Right. Fun."

"The goal for the night is to be creative." The teacher turned and gestured to a table piled high with different supplies. "There's a stack of magazines in the front of the class. There are markers and paint to the left. Let your imagination flow, wander the room, and see what speaks to you. Then let it take you wherever it wants without worry or judgment. Now, let's make some art!"

Marissa leaned over to me. "Did you notice everyone else in this class is like fifteen?"

I chuckled. "Yeah. Goal exploration is wasted on adults." I shrugged. We joined the throng of youth heading to the front. I had no idea how to paint, but I knew what my goals looked like. This would be so easy.

Marissa followed me to the front of the room. Grabbing a few magazines, colored pencils, and markers, she sulked back to her seat. Her shoulders drooped inward. Maybe I shouldn't have done this as a surprise. Marissa looked like she would rather be anywhere but here.

She watched as kids crowded for markers and paint, their faces eager. I put my focus on my board. Maybe she didn't want an audience.

I thumbed through one of the business magazines I had grabbed.

Nice!

There was a picture that looked close enough to my car. I began cutting it out.

I looked further into the magazine and continued ripping page after page. A list of Michelin-starred restaurants. Then I caught sight of a limited-edition Rolex. My breath snagged for a minute as I glimpsed a penthouse with a view of a cityscape, and I debated a moment before adding it to my board.

After several minutes, I peeked over at Marissa as she thumbed through the pages of a magazine. She hadn't torn out anything. She tossed the magazine to the side and watched everyone around her laugh and splash color on their boards.

"Focus on where you picture yourself in five, ten, or twenty years. Let the process take over." The teacher threw her hands in the air.

Marissa picked up some colored pencils and hovered over the board, staring at it. She closed her eyes and rubbed her forehead.

"Hey, are you okay?" I set down my scissors and glue.

The teacher came to Marissa's side. "You okay, love?"

"Yep."

Marissa opened her eyes and smiled, but the teacher must have seen through the facade.

"It becomes harder to dream the older we get. Life gets muddier and harder to see through. Maybe don't focus too far ahead." She put a hand on Marissa's shoulder. "Or, sometimes exploring our fears can tell us just as much. Try not to judge the process. Just do whatever speaks to you at this moment."

Marissa nodded and picked up a green colored pencil. I grabbed my scissors and paste and began making a collage of ideas about the future.

After about thirty minutes, the teacher made her way to the front of the room. "Alright class, now this part is different. I want you to write some words on your board about how your future makes you feel, or you can make a wish for your future self." She turned and pointed to a section of the table with highlighters, markers, and pencils. "Words are powerful, and this is a space to dream and pretend. Reach for the stars!" The woman resembled Ms. Frizzle as she handed out stickers, highlighters, and stencils to random groups.

Hmm, what words did I want to represent my life?

Prestigious.

Recognized.

Proud.

Important.

I looked at the board covered in my future. It was perfect, and I was so close, I could almost taste it.

I looked over at Marissa's. But before I could glance at the words she wrote, she tilted it away from me.

"Hey." She glared. "Eyes on your own paper." At least her pencil was moving. I worried maybe her poster would end up blank.

At the end of class, we thanked the teacher and left. Marissa pressed her canvas against her body as we walked into the parking lot.

"Well, any clues for London?" I walked next to her as we headed towards her car.

"Hm, nope. Sorry." She shrugged.

"Well, can I see it? It might help give me some ideas."

She stepped further away from me.

"It's not a big deal . . . it was for fun. Plus, I'm curious."

"Then show me yours."

I turned my canvas so it faced her, and watched as she scrutinized my future. Would she be proud of my dreams? Or think I was vain?

"Looks like you know what you want." She gave a nod as she stepped closer. Her finger traced along the different objects. "I hate to break it to you, but working in Hillsdale won't get you most of these."

I chuckled. "True. My dad believes things will just *work out*." I emphasized with air quotes. "But I think you know my feelings about Fate." Would this hurt my chances with Carol if I were honest with her? I might need to tread carefully. "I don't plan on staying here forever. I never planned to be here at all though . . ."

"Why are you here now?" I couldn't tell if she meant in a Hillsdale law firm or standing there with her. I leaned against her car next to her and chose the easier option.

"My father was a friend of Harry's from law school and wanted to allow him to be with his wife. I was included in the package. I plan on getting things fixed up and letting another employee take over."

She tipped her head to the side. "Where were you before that?"

"Fixing my father's firm."

She bumped me on the shoulder. "I'm sensing a pattern."

"I know, I know." I sighed. "I won't ever get what I want if I can't put myself first, but I'm weak when it comes to them."

"I'm not sure weak is the word I would use." Marissa tipped her head to the side.

"What would you use? Broke? No backbone? Or a glutton for punishment?" I scoffed as I kicked a stray pebble with my shoe.

She tipped her head to my shoulder. "I was thinking more like loving and dependable."

"You make me sound like a dog." I rolled my eyes.

She laughed. "That's not what I meant." She leaned her head on my shoulder, and I felt the urge to stand a little taller. "Well, I hope you get everything on your vision board," she paused in thought, "and that it brings you the happiness you think it will."

What did she mean by that last part? "Thaaannks." I looked down at her. "Why wouldn't those things make me happy?"

Marissa shook her head. "What?"

"You made it sound like those things won't make me happy." I stepped closer to her, eager for her explanation.

"I think those can lead to happiness." She looked down at the parking lot. "I guess it might depend on why you want those things. Sometimes, the shiny life just feels empty."

My entire future was under attack. I counterattacked. "What would you know about the shiny life? You live in a small town, drive a run-down car, and wear a threadbare jacket."

She bristled. "Wow. Okay." She turned away from me, opened her car door, and threw in her canvas.

She was leaving.

"Ugh, wait Marissa. That's not what I meant." She turned back to me and waited for my explanation. What was my explanation? I rubbed my forehead. "I guess I felt like you thought everything I've been working for and dreaming about for my future was shallow. I often have to defend my choices to my family, and I lashed out. I'm sorry."

Her eyes searched mine and I think we were both surprised by my honesty. She sighed and her shoulders relaxed. "That isn't what I meant, and I'm sorry if I hurt your feelings."

"What did you mean?"

"Before I lived with my grandma, I had nice things. My dad was very successful, and my mom made pretty good money too." She leaned against the car. "We owned a nice car, went on trips, and I had all the right clothes. I can tell you it's not the stuff I miss."

What happened in her past?

She shrugged. "Nice things can be great. Money right now could help me have great vacations, great food . . ."

What had she put on her vision board? "Can I see your poster?"

She looked hesitant, warring within herself.

"You saw mine, and it obviously doesn't match with yours. Now I'm curious."

She grimaced. "Oh yeah, trust me, my future is not one you want to shoot for." She reached into her car and handed me the canvas.

My mind emptied. Where my board was full, bright, and flashy, hers was practically empty. It had one girl standing with her back to me on a path that branched in different directions into a forest of trees. The words penciled above them were hard to make out.

Alone.

Afraid.

Unlovable.

I had somehow glanced at what was beneath Marissa's vibrant, cheerful surface and got an off-limit glimpse at the turmoil underneath.

"The teacher said I could do fears, that one felt easier." She was pulling on her shirt and looked ready to run as she reached for her poster.

"I admit, I'm surprised. Why would you feel those things?" I ran my hand through my hair. "So far, everyone who comes in the office wants to see you, not me."

She rolled her eyes. "That's different. I don't really want to talk about it." Marissa rested her head on her car. She seemed worn down, and I wanted to make her smile.

"Hm, Yeah . . . mine might be shallow." I tried to lighten the mood. "But yours is not giving me happy vibes . . . I'm thinking I'll stick with shallow." I grinned, hoping she could tell I was joking.

She laughed and grabbed her poster back. "Yeah, maybe stick with yours."

"Yeah, I will keep my vain, shallow life. Thank you very much."

She swatted at my shoulder and her stiff posture had relaxed. "I didn't say that."

I no longer felt like she was ready to bolt. Tonight, Marissa felt different. Vulnerable and real. She still had the smiles and sassy banter, but with a glimpse at the real her, I felt drawn in like a fish on a hook.

"Well, thanks for the interesting night." She grinned and turned back to her car.

"Hey, how about we go get some pizza?" I wasn't ready to let her go. "I'm starving." I nodded at the restaurant.

She slammed the door shut and came up to my side. "Alright. I could always eat." Her bright countenance was back, but it shined a little truer than before.

We walked into the restaurant. It had black and white tile floors and fluorescent tube lighting above. Stepping up to the counter, a teenager looked up from her phone, popping bubble gum. "Hey, what can I get you?"

Marissa ordered a slice of chicken Alfredo pizza and a Dr. Pepper and paid before I could even offer. Not that I would. I didn't want to send her running. Although I wouldn't mind it being a date.

I ordered two slices of pepperoni pizza and Sprite and followed Marissa towards a little table with red benches near the front window.

"How are things with Carol?" She looked up at me over the cup, straw in her mouth.

My stomach stirred with guilt. Tonight, Marissa was showing part of her true self, and I didn't want to lie to her, but I also couldn't put everything I was working for at risk. "Let's talk about something new. Not Carol, work, or London."

She sat up and leaned back in the booth. "Well, what should we talk about then?"

"I don't care. You start."

"Hmm." She tipped her head back and forth. "Favorite color?"

"Green, maybe?"

"Why?"

My immediate thought was because it reminded me of her eyes, but that was way too creepy. "Maybe because it seems full of life? Not sure. What's your favorite color?"

"Purple."

"Why?" I countered back.

"Umm," she turned the cup on the table. "because it reminds me of my mom. She really liked purple. She smelled like lavender, wore the color, and her favorite flower was lilacs. I miss her . . . when I see purple, it's like my mom saying hi."

I thought about the scars on her stomach and references to being raised by Nan and talking about her parents in the past tense. It was obvious Marissa had some big trauma in her past.

"What happened to your mom?" I asked.

Her finger traced dings on the table. "Car wreck. Both my parents died. That's how I got the scars." She glanced up at me.

Whoa, I wasn't sure she would answer and didn't expect the bluntness of the statement. "I'm really sorry, Marissa. How long ago was it?"

She shrugged and refused to make eye contact. "Long time ago. Seven years this next January."

She was so young.

"You were what? Sixteen?" I thought back to when I was sixteen. My biggest fears were the debate team and if someone noticed my worn-out shoes.

"Fifteen."

Was this why she was afraid to plan for the future? Because her parents died? I thought of my loud, overwhelming family. What would it have been like to be raised without them? Who would I even be? Changed for sure.

Without being prompted, she continued, like a door had opened and she was afraid of what would happen when it closed. "I was raised by my Nan, my mom's mom." She turned and looked out the window. "It wasn't easy to come to a small town with a tragic story like that. I couldn't escape the stares and questions. Even now, I'm worried someone will bring it up or ask about it. I can't move on while I'm here, you know?"

I thought about what it would be like to be a teenager and find yourself in the center of the Hillsdale gossip chain and have your entire world ripped from you. My view of Marissa as carefree sunshine was not accurate at all. I always assumed her life must have been light and breezy to make her cheerful, but it seemed like it was the opposite.

She had to be overly happy so people wouldn't pity her for being sad.

I nodded as another piece of the puzzle fell into place.

"That's why you don't like to plan . . ."

Marissa smirked. "We had lots of plans. My mom loved to travel. We would be on one trip, and she would already plan the next. We were going to London when I graduated. Planned to spend months backpacking through Europe. That's where my parents honeymooned. She wanted to show me. No one knows what will happen. If you plan, it'll hurt more if it doesn't work." She took a sip from her drink.

London. Another piece of the puzzle.

"I almost went after graduation, but Nan got sick and then had hip surgery, and she had always taken care of me. Then there was Harry. I was a mess when I arrived in Hillsdale. I made his coffee without a filter for three months before he told me I was doing it wrong." Marissa chuckled. "Hillsdale has challenges for sure. Everyone is in everyone's business, and everyone has an opinion about everything in your life. My Nan would know about stupid high school stuff before I even got home from school . . ." She leaned back in her seat and looked at me. "But when tragedy strikes, the people in Hillsdale come together. It's annoying here but also kinda beautiful . . . sometimes." She shook her head and picked up her pizza. "Trust me when I say I get not fitting in with Hillsdale." She took a bite of pizza and chewed.

I reached across the table without thinking and grabbed her hand, giving it a gentle squeeze. Her hand was soft under my mine. My knee jerk reaction to comfort her surprised me, but I didn't regret the decision to reach out. And I didn't want to take my hand back.

She shook her head, coming out of the daze of her past, and pulled her hand gently away from mine and tucked it under the table. "Wow . . ." She shook her head. "Sorry, that is way more about me than you bargained for." Her cheeks flushed. "Tell me something about you now. Please, stop me from talking."

The time for a change of subject was obvious. The door to her past was now shut.

"Thanks for telling me." I smiled at her, trying to lighten the red in her face. "I'm glad you did." She nodded but wouldn't look in my eyes.

"I didn't have a great high school either, although it had nothing to do with being the new kid and all with being the poor, nerdy, awkward one. That and my perfect twin brother was always everything I couldn't be."

Her eyebrows scrunched down. "You?"

"I had these embarrassing thick glasses and oh man, it was bad. This one time, before my parents realized I needed glasses, I walked into the girls bathroom when I was upset and my third-grade crush found me in there crying . . . She told everyone. My defense was to deny it. To this day, if that story ever gets brought up—and trust me, with my family, it gets brought up—I say it wasn't me." I continued to tell her every embarrassing thing about me I could remember. It seemed only fair.

The rest of the night, my mission was making Marissa smile and laugh. And I succeeded. As she got into her car, she had a soft smile on her lips as she looked up at me. Mission accomplished.

"Thanks for tonight."

Chapter Fifteen

MARISSA

I punched my pillow, blaming its uncomfortable lumps on my restless night. I flopped back onto my bed and rubbed my tired eyes.

Why had I told Scott all those things about my past?

I never talked about the past to anyone. Why did I start now? Why with Scott, the man I see every day?

Would he make it weird at work today? Would he pity me now?

I flipped over and checked my phone. Six-thirty a.m. *I could finally get up without having to give Nan an excuse.*

I sat up and stretched out my neck.

My phone vibrated with a new text. If it was the group chat, Rose would kill Faith for texting at this hour. I unlocked my phone.

Huh, weird. An unknown number.

I clicked to open the message.

Morning Marissa, this is Scott.

Scott! I felt a tickle of butterflies in my stomach.

Whoa, settle down there. I patted my stomach. Just friends, no need for flutters.

Scott: I hope you don't mind that I have your number. Harry gave it to me for emergency purposes.

What happened?

Marissa: Oh no! Is there an emergency?

Scott: Sorry! No emergency. I guess I should've started with that.

I sighed and tried to calm down my heart *and* my stomach. This man had way too much power over my body systems this morning.

Marissa: Well, now that my heart is racing, good morning to you.

I watched the dots appear as he typed and then vanish.

What was he going to say?

I hoped it wasn't about all the personal bombshells last night. I would rather not dive back into that pool this early . . . or maybe ever. But part of me felt a little lighter knowing I told him on my own terms.

Scott: Um, I guess I just wanted to make sure you had my number too, in case of emergencies.

I couldn't keep my grin from growing. We were work friends. This made total sense. Right? Like you know, as friends . . . sharing phone numbers.

Marissa: Thanks! I feel fully prepared should we have a law office emergency. =)

I hope the smile conveyed I was joking.

Scott: Thanks again for the help with Carol. It has been amazing not sleeping on the air mattress in the office or having you scare me awake. Still feel terrible about the bloody nose.

I grinned as I pictured Scott and his nervous expression rushing around the office trying to get me tissues and ice.

Marissa: Yes, let's avoid the nose bleeds.

Scott: And you catching me with my shirt off . . .

I felt my cheeks heat as I pictured his arms flexing when he shoved the mattress into the box.

Marissa: I don't know, that wasn't so bad.

Wait! Crap! Unsend, unsend, unsend!

Scott: . . .

The typing dots appeared and then disappeared from the screen.

Marissa: Wait, that wasn't what I meant.

Scott: So, you don't like to see me with my shirt off then? Was it that bad?

Marissa: No, it was great . . .

Ugh. Not helping.

Marissa: New idea— let's change the subject . . . NOW!!

Scott: About my shirt . . .

Marissa: Ugh! Whatever, I'll see you at work.

I set my phone on the side table as it vibrated with a response. I wouldn't look at it. If I looked at it, I would have to answer. It was best not to look.

I stood up and went to my dresser and I did not look at my phone while I got dressed for the day. Then I brushed my teeth, not thinking about Scott or what he had said. I tied my shoes, not thinking about Scott.

Ugh. This was worse than reading it. If I read it, I could get it out of my system. I rushed back to my bed, sat down, and opened my phone.

Scott: See you at work.

Well, that was anticlimactic.

Which was perfect. Friendly, no talk about missing shirts. Exactly what I wanted. Right? Why did I feel disappointed?

I lay back on my bed and closed my eyes. Something clanged outside my bedroom window. Was the apple tree hitting the siding again? I didn't think it was windy. I sat up and looked out my bedroom window. The leaves weren't blowing, but now sounds were coming from the roof.

Crap!

I rushed to the window. The ladder was leaning against the house, and, to my horror, Nan's pink slippers were in line with the top of my window.

Crap!

Nan was on the ladder! I bolted for the front door. The last thing I needed was for her to take a fall from that height. When I rounded the corner of the house, there she stood on the top steps of the ladder, waving a hammer in the air.

"Nan!" I rushed and steadied the ladder.

Nan screamed, and the hammer launched into the air, falling to the ground a few feet from me. She clutched her heart as her fuzzy bathrobe flapped around her.

"Darn nabbit, Mar! What in heaven's name are you doing rushing up behind an old lady on a ladder? You very well could've given me a heart attack!"

"I think you already gave me one." The pounding in my chest was on rapid fire. "Please come down."

"Not yet. I need to fix these shingles."

"I'll fix all the shingles tonight, I promise."

"It's not a problem . . ."

"Nan, *please* . . ."

She huffed as she straightened her robe. "Oh fine, but I can handle it, you know."

I PULLED INTO THE PARKING LOT, PUT MY HEAD ON THE headrest, and closed my eyes. This had been a doozy of a morning. I checked my rearview mirror, making sure that the ladder was, in fact, compressed down and folded into the back seat. Stinking Nan, she never even told me about that section of shingles. I rubbed the crease on my forehead, hoping to ease the panic that had been racing through my veins all morning.

First, I slept terribly, then I told Scott that I like him without his shirt on, and then Nan on a ladder. Was eight A.M. too early to beg for a do-over, or at the very least, a sprinkled sugar cookie?

A small knock sounded on my driver's-side window, jump-starting my heart again. I looked out to see Scott's worried expression. His glance bounced between me and the ladder in my backseat. I shooed him away and pushed hard to open my door. It didn't budge. I leaned into it this time, causing it to spring loose and barrel off toward the passenger-side door of his car. I swore and flinched as Scott used his body as a human shield against the hurtling metal.

"Whoops . . ."

Scott rubbed his side. "I think that might be an understatement. We should probably oil your car doors or something, for everyone's safety."

I reached for my purse, climbed out, and slammed the door shut. "If that was the case, where would I take out all my aggression?"

Scott flinched. "Remind me to never make you angry. I should make a list. Beware of pumpkins, never stand between Marissa and cookies, likes me with my shirt—"

"Shut up!" I pushed him and Scott laughed.

"You're just proving my point."

"Whatever." I headed to the office front door with Scott right behind me.

"Okay, seriously though, I have to ask, or it will haunt me all day. What are you doing with that ladder in your car?"

"What do you mean?"

"Well, the worried expression on your face and then the ladder in your backseat . . . it can't be good." He grimaced.

"You worry too much." I grinned as I stepped into the office. I froze. There on my computer desk, where the old paper pumpkin used to be, was a vase of lilacs.

Purple. Mom.

Scott?

I turned around to Scott. He was rubbing the back of his neck with his right hand and staring at the ground.

"Was that you?" I pointed to the flowers.

He shrugged. "Wasn't a big deal. They aren't real or anything. I saw them in a box in Carol's garage and she said I could have them." He was talking fast, and his cheeks turned red. "I wanted to say thank you for talking to me last night. I washed them though, hopefully I got all the dirt off . . ."

This was what I needed this morning, a hello from Mom. I turned and threw my arms around him. He stiffened.

"Thanks for remembering."

His arms softened and rubbed my back. It was comfortable here after a night of no sleep. I could stay here forever. *Whoa. No.*

I bolted out of his arms and went to the vase. I touched one of the small, dainty petals. "Now lilacs will always remind me of my mom, and you."

Scott cleared his throat. "Anyway, don't change the subject . . . about that ladder."

I went around my desk and turned on the PC. "Nothing nefarious. I'm hiding it from Nan."

His eyebrows pulled down in question.

I sat in my chair and sighed. "Turns out we have some shingles loose. Nan picked the lock on the shed and attempted to fix them herself this morning." I shivered, remembering her wobbling on top of the ladder. "Stinking woman can't be trusted."

"How old is Nan?"

"Eighty-three," I answered.

"What? Umm wow . . ."

"She is so determined. She did this ten months ago, and I had to lock up everything in the shed. It's like she thinks she is still in her fifties or something." I rubbed my eyes. "I will have to fix them tonight before she gets too antsy."

"So, you'll be on your roof fixing shingles tonight? Alone?" He flinched. "Do you have someone to hold the ladder . . . other than Nan?"

I waved it off. "No, but I can lean it against the siding and it should be fine."

"Should . . ." Scott stood rigid. "What time are you working on it?"

"Right after work. I can't risk Nan getting back up there."

He nodded. "Sounds good. I'll grab some of my tools and meet you there."

I looked up at him in shock. "Wait . . . meet me there? Meet me where?"

"At your house." He folded his arms and looked down at me in my chair.

I held my hands up in protest. "You don't need to come. I can handle it." I wasn't sure if I was more worried about Nan's reaction to him, Ashley seeing his shiny car at our house, or seeing him fix our roof and having more fuel for my dreams. All options were very dangerous.

Scott chuckled. "I know. It's not for you, it's for me." He turned and started walking to his office.

"Wait, how can it possibly be for you to help me fix our roof?" I followed him.

"That way I won't have nightmares about you falling off your roof." He chuckled, proud of his joke.

I folded my arms. "I've climbed on that roof for the last ten years."

Scott shuddered.

"Whatever."

Scott turned back to face me and rested his hands on my shoulders. "Marissa, please, let me help. My father would disown me if he ever found out I let you do it alone." He gave my shoulders a squeeze. He studied my face. "Please," he whispered, and my insides melted.

Ugh. There was no way I was saying no to those eyes. It was

like I was being pulled out to sea and tossed in its depths. "Fine," I agreed and looked away, re-centering myself. "I mean, if you really want to, but—"

Scott grinned and cut me off. "Thanks. And I know . . . you've got it." He strolled to his office.

What did I get myself into?

Chapter Sixteen

SCOTT

After work, I hurried back to the B&B, changed into a t-shirt and jeans, and grabbed the compact box of tools I had gained from completing minor projects without Carol's knowledge. I was determined to fix up Carol's place. I knew she would refuse the help, but she was tired. Plus, resale values and all that. Win-win.

I rushed to my car. Who knew how fast Marissa would get that ladder up without me there?

I pulled into the short dirt driveway next to Marissa's beat-up car. The house was quaint, surrounded by a short fence, a small wooden porch, and a navy-blue door. I found Marissa on the side of the house, dressed in a sweater and jeans and already halfway up the ladder.

I swore under my breath and hurried out of the car. "I thought you were going to wait for me," I hollered as I rushed over to steady the ladder that was tipping back and forth with each of her steps.

"Yeah, well . . . like I said. I've got it." Marissa grinned down at me, her brown hair framing her gorgeous face, and climbed the rest of the way onto the roof. Tension built in my shoulders. What if she fell? She reached into her back pocket. "Shoot, I forgot the nails." She turned to head down the ladder.

"No wait there. I'll grab them. Where do I go?"

She pointed to the front of the house. "They should be in a box on the left side of the porch. Nan can show you if you need her to."

I nodded. "And you'll stay where you are . . . right?"

She chuckled. "I won't touch the ladder."

I moved towards the porch. An older lady huffed as she reached over and grabbed the box of nails. Gray hair curled around her face, and her back curved beneath a worn flannel jacket.

I reached for the box she'd extended in my direction. "Thanks," I said as I grabbed the nails. "I'm Scott. You must be Nan. I've heard a lot about you."

Her eyes sparkled as she looked me up and down. "Marissa said her boss was coming over, but had I known I was going to get to watch *you* work on my roof, I would've popped popcorn." She chuckled.

What was I supposed to say to that?

"Nan, leave him alone," Marissa hollered from the roof. Nan grinned, and I could see where Marissa got her smile from. And while their eyes were different—Nan's were blue, not green like Marissa's—they held the same shape and combination of kindness and mischief.

"If you are getting on the roof, I'm going to need a different chair." Nan turned and waddled back into the house.

I grinned as I went back to Marissa. I could already tell I was going to like Nan.

I made sure the ladder was braced against the house and made my way up the ladder. Marissa looked at me over her shoulder, her hair blowing in the soft breeze that teased it. "Alright Suits, let's see if we can get done before Nan embarrasses me some more."

Marissa grabbed a few nails from the box and as she leaned down, her feet slipped. She braced herself on hands and knees, and I hurried to plant my feet behind her shoes so she couldn't slide further. *This woman was going to kill me.* My palms were sweaty, and my heart raced.

My hand shot toward her, and she took hold of it, steading herself before she stood and turned to face me.

"Whoops." Marissa's voice was breathy.

Her cheeks were pink, and she was close enough I felt her breath on my face. Her fingers were soft in mine, and they trembled in my grasp. I wanted to kiss her. The thought somewhat surprised me, but it held true. Her green eyes staring up at me, the full pout of her lips, and her hand still resting in mine made my heartbeat erratic. Nothing wrong with enjoying time together for a bit. It could be fun and temporary. Plus, she was gorgeous, and I couldn't help the way my hands always itched to touch her, or the way my body was drawn to be near her. Her eyes flicked to my lips, and I wondered if she felt the same. I reached up and brushed her silky hair back from her face, electricity shooting through my hand as my finger grazed her skin. When her eyes found mine again, they held a combination of excitement and fear.

She stepped away and cleared her throat. "Thanks." She looked down at her feet.

What was I thinking? I was her boss. Being anything more than friends would be dangerous and unethical. I took a few steps away until my body could remember this was a dangerous idea.

"Alright, let's fix this roof, so I stop thinking of you falling off." I smiled, trying to ease the tension. She looked at my lips and I had to remind myself not to pull her into my arms.

"Deal." She grabbed the nails and picked up the hammer. I helped but stayed between her and the edge of the roof. Just in case.

The next thirty minutes went faster than I hoped. We were a

good team, but now that the project was done, there was no reason to stay around.

I came down the ladder first to hold it for Marissa. She grinned and humored me.

I rested the ladder on the ground, trying to miss the scattered soft apples. "Where to with the ladder?"

Marissa was standing next to Nan, who was in a camping chair, wrapped in a blanket, eating popcorn.

"I've got it." Marissa stepped towards me.

"I'm happy to help."

"In that case . . ." Nan chimed in. "There are plenty of projects around the house that we would love help with. Bert tries, but he isn't much better on a ladder than me. What I wouldn't do for joints like yours." She whistled.

"Nan! Stop!" Marissa pleaded. "What would Bert say about you gawking at Scott?"

"He would join me. Did you see how fast he climbed up that ladder?" Nan waved Marissa off. "I'll make you dinner . . ."

A home cooked meal and more time with Nan and Marissa? "Sold."

Marissa rolled her eyes and walked next to me. "Really, we're fine. She can bulldog anyone into getting her way. Don't feel like you need to do any of this." Her cheeks were flushed, and I clenched my hand into a fist to keep my finger from running along the color.

I picked up the ladder and walked beside Marissa to the shed.

"She's hilarious."

"She thinks so. Thanks again for your help. That went way faster than I thought it would. You're better at home-improvement stuff than I expected for a suit." She smiled, letting me know she was joking.

"Of course." I leaned against the wooden wall of the shed. "Like Red Green says, if the women don't find you handsome, they better find you handy."

"And what happens when they find you both?"

Whoa.

That was the most Marissa had ever flirted with me, and I liked it. I didn't want to scare her off. The tips of her ears were turning pink as she locked the ladder in the shed.

I looked over at Nan, who was taking her blanket back to the house. "It's almost like I'm looking at you in the future. Full of fire and energy. Plus, some home-cooked meals sound fantastic."

Marissa leaned against the shed beside me. "Are you thinking that I'll still drool over you when I'm eighty?" She chuckled. "I mean, Nan obviously does . . ." She grinned.

"That's true. I have quite a way with older ladies. They can't resist me."

Marissa glanced at her watch. "Oh shoot! I need to go. I have dinner plans."

She did? With whom?

What happened to the no-dating rule? She took a few steps back to the house and then turned back to me, unsure of what to do.

Nan stepped next to me and looped her arm in mine. "Don't worry, it isn't with a guy. It's Rose's birthday night out."

Apparently, my expression was showing on my face more than I wanted. Nan nodded at the house. "How about you come fix my sink and I'll make you dinner? I need someone to beat at Jeopardy tonight, since Marissa will be gone."

Marissa sighed. "Nan, leave him be."

"Dinner and Jeopardy sounds great." I smiled. A night with Nan was sure to be interesting.

Even though Nan's house differed from the house I grew up in, when I walked through her front door, it felt like coming home. It was smaller and simpler, but the worn floors were the same—and they held years of stories and wear. I looked over at the pile of cut timber by the wood-burning stove. It wasn't very full. Was this their only source of heat? There was a shelf that held pictures above the stove. I wanted to stop and examine them but didn't want to pry.

"In here, lawyer boy," Nan called out to sound like "lover boy" and I chuckled. I walked past the old China hutch, my feet causing it to shake and groan. In the kitchen, the linoleum floors were chipped, and the counters covered with mason jars. Nan was tying on a "Life's better with butter" apron.

"I'll start on peeling the potatoes if you start on that sink." She nodded to the left. "The thing takes forever to drain."

Great, plumbing. I hated plumbing. I looked under the sink at the neck of the plastic PVC pipe, at least it was PVC and not something older. Maybe it just needed to be cleaned out. I turned the knob under the sink, made sure I turned the water line off, and began unscrewing the pipe. As always with plumbing, the smell was atrocious and made me gag. The pipe seemed to be plugged with some type of hardened grease. After cleaning it out into the bucket Nan had provided me, I stepped outside, looking for a hose connected to the house to spray the remaining gunk out. I found a pump, pulled the lever all the way up and stuck the pipe with hardened grease underneath the nozzle.

The water pressure was something of legends as it rushed out into the pipe, blasting out all the gunk and sending water mixed with chunky grease everywhere, including my t-shirt.

Ugh. Sick!

The smell assaulted my nose. I ripped my shirt off. I would let Nan know I would be back for dinner after I changed. I would not wear this soggy, greasy shirt a second longer. I continued spraying out the gunk, then headed back into the kitchen. I reassembled the pipe, making sure I got it on tight so it wouldn't leak, and turned the water back on. I tested the drain in the sink. Not perfect, but much better. I used the kitchen towel to dry my hands.

"Oh, wow!"

My back stiffened. That was not Nan's voice. How was I going to explain my reasoning for taking my shirt off to clean the sink?

"Close your mouth hun, don't want to catch flies." I heard the humor in Nan's voice as I turned. Marissa's cheeks were pink. Her hand covered her mouth as her eyes roamed up my chest and back to the sink.

"Sorry. My shirt got all gross."

"No apologies necessary, trust me." Nan chuckled and came the rest of the way into the kitchen.

Marissa lowered her hand, and I watched her cheeks changed from pink to red. She looked away. Now it was my turn to gawk. She was in a black, short skirt with black strappy heels, and an orange sweater that made her skin look amazing. Her lips were brighter than normal, and her eyes were a bold color of green beneath the dark lashes that framed them. Wow! I was instantly grateful she wasn't going out with a man.

"Oh, don't you start now," Nan whispered and bumped me with her hip. "Close your mouth and walk her out."

I shook my head to clear my foggy brain. Marissa tucked her hair behind her ear and gave me a shy grin. All thoughts of shirts and leaving Hillsdale fled, and all I could think of was Marissa. I wanted her to stay here with me for the night instead of going out, but I walked her to the door instead.

Chapter Seventeen

MARISSA

I rushed towards my car, refusing to look back. Was Scott standing in the doorway looking at me? What would I do if he asked me to stay with him with his shirt off? I wouldn't be able to control myself.

Leaving was safer. Other than I was leaving him with Nan and who knew what she would say.

I felt my phone vibrate again. I unlocked the screen and saw I had three unread messages in the group chat.

Rose: Mar we are leaving in ten minutes for my birthday dinner and dancing.

Rose: Five minutes . . . where are you?

Rose: Mar, so help me. If you bail on my birthday dinner, I will come slash your tires and then kidnap you. Remember to dress up and you both have to go dancing with me.

We were going to Clifton to The Stuffed Olive and then out dancing. Faith was not one for social crowds, but she would do anything for Rose on her birthday.

I typed my reply.

Marissa: Sorry, on my way!

Faith sent a bunch of dancing emojis and hearts.

I drove the ten minutes to the little duplex they rented and grabbed my jacket and Rose's gift bag off the passenger seat then shut the car door with a thud.

Rose and Faith must have heard me coming because they were already out the door.

Rose had large gold hoop earrings and her long dark hair in a tight high ponytail. She had black tight pants, and her crop top had gold sequins. Her dark eye makeup and red lips completed the look.

"Alright birthday girl! You look *hot*!" I ran the rest of the way to her, trying not to roll my ankle in my heels, and pulled her into a hug. "I'm so sorry I'm late. Nan was trying to get on the roof to fix the shingles. I figured I better fix it before she got any ideas."

Rose chuckled. "I love her. Alright, let's go ladies, let's party!" She pulled us both into a side hug. "Twenty-four has never looked so good!"

Faith gave a soft smile. "You both look amazing."

Faith's blonde hair was curled, and she had some silver dangle earrings. Where Rose was sequins and bold, Faith was subtle and soft. She had a loose-fit cream-colored yarn sweater with a knee-length flared dark blue skirt. I had no idea what brand her heels or purse were, but they looked expensive. She must have scored those thrifting. Teachers were tragically underpaid.

"Want me to drive?" I pointed to my Honda.

Rose laughed. "No, I want to actually get there and back. Faith already volunteered."

"Ouch." I laughed. "Respect your elders." That car had seen me through a lot of things. When Carol said she didn't want it taking up space in her parking lot anymore, I knew it was most likely a lie and that she was trying to be nice.

We climbed into Faith's car, and she pulled onto the main highway.

"So . . . are you dressed up like this for tonight? I mean, I said to dress up, but I was curious if this was because of a certain someone helping fix the roof?" Rose turned in her seat.

"What the . . ."

Rose was the queen of the gossip chain. She didn't spread it, but she was always in the loop. I think it's because she owned the only salon in town, and everyone was always trying to be on her good side.

Rose held up her phone with its bedazzled case, showing me a picture. It was Scott and I on the roof, my body pressed against his. I felt my breath catch in my throat. How was I going to explain that?

She swiped again and showed one of us against the tool shed.

Another picture. Okay, this was borderline creepy.

"Geez, where's the paparazzi?" I shouldn't be surprised.

Rose pursed her lips. "Ashley sent them to Nancy, who then sent them to me."

That woman needed some more hobbies or cats or something. "We're just friends, nothing more."

"Faith is a friend, and she has never held me like that . . ." Rose smirked.

Faith flinched. "Oh no, don't bring me into this. I told you to leave it alone and let Mar tell us when she was ready."

Rose shook her head in Faith's direction. "Boring."

"Scott is helping me leave. That is hardly a source of relationship."

Rose's nose crinkled. "Who said anything about a relationship? I was just implying a little fun." She winked.

Scott would be fun. It would be no-strings-attached. No worry about futures and tricky conversations.

"I'll admit he is hot! You should see him without a shirt." I gave the girls a chefs kiss for emphasis. "And the thought of kissing him might have crossed my mind tonight."

Faith squealed and started clapping her hands before she grabbed the steering wheel again.

Rose grinned and looked down at my legs. "So, did he like the outfit?"

I chuckled and matched her sass. "I mean, what's not to like?"

She laughed. "Yes girl!"

Talking about Scott was not what tonight was about. I had no idea if the PTO mom was still bugging Faith and last I heard Rose was fighting with her sister again.

"Alright, no more about Scott. Tonight is about you, Rose. And giving you the best birthday ever! Wait till you see what I found." I grabbed the black gift bag with gold stars and handed it up to her. She brushed her hair off her shoulder and laughed as she pulled out the tissue paper.

Chapter Eighteen

MARISSA

I sat in my car in front of the B&B. I had come here once or twice a week the last couple of weeks to help with the trunk-or-treat, and each time the pain in my chest eased a bit. When I looked across the field, I remembered picnics with my parents when we would visit Nan, and Christmas pageants on the stage in the barn. I remembered eating fluffy pancakes with Carol and Mom as they laughed and gossiped. There were still moments from their funeral imprinted on my brain, but mixed in with the pain, moments of sunshine were breaking through.

Today we were meeting to finalize all the assignments and finish any last-minute problems. The trunk-or-treat was in seven days.

I didn't want to take this event on, but I had to admit, I was enjoying the work. Watching people come together and work towards something beautiful, not for money or pride, but for their neighbors, was touching.

The meeting started in twenty minutes. I needed to set everything up. I shut my door with my trademark strong hip thrust and started walking across the parking lot. Around the corner, I saw a small pad of concrete and a basketball hoop installed in the ground.

That wasn't there last week, was it?

I saw the group of boys passing the ball and laughing. It looked like it would get plenty of use.

"Hey, boys," I called in their direction.

They grinned and waved and went back to dribbling. The back door to the B&B swung open. Scott came out and began walking to the community barn. The boys' eyes lit up, and they all grinned.

"Scott!" they hollered.

"Hey Scott, do you have time for drills?" Ethan asked.

Even Josh, who didn't talk to anyone, wanted to talk to him. "Hi, Scott! Watch this!" The boy dribbled the ball between his legs.

Scott grinned at the boys. "That's awesome!" He rushed over and gave Josh a high five. Scott's smile grew as he spotted me. "I have a meeting with Marissa now, but we'll play later."

The boys made kissing noises. "Scott and Marissa sitting in a tree . . ."

Scott laughed and jogged to meet me, and we headed to the barn together. "Don't forget you have twenty minutes until you have to come help me," Scott hollered to the group as they started passing the ball.

"You seem to have made some friends."

He chuckled. "They're good kids. We're almost done painting our fishing booth for the trunk-or-treat. The booth was Josh's idea."

"Was the basketball hoop there last week?"

A hint of a smile. "I don't know, I think so."

It was obvious I wasn't getting any information from him. I would ask Carol later. "Hope Nan wasn't too ruthless with Jeopardy last night. She likes to win."

Scott grinned. "Yeah she does. She actually faked a heart attack when I started to win. Scared me half to death."

I gasped and covered my laugh. "I'm so sorry."

"I'll get her next time," he chuckled.

Was he planning on a next time?

"How are you feeling about tonight?" Scott walked beside me along the path.

"Pretty good." I shrugged. "We'll see how the meeting goes. How are things going here?" I looked back at the bed-and-breakfast.

"Pretty good. Hey, I was going to ask, were your parents married here? There were these pictures on the kitchen wall and the bride looks a lot like you."

The fall trees were dropping their leaves; I focused on the ones around my feet. "Remember how I said things were complicated with Carol?"

Scott's forehead creased. "Yeah."

"Well," I sighed. What could it hurt if he knew? "Carol and my mom were best friends. This place holds a lot of good memories for me with my parents . . . but it was also where we held their funeral. Until Carol forced me to help plan the trunk-or-treat this month, I'd stayed away since."

Scott stopped walking and took my hand. "You came here just to help me find a place to stay?" He looked humbled.

I didn't want it to be a big deal. "That and because I want to escape Hillsdale and you're helping me plan that." I smiled. "Carol has the crazy idea in her head that I can take this place over for her." I laughed. "Can you even imagine? That requires *way* too much planning."

Scott went quiet. It must be because he feels guilty about having me coming to the B&B.

"But this has been fun." I looked around at the trees, the colored leaves, this beautiful place. "I think it's magical." I bumped Scott's shoulder, trying to ease the mood. He had become stiff and distant. I didn't want his pity. "It's been good making fun memories here again, and remembering the good that existed here before. Please don't feel bad. It's healing for me."

THE MEETING WAS ALMOST OVER, AND EVERYONE'S booths were looking amazing. Hopefully, the community would have a good turnout for the decorated trunks. I walked through the group, examining different projects and their status of completion. I pretended I was giving them all equal attention, but I checked on Scott and the boys more than the rest.

Just in case they needed help, I reminded myself and the butterflies in my stomach as I watched Scott interact with the group of boys.

They were painting a big piece of particle board with holes cut into it. Most of the boys were laughing and goofing around, but Josh stood still, staring at the section he was painting. The way he was mixing paints to make the color of the ocean was sweet and showed his obvious care for this project. I wondered if he got the opportunity to paint much. I stepped near the painting and examined it. "That looks great."

"No it doesn't." He huffed and glared. "I can't get the color of the water right. I know it needs to be darker, but none of the mixes feel right."

Scott's hand froze midair as he was painting his section of ocean neon blue. "Um, am I ruining this for you Josh?"

The boy shook his head. "You can paint your section how you want."

Scott stepped a little closer to him and rested his arm on Josh's shoulder. My insides melted. "Well, if it was your section, how would you paint it?"

Of course, he would be great with kids . . . not that it mattered.

We're just friends.

I was leaving.

Without missing a beat, Josh answered, "Your ocean is too bright, your fish too orange and your bird isn't thick enough."

Scott's eyes widened, and I chuckled. The rest of the boys were now in the middle of a leaf fight. Scott might need reinforcements. I stepped in. "Tell you what, Josh. How about you give both of us tips and we can try to fix it?"

Scott smiled and Josh nodded.

I picked up a brush, and Josh fixed my grip. For the next fifteen minutes, I learned more about painting than I ever could have imagined.

Maybe we could start an after-school art program at the B&B? Well, not me, but Carol, or someone.

The leader of the group of boys, Ethan, appeared at our side. "Josh, it's getting dark. Better get you home before your mom comes looking."

He stilled and nodded, dropping the brush in the mason jar filled with water. "I can give you boys a ride."

"Nah. We're good." Ethan gave Scott another obnoxious kissing face when he thought I wasn't looking.

Josh looked between Scott and me and gave a shy grin. "Yep. All good." The group ran off, leaving Scott and me alone.

"If I didn't know better, I would think those boys are trying to play matchmaker." I grabbed the brushes. "I might ruin this painting without Josh's supervision." I nodded toward the board.

Scott grinned and began closing the lids on various paints. "I had no idea he enjoyed painting that much. Pretty sure he was less-than-pleased with my efforts."

I laughed and Scott's eyes met mine, then they traveled to my left cheek. He set down the paint and closed the distance between us.

"What?" I sounded breathy. I cleared my throat and tried again. "What?"

"Here, you got a little something." Scott grabbed a paper towel and, taking my chin in his hand, he tipped my face slightly. He gazed into my eyes and took a step closer.

My throat went dry, and I forgot to breathe. His eyes glanced at my lips.

Was he going to kiss me?

I know it's cliche, but I couldn't help it. I licked my lips. His eyes flashed back to mine, no longer passive but on fire.

He stood frozen, seeming at war with himself, and I waited for him to decide, unsure what outcome I wanted him to choose. Scott shook his head and softly wiped the blue paint from my cheek. He smelled like cinnamon and autumn leaves. I looped my thumbs through the belt loops of my jeans to stop myself from wrapping my arms around him. He was cleaning the paint off, that was all.

Which was what I wanted. *Right?*

When he was done, Scott looked at my lips once more, and dropped my chin. He picked up the brushes and walked over to the box of paints without looking back.

I stood rooted to the spot, urging my feet to move, but they somehow had grown roots. Wow . . . okay. I tried to shake the mental fog. I was standing still like an idiot.

"You know," Carol appeared at my side, wrapping an arm around my waist, and nodding to Scott. "That boy put that basketball hoop in for the boys. He asked me, of course, but it was all him."

"He did?"

"Yep. Had his dad come help too. He's always fixing little things around my place too. Thinks I don't notice." Carol shrugged her shoulders. "He might be alright . . . for a city lawyer." She left.

I wanted to run to him and give him a hug and let him know how much it meant to me he cared. About the boys, about Carol, and about me.

If I ran after him, I wasn't sure I would stop at hugging. That thought made my stomach drop. *What was I thinking?* I needed to get out of here, and fast. I practically ran to my car.

No, no, no. Not good.

Just friends, nothing more. He was a hot, caring, amazing man who was a friend. But just a friend.

My phone vibrated in my pocket.

What if it was Scott? What would I say? Sorry I almost kissed you, or sorry I ran away without saying goodnight? I wasn't ready to answer anything.

I drove home. Best to not have the temptation too close. Once I pulled in front of the fence, I pulled my phone from my pocket.

Not Scott. Rose. On our group chat. My heart dropped with disappointment. No wait, it didn't drop because this was what I wanted.

Chapter Nineteen

SCOTT

I SAT AT THE CHIPPED WOODEN BREAKFAST TABLE, scrolling through TripAdvisor's top ten things to do in London. There was a Harry Potter immersive experience. Would Marissa even like that? I had a stack of brochures and papers spread over the table. Hopefully Carol and the other two random guests staying at the B&B wouldn't mind my mess. Marissa kept her end of our deal with getting me a place to stay, and I needed to make sure I kept mine. After all, planning was no joking matter.

My stomach was a jumbled mess after Marissa opened up to me last night. Carol wanted her to take over the B&B? *But she didn't want the business, right?* I was certain Marissa had never mentioned running the B&B before.

Carol sat down with her cup of coffee and glanced at the papers. "Those for you?"

Oh great, she was going to think I was running off. "No, for Marissa."

She raised one eyebrow. "So, you and Marissa are a thing?"

I needed to stop that rumor before it caught and spread. "Nope. Just friends."

Okay, not just friends based on how often I thought of kissing her, but either way, nothing serious.

"Is she having you plan a trip for her?" Carol nodded to the brochures and blew on her coffee. "Are you going too?"

"Nope." I stacked the papers into even piles. "I offered to help her if she convinced you to let me stay here." I flinched. That didn't sound good. "It was for her own good, though. Did you know she was planning on leaving? Going to another country with zero plans?" I shuddered at all that could go wrong. "Just winging it?"

Carol chuckled. "That doesn't surprise me. I think she believes that if she doesn't plan life, it will hurt less if it doesn't work out how she wants." Carol picked up a printout about Buckingham Palace and the changing of the guards.

I thought back to the scars across her stomach. Life had not been easy for Marissa. "Is that because of the accident?"

Carol's eyes widened. "She told you about the accident?" The paper stilled in her hand. "Or was it someone else?"

"She told me, kinda. She only said that her parents died, and that's how she ended up living in Hillsdale. I could tell she didn't want to talk about it more. I didn't press."

Carol raised her eyebrows. "She never talks about it. To anyone. Except maybe Rose. Even then, I doubt it." She set down the palace paper and picked up one about the tour of Bath. I went back to scrolling my computer, saying nothing. I resisted the urge to use Carol to find out more about Marissa's past. "She is tricky, that Marissa." Carol thumbed through more papers. "Wow. You should have her try this."

Carol pulled out a paper with a "Meet your Match" romantic getaway package. There was speed dating, dancing lessons, making pasta, the whole thing. Heat rushed through my chest as I imagined her dancing through Europe in some random man's arms. He would probably wear a wool scarf, have an accent, and be a duke or something ridiculous.

I closed my eyes, trying to clear the image and my unexplained anger away. I opened my eyes to Carol's smug smile.

"Interesting . . . friends . . ."

I groaned. "Carol, it's nothing."

"Doesn't look like nothing." She smirked, finished her coffee, and stood from the table. I shook my head and grabbed my plate with remnants of bacon and eggs and followed her to the kitchen. I looked around the worn space. It had a safe, welcoming vibe. I hoped the investor would be good to the property when they took it over.

Carol glanced at me sideways as I started filling the kitchen sink with warm water. "I'm still not sure if you are here to stay or for something else . . ."

I froze. What did she mean? I hadn't said anything about Raymond & Johnson Law Firm out loud, right?

"But I noticed the repairs around the house are magically fixing themselves, and I appreciate it. I don't even know how you reached the light over the stairway. That one has been out for three years."

I knew the one she referred to. Even with my height, I needed to use a ladder and lean precariously on the banister. "It would be easier if I didn't need to sneak around and guess what needs doing." I nodded to her. "Maybe you could give me a list?"

Carol turned to face me. Her eyes bored into mine, pleading. "I'll see to a list, but Scott, do not hurt those boys. Or Marissa." Carol's eyes were full of emotion and I couldn't look away.

The air caught in my lungs and my chest tightened. Somehow that group of boys and Marissa had made it past the boundaries I put up to keep them at a distance, and the thought of hurting them made me feel sick. "I don't plan on it, Carol. Promise."

Carol nodded, grabbed a towel from the stove and dried her

hands off. "Let's talk about rent too. How about $250.00 and whatever time you can give to help me around the B&B?"

"That would be great. Thank you."

Carol nodded and looked out the window. There was an older woman in a puffy jacket walking around outside shaking a bag of cat food. "Alright, I got to go help Betty Ann. Seems that she lost her cat . . . again." And with that, Carol sighed. "I better go before she gets it in her mind she can climb trees." She hurried out of the kitchen.

I stayed and finished rinsing the dishes. Outside the kitchen window, the large maple trees in the yard had dropped piles of orange and yellow leaves. A mom and her child threw the piles of color back and forth, laughing. If Carol sold the property, would this still be a place where people could come and enjoy all the grounds offered, or would they only belong on the property as employees and not share in its beauty? That would be a shame.

Tonight, the town would come together as ghosts and goblins here at the B&B. A place where they belonged, because Carol had always made sure everyone in this town had access to it. The boys thought of this as a second home. Marissa had taken to planning the trunk-or-treat and shined. I loved watching her excitement in it all. I loved watching her, period. She said she couldn't imagine herself running this place, but I could.

I felt that thought drop like a stone in my stomach.

But what about my goals? What about my office? I needed Carol to sell the B&B for me to reach my goals. Marissa wanted to leave me far behind. Anyway, why should I avoid convincing Carol to sell? We would both be getting what we hoped for. The imaginary British gent flashed in my mind again, and I considered skipping planning her trip all together.

I felt my phone vibrate in my front pocket and dried my hands. It was a text from Marissa.

Marissa: You ready for tonight?

Scott: Yep, the fishing booth is painted and dry and has people to run it. I was thinking maybe we should do a trunk for the law firm. Only if it wouldn't stress you out. I know you already have a lot going on. I could do it by myself.

Marissa: That is a great idea. What should we decorate the trunk as? Do you want to do costumes?

Nope, of course, I didn't want to do a costume. But Marissa would love it.

Scott: I think costumes sound fun.

Marissa: You do? Fun! How about Peter Pan? I have a Tinker-bell costume from a few years ago somewhere. Could do a clock face or something for the trunk for Big Ben?

Right, Big Ben, in Europe. Because she was leaving.

Scott: Right, since you'll get to go see it. Great idea.

Marissa: Right, because I'm leaving soon . . . I guess we should figure all those details out.

I could not read enough into her text. Was that like *right, because I'm leaving and super excited so don't get attached . . . or like right . . . because I'm leaving but would rather stay here with you?*

Text had to be the worst way to communicate.

I was sure it was the first way. That was what she had always wanted. She didn't want to stay, and neither did I.

Scott: I'm fresh out of Peter Pan costumes . . . but I will figure something out.

I would figure it all out.

Chapter Twenty

MARISSA

Suggesting the matching costumes might have been a bit much, but I couldn't resist the opportunity. I loved these sparkly wings, and I was pretty sure this skirt with these tights made my legs look longer than they were, which, at my height, was always a plus.

I wasn't dressing up to impress Scott; I reminded myself as I adjusted the little star gems near my eyes and made sure I had no stray hairs from my bun. I reapplied my berry lip gloss and took a deep breath.

Hopefully, everything went well, and the neighborhood didn't form a revolt against me.

He said he would have everything prepped for the law firm's trunk. I decided to check on Carol. The last few times I saw her, she'd looked minutes from falling asleep where she stood. Was I not doing enough to help?

Maybe running these community events was too much for her. Would I want to run them for her?

And where would that leave London and finding myself?

I walked across the field towards Carol, the fallen maple leaves crinkling under my feet.

"Oh, there you are." She sighed and handed me some string and clothespins. "Will you take this over to the boys running the fishing booth and remind the basketball team that the haunted Red Riding Hood trail needs to be kept at a PG level of scary?"

I reached over and gave her a hug. "I got it. Give me the clipboard of things that need finishing and go sit down. Or better yet, get a donut first, then relax. I've got this." I felt sure. I could do this, and a small surge of pride trickled through me.

Carol rubbed the back of her neck. "I'm not as young as I used to be. It's becoming too much for me. Especially since John died. I don't think we would've pulled it off this year without you. Honestly, Marissa, you have a gift for organization and loving the people in this town." I walked Carol over to the bench near the pond. She needed to sit.

Carol leaned back against the seat; her shoulders slumped. "I know I promised I wouldn't ask, but I would love it if you took this place over. With your mother gone, and no babies of my own, I always kinda thought of you as mine." Carol reached over and grabbed my hand in hers. Her eyes started to tear up. She was never emotional. This was too much for her.

I pulled her into a hug and, instead of comforting her, I felt safe in her arms. She was the closest thing to my mother I had. I wondered if that was why I pushed her away. The reminder of Mom was too much. My heart swelled.

"That means a lot Carol, you have always reminded me of Mom. I think that scared me." I took a deep breath to calm my heart.

Carol reached up and patted my cheek. "I know that Mar, and that is okay."

I looked around at the gathering town and loved what I saw. "Honestly, I kinda enjoyed doing the trunk-or-treat. I loved being here again. Thank you for forcing my hand a bit." I grinned at her.

"I'm still planning on a trip to Europe." I needed to leave Hillsdale. I'd had thoughts about leaving for so long, but I hadn't thought about what I would do after. Maybe that *could* be the B&B? "I'm not saying yes." I looked at Carol to make sure she understood. "But after Europe I will think about the B&B." I smiled as I realized this was the first thing I had ever planned on for after Europe. It used to be my all-or-nothing. All I wanted or could think of was running there, but I couldn't picture anything after it. And now, although the picture was fuzzy around the edges, and blurry in the middle, something colorful in my future was taking shape. And I didn't hate it.

Carol sighed and leaned against me. "Thanks for at least considering it." She bumped my shoulder. "Scott mentioned you were heading to Europe."

"He did?"

"Yep, he was going through a list of activities this morning for you."

"Oh . . . That's great. Did he sound excited?" My voice forgot to convey my excitement. It was a good reminder that he was planning on me leaving, and he was leaving too. Nothing permanent.

"I'm not buying it, missy." Carol crossed her arms. "Never mind that though," she waved me off. "We'll talk pleasantries later. Let's get through tonight first."

I hugged her again and relaxed into her motherly arms. "You stay sitting down." After I was sure she wouldn't bolt, I headed back to the groups of people. I looked down at her list.

Here we go.

THE TRUNK-OR-TREAT WAS STARTING IN TWENTY minutes, and if I had to guess, I had already walked twenty thousand steps. Nearing one of the few shiny cars in the field, I smiled as Scott pulled his into the lineup. I had offered to use my Honda, so he didn't have to worry about sticky fingers touching his car, but he said he wanted to use his. Weird.

The group of boys spilled out of his back seat. With Scott dressed as Peter Pan, they looked like his group of lost boys. I looked Scott up and down. His green tights only reached his knees, his shirt fighting to cover his long torso. It wasn't winning. He lifted his hands over his head to adjust his hat, exposing his toned stomach. He was hot. I would never have a stomach that looked like that, but that didn't mean I couldn't enjoy the view. Points for effort, and extra points for the hotness factor.

When Scott saw me coming, he turned bright red. "It was the only thing I could find . . . the package said adult." He frowned and pulled his shirt longer.

He still wore it. Even though it didn't fit, and he would've been more comfortable in a suit and tie. My heart grew as I looked at him, awkwardly shifting from side to side.

"Looking good there Peter, even though you are waiting for a flood." I was hoping the teasing banter would ease the tension.

Scott rolled his eyes. His gaze then traveled up my legs, which were covered in green tights and a miniskirt that hit mid-thigh. I had to remind myself I was in fact covered, but I'd never felt as exposed as I did now, watching Scott's eyes glide up my legs.

"If I'm waiting for a flood, then you are waiting for a monsoon." His eyes drank me in.

I laughed and swatted him on the shoulder.

"I cannot believe I'm wearing this." He gestured to his stretchy pants and bright green hat.

"Aww, come on. It's for the kids. Besides, I like it on you."

Scott grinned. "Oh yes, Peter Pan is my most manly look."

I closed the distance between us and gave him a kiss on the cheek, surprised by my actions but not regretting them. I was grateful for all he had done for me.

"Well, if I knew you liked it that much, I would've worn this a long time ago."

I chuckled and my cheeks warmed, as he pulled me into a tight hug. I leaned into his hug and felt his heart beating in his chest.

"Thanks for doing this," I whispered into his chest.

Scott looked around at the gathering crowd and smiling faces. "You know, I started it all to avoid sleeping on the floor, but I've enjoyed it."

"Me too. Maybe it won't be so bad." I looked up at his stubbly jawline. I grabbed the edge of my miniskirt to keep from reaching up and rubbing it. His eyes dropped to my lips and paused.

What would happen if he kissed me here, in front of everyone? Really kissed me. Not my version of a short, sweet peck on the cheek. He brushed a loose hair away from my face and the breath got stuck in my throat. The tension between us was like a magnet. I couldn't break it or decide what to do next if I wanted to.

All it would take was a little flip of the magnet and everything would change.

Nope, time for a new subject, and fast. I glanced to the side and saw the Lost Boys making obnoxious kissy faces. That did it. I nodded at them and forced myself to pull away.

"Alright boys, go man the fishing booth," Scott said. "If Carol catches you goofing off, she won't let you use the hoop for a week." He gave a soft smile as the boys ran off.

He popped the trunk and pulled out a cardboard painting with a clock face to look like Big Ben. "Josh helped me paint it." Setting it against the trunk, we admired it. "Okay, I asked for his help, but before too long, he kicked me off the project." Scott grinned, looking at the painting. "Josh sure has a thing for paint."

"Maybe you really are Peter Pan. You have helped that band of Lost Boys more than anyone. How did you get them to open up?"

"I convinced my dad to help me put in a hoop for them." Scott shrugged it off like it wasn't a big deal, but I knew. It was a huge deal. He reached into the back seat and grabbed a half-empty bag of candy. "Ugh! Those hooligans ate half the candy already."

I laughed and wrapped my arm around his. "I bought a few

extra bags. Let's go grab them." We wandered into the barn to get the candy.

"If I'm Peter Pan, then maybe you should've dressed up as Wendy."

I scowled. "Why be Wendy? Tinkerbell can fly and has magic." I shimmied my wings for emphasis.

"Yeah, but Peter likes Wendy." He winked down at me. "But with that skirt on Tink, I'm pretty sure he would've changed his mind."

I blushed and had the urge to fan my face. Luckily, my hands were in reach of the bags of candy. I grabbed them to keep my hands busy. If thinking happy thoughts and pixie dust caused a person to fly, I should've been soaring at the tops of the maple trees.

"Alright, Tink. Looks like this party is starting." He nodded to the kids and parents making their way up the street.

We joined the line and started passing out candy to what felt like every cowboy, monster, and princess in town. I was pretty sure I saw a few of the high school kids twice. If they took the time to wait in this line twice, they could have all the candy they wanted.

"Are you Tinkerbell?" a cute little girl with blonde curls dressed as a princess asked. "I almost came as a fairy, but Mom said I couldn't buy a new costume."

The woman behind in a matching costume sighed. "I had already bought this one." She grinned as she looked at her daughter. "That was even after the double pinky promise you wouldn't change your mind . . . again." The woman blushed as she nodded to her pink satin dress. "She wanted to match."

That was so sweet.

"Well, I wanted to be a princess, but this guy insisted on Peter Pan." I elbowed Scott.

Carol walked toward us with Betty Ann and I saw her resemblance to the blonde princess in front of me.

"Oh, is this your granddaughter?" I asked Betty Ann. I reached forward and put an extra candy in her bucket with a wink.

Betty Ann stepped up near her granddaughter. "Yep, this is Millie."

Carol bent down and looked at the mini princess.

"Oh my goodness, she is a doll."

"I think your Peter Pan costume is too small." The little girl giggled as she glanced up at Scott.

Her mother turned red. "Millie! What did we say about thoughts?"

"Sometimes they should be inside ones." She continued to stare Scott down.

He chuckled and bent down so he was at eye level with her. "You're right. I think the suit is magic. I put it on, and I grew eight inches."

Her eyes turned wide. "Really?" She eyed his costume with more interest. "So it's magic?"

Scott nodded. "It must be."

Ugh. Of course, he would be cute with kids. But his vision board had no kids on it.

Not that it mattered. We were both leaving.

Did it matter? I shook the thought away.

Scott stood next to me and nodded to the retreating girl. "I think that will be you someday."

I felt my stomach drop with panic. "What do you mean?"

"I can see you dressing up your kids and doing the big family matching costumes." His grin was wide.

Crap! No, no, not having this conversation.

The sensation of ice water rushing through my veins over-whelmed me. Carol looked at me with raised brows. I shook my head.

No. No. I hadn't told him, and I didn't need to, right? We were leaving.

Carol nodded and kept walking down the line.

I stepped further away from Scott. "I think I should go check on everyone. Make sure they have enough hot dogs and all that . . ."

"Hey, are you okay?" Scott moved near me. "You are looking a little pale. Do you need to sit down? Did I say something?"

"Excuse me!" A little cowboy held out his bucket, but Scott only watched as I retreated from his car.

"Excuse me!" yelled the child, holding out his bucket further.

"Marissa." Scott set down the bowl of candy. The young boy decided that meant it was all fair game. Scott came beside me. "Can I get you anything?"

"Yeah. I mean, no." I stumbled on a tree root, and he reached out and steadied me. "What I meant was no, I don't need anything. I just realized I needed to check on everyone." I shook out of his hold.

I could tell he didn't believe me, but he didn't press, so I turned and left Peter Pan and any questions behind.

Luckily, the rest of the night I had plenty to do other than think of Scott or kids or any conversations that wouldn't be happening tonight.

After cleaning up with aching feet, catching two sets of high schoolers making out, and tracking down two lost Power Rangers, the night was finished. I leaned up against my car and sighed. That was a lot. I wasn't ready to do it all over, but it was awesome.

Someone leaned next to me, and the smell of cinnamon surrounded me. I peeked up at Scott.

"Wow . . ." Scott had a goofy grin on his face. "You did it. This whole thing was amazing."

"It was great. Thanks for all your help. It wasn't me, really. Carol has done it for years and had most things figured out." He turned to me and looked at my face.

He wasn't going to bring up the kid thing again, was he?

His eyebrows were down, and he was watching me. The silence stretched and pulled around us. "Are we okay?" he asked.

"Of course. Why wouldn't we be?" My voice was too high. I cleared my throat.

Scott tipped his head to the side but didn't press. He leaned back against my car and looked up. I followed his gaze. It was a clear night, and I could see Orion's belt. Maybe I could find Cassiopeia. It was one Mom always pointed out.

Aww, Mom.

If she and Dad were here, they would tell me what to do with everything; Scott, London, the B&B. How do I navigate life without them?

"The stars here amaze me. I still can't get over it. They are so bright." He pointed to the sky.

"Yeah." I shrugged, looking at the stars. "Yes, found it."

"What?"

"Cassiopeia."

His body turned, and he began studying me instead of the night sky. "What's Cassiopeia?" I felt him shift his weight closer.

Even on the chilly October night, heat rushed through me.

Stars. Just keep it on the stars. "A constellation." I pointed up above the barn. "Look."

He leaned his head down closer to mine to have the same perspective. His warm breath danced across my arm. I sighed.

Out loud.

Ugh. Keep it together.

"See those bright stars right there?"

Scott's chest pressed against my side. I cleared my throat.

"It makes a wide W with the brighter stars." My finger shook as I followed the pattern again. "Can you see it?"

I turned my face to his, only to find his eyes searching mine and not the stars. I stilled and stared at his face. He grabbed my extended arm and ducked under it, putting himself even closer to me.

His eyes dropped to my lips and didn't jump back to my eyes. Goosebumps ran up my spine. *No, don't look at his lips.* I focused on his chest instead, watching the rise and fall of each deep breath he took. I was sure his chest was the safer bet, but as I watched it catch, my hand reached up and rested over his heart. *Stupid hands!*

Feeling a whisper of fingertips under my chin, I looked back up at his face. His eyes showed intensity and passion as he leaned his head to mine. His lips parted a breath away from mine. *He's going to kiss me! Oh, my gosh! Is this what I wanted?*

His eyebrows rose a fraction. I knew what he was asking. Can he kiss me?

What about England? And my future plans?

I bit my lip and heard a groan in the back of his throat. Plans weren't my thing anyway, and I desperately wanted him to kiss me.

I took my free arm and wrapped it up around his other shoulder and twirled the little curl at the base of his neck. My mouth went dry as Scott leaned into my touch and closed his eyes.

Raising up on my tiptoes, I brushed my lips against his. The touch wasn't fiery or out of control. It was more like a whisper. A whisper of what-ifs and who-knows. My hand grazed the light stubble on his chin. The left side of his mouth turned up in a self-satisfied grin.

"Maybe Peter ends up with Tink after all." Scott whispered as his fingers brushed down my jawline.

I felt a breathy laugh come out of my throat. *What was he saying?* But before I could ask, he wrapped his hand around the small of my back and pulled me to him, removing any distance between us. I could feel his heartbeat hammering, matching my own, fast and erratic.

"You have kissed me twice tonight." He gave me a wolfish grin. "My turn," he challenged. He leaned down and placed a soft kiss near my ear. His warm breath sent shivers down my spine and my breath hitched. My senses were overwhelmed.

His kisses continued.

My ear.

My cheek.

The left side of my mouth.

My lips. I felt the tip of his tongue trace along my bottom lip.

The trail was fire and ice and I shuddered. I grabbed his shoulders and deepened the kiss. If I didn't know better, I would've sworn we were flying, and I never wanted to land.

"Alright, Tink." Scott leaned his head back, breaking the kiss. Both of us were a little winded and flushed. He slid his hands down my arms, rubbing the goosebumps that had erupted all over me. "You better get home before you get sick." He thought I was cold, but I was far from it. My insides were on fire.

But fire burned, fire destroyed. My throat tightened and I leaned away.

"I will see you tomorrow." He kissed my forehead and opened my door. I slid into the driver's seat. I was there, but also floating in the clouds. Scott closed the door only to have it bounce back toward him.

I shook my head, waking from the stupor. "Oh, I've got it. You really have to slam it." Scott stepped back, and I opened the door and pulled it shut with all my force. Then I turned and smiled at Scott. He was chuckling and shaking his head. I put the car into drive and drove off before I did something stupid like ask him if he wanted to be more than friends.

Chapter Twenty-One

SCOTT

My squeaky bed groaned as I flipped over and stared at the ceiling. If there was a perfect night, it had to be last night. I had always felt like I was missing something, like there was a hole that needed patching inside. But with Marissa in my arms, looking up at me, and kissing me, the hole was closing.

I silenced my alarms, went to my email on my phone, and began sorting messages into the right folders.

What am I going to do about Raymond & Johnson Law? What do I want my future to look like?

With all her no-dating rules, was Marissa interested in a serious relationship with me? Why did she get nervous with the question of matching costumes with her kids one day? That seemed like something up her alley.

The canvas board of my goals sat in the room's corner. Stepping out of bed, my feet moved along the cold wooden floor. I grabbed the canvas and returned to my bed and stared at my vision board. Everything I wanted. But was it enough?

What did I want now? And why was I questioning everything after one kiss?

My phone vibrated with a notification. Maybe it was Marissa. I grinned as I tossed the canvas aside.

Not Marissa. It was an email from Clyde Johnson. My finger hovered over the envelope icon, as if I was standing at a crossroads. That's ridiculous. It was just an email. I clicked it open.

Scott, I haven't heard from you in over two weeks. I'm missing the frequent updates. How are things with the bed-and-breakfast? Don't forget, your future is on the line. Please update me TODAY.

Clyde Johnson

I tossed my phone to the side. My stress was climbing to new levels. Yeah, that was a mistake. The smell of Carol's pancakes downstairs found my stomach. I probably just needed to eat. Everything seemed less dramatic when I wasn't hungry.

I grabbed my flip-flops, pulled on a loose shirt, and headed down the stairs. The fourth step creaked in protest.

"I was going to fix that, but then I found I liked the warning," Carol called from the kitchen.

I grinned and stepped through the dining room into the kitchen and grabbed some plates from the cupboard.

The paint was peeling, and one cupboard door hung crooked. I tested it to find that all it needed was a new hinge.

I set the dishes down on the faded yellow tablecloth.

Carol sat down with a sigh, gesturing around the kitchen. "I'm just tired. This was always more my hubby's dream than mine. Then we thought we would have kids that might continue running it, but that didn't happen." She stabbed a pancake, bringing it to her own plate. "This home is full of wonderful memories, but hard ones too." She looked around the round table full of empty chairs. "Sometimes I wonder if there is a simpler life for me."

Warning signs flashed. *Proceed with caution.* Was she saying she wanted to sell? "It's a lot to run. I don't know how you've kept it up by yourself. It's not a one-person project."

Carol rarely let her exhaustion show, but in this moment, she couldn't keep the agonizing burden off her face. She wanted something else. At least some part of her did.

"I've had a lot of help . . . but never quite enough rest." She sighed.

I took a bite of pancake.

"Carol, do you want to run the B&B?" I wasn't sure how I wanted her to answer. I respected her and wanted her to have the life she wanted, but I also had my job on the line.

"No . . . I don't know . . ." She eyed him. "Don't go running off to the Raymond & Johnson Law firm on me."

My hands raised in front of me. "I wasn't planning on it . . . wait. What?" I leaned back in my chair.

Carol huffed. "The second you walked on to my property, I knew they must have sent you. You look exactly like the rest with shiny shoes, stiff suits, and flashy cars. I only let you stay because I would do anything for Marissa."

I didn't confirm or deny her claims.

"I'm curious. You've had offers. If this isn't what you want . . . why not sell?" I looked around the room. "This place is beautiful and has a story everywhere I look. But it's also a huge amount of property for one person . . . If you sell, you could—"

"Don't you start too. You sound like Betty Ann." Carol set down her fork with a thud. "She thinks we should all move to Florida."

I could see her walls snap back up. I had pushed too far. "Sorry, didn't mean to pry. It's a lovely place and I'm happy to help fix it up while I'm here."

I watched as Carol's frosty exterior melted.

"No, I'm sorry. I didn't mean to snap. Honestly, I would love to sell the place and rest these old bones."

The firm's offer would be more than enough for the dream she wanted. "Then why don't you?"

Carol looked around the kitchen, to the pictures all over the wall and scuffs and dings around her. "John loved this house and this town. I know what the place is worth. If it was all fixed up, it could be a nice resort. With the grounds and hot springs and all . . ." She paused and closed her eyes. "If I sell, some outsider is going to come in, change it all up, and make it all nice and fancy, which part of me wants . . . but then the people that live here, that work here, the ones that have their weddings on the lawn, their church BBQs, and then there are the boys." She shook her head, reaffirming her decision. "They wouldn't even have the money to use the place. They would have jobs here but not be able to use it with their families on their special days. I won't sell it because they need it. And John wouldn't want that, and neither would I. This summer Letty's daughter had her wedding here. I know they couldn't afford any of the venues nearby. It's important."

She was right. Everything would change. It would change her life. It would employ the town, but this would no longer be a community place. It would be a resort for visitors, not the locals. Unless . . .

"I wonder if, when you choose to sell, you could put certain stipulations in place? Maybe a certain percentage of the property has to be set aside for town use?"

She rolled her eyes. "I tried that once. They wouldn't even take me seriously. Plus, how can I trust them?"

True. "Right, but I'm a lawyer too. Maybe I could help you?" I wasn't sure how this would work since I was supposed to be getting it for Raymond & Johnson Law.

She angled her head to the side. "Do you think they would honor it though?"

I tipped my head back and forth. "It would depend on if they had to." And what I wanted for my future. I felt a pull at my conscience. I couldn't represent them both. I technically wasn't a part of their firm yet, and never would be until after the sale of Carol's property. A bit of a gray area, but I think I could make it work. Had she given up having Marissa run it?

"I'll think about it. If you promise to help me and make sure the town is taken care of, I'll consider it. Or maybe someone from the town would be interested?"

Would someone from town want it? Did Marissa want it? I doubted anyone could offer Carol what it was worth. "Perfect. Let's talk about it tonight after work." I stood and took my dish to the sink. This would be an awesome update to give Clyde Johnson to show the progress I was making, yet odd that I didn't want them to know yet that Carol was thinking about selling. This was the most progress I'd made in a long time. I decided I would wait to email him until I knew what Carol wanted.

I was early to the office and didn't know where to focus my building energy. I paced as I waited for Marissa to show up and was annoying even myself. I felt pulled in so many directions. Pulled to help Carol sell and get what she needed to retire and live the life she wanted. Pulled in the opposite direction to have the life I wanted. Pulled to the town's sense of community, and the boys need for good mentorship. Pulled toward Marissa and that kiss.

How would she act now, after the kiss? Would she push me away or let me in?

The front door ding and I wiped my hands on my suit pants. Stepping into the foyer, I watched as Marissa hung up her coat. I leaned up against the door frame, folding my arms tight and trying my best to imitate my brother Michael and his persona. How did he tilt his jaw? Right. Confidence. I took a deep breath as my arm brushed the fake plant outside the door, sending years of dust into the air and right into my throat. I felt a tickle in my nose and my eyes watered. There was a cough deep in my throat. I held it, pushing it down. Unfortunately, that made it so much worse. My chest seized, and I bent over coughing, trying to get air into my lungs.

I felt Marissa rush over and slap me on my back. "Scott, are you okay?"

I nodded but continued to cough. Oh sure, Marissa looked at me now.

She rushed over to the water dispenser and filled a cup.

Downing the water Marissa handed me seemed to help.

"Thanks." I smiled at her, with tears streaming down my cheeks.

Nailed it. Ugh.

"No problem." She wiped a tear from my cheek. "Are you feeling better?"

"Much." I realized I was feeling better, and more than just my lungs. My nervous energy from before had settled with Marissa this close. "Will you go out with me tonight?" I reached up and felt the soft ends of her hair in my fingers.

"Like as a date?" She bit her bottom lip, and I suppressed the urge to lean down and kiss her.

"I don't care what we call it. We can work on your London plan." I stared at her lips again. "I just want to spend time with you."

The front doorbell dinged.

"Elliot, where are you?"

My eyebrows rose. "I think that is the first time someone has come in here looking for me." Something like pride grew in my chest as I looked at a woman with a scowl, holding a scary-looking cat in her arms.

"Morning, Ashley." Marissa stepped up to my side.

"There you are." Ashley angled her nose at me. "Will you be a pie judge at county weigh-in day?" She reached up her hand and brushed my arm.

"What happened to the fair board judge?" Marissa stiffened.

"Letty paid that teenager last year, I know it. I think a big city lawyer would be the perfect impartial judge." Ashley sneered at Marissa. "As long as you aren't entering."

Marissa's eyes narrowed. "I'm not entering, but it wouldn't matter if I did."

"Right." Ashley rolled her eyes.

"I heard you are taking up photography. You shouldn't take pictures of people and send them without their consent." Marissa folded her arms and glared at Ashley.

Ashley turned from Marissa. "Mr. Elliot, will you do this town the great service of being a pie judge at the fair?" Ashley looked up at me, fluttering her eyelashes as her cat hissed in her left arm.

I felt like I was standing on the outside of a storm and did not know what to do, where to take refuge.

Marissa stepped closer to my side, and I liked this sudden show of jealousy from her.

"I enjoy pie. When is it?"

Ashley giggled. "Silly boy." She swatted at my shoulder. "It's always the first Saturday in November, sugar plum."

I could be mistaken, but I think Marissa might have growled. I grinned.

"Ok, yeah . . . I can make that work."

"Oh, thank you so much." She winked and sauntered out the door.

Marissa shook her head. "Be careful."

I smirked. "With Ashley or the pies?"

"Both." Marissa bristled. "Definitely both."

Chapter Twenty-Two

MARISSA

I put on another layer of deodorant. It wasn't anything serious. Scott wanted to plan my London trip, which meant he wasn't thinking of me staying. I grabbed my pink lip gloss and ran my fingers through hair I had taken the time to curl, even though I knew it would be flat in an hour.

Did I want tonight to be a date? It was safer if it wasn't. The front doorbell rang. *I better get that before Nan pesters him.* I ran through the living room and threw the door open.

"Hey." It came out breathy. I cleared my throat. "Hey, come on in, I need to grab my jacket."

He looked amazing. He wore a light-blue button up with khakis and his hair was gelled. As always, his scent wrapped me up like a warm cinnamon roll. I held the door open as he passed and, I admit it, I checked out his backside and was not disappointed.

Nan came hustling in from her bedroom to the front door.

"Good evening, Nan." Scott walked toward Nan and gave her a quick side hug.

"It is now," she wiggled her eyebrows at him, causing Scott to chuckle.

I grabbed my jacket and gave Nan a hug. "I'll be home soon. Let me know if you need anything. I know Bert is out of town until Thursday."

Nan rolled her eyes. "I'm not an invalid. Now go have fun on your date."

My cheeks flushed as I checked Scott's expression. He gave away nothing. "It's not a date, Nan. I told you Scott is helping me with my London trip." I glanced at Scott, but his face was stoic.

Nan peeked around me and looked at Scott. "Oh trust me honey, it's both."

Scott grinned, and I tried to keep the jitters down. It had been so long since I had felt this excited about anything. Especially considering the *date* word kept coming up.

Scott walked me to his car and opened the door, helping me in. He rushed around and climbed in his side.

I tucked my hair behind my right ear. "Sorry about Nan."

"Don't be. I love her spunk." Scott put the car into drive and turned down his talk radio. It made sense that Scott listened to talk radio. All practical and serious. I smiled. "What, not wanting to listen to a fiscally-responsible and maze strategy podcast?"

Scott shook his head. "I already listened to this week's episode."

Wait, was he serious? Was there a podcast about that?

He chuckled.

I grinned and smacked his arm. "Ha ha. What's the plan for tonight?" I shifted in my leather seat to see him better.

Scott shrugged. "Movie and dinner? Figured we could talk about what you want to do in London on the drive." He looked nervous. "Is that too boring?" His lips pulled down in a frown.

"Nope. Sounds fun. What movie?"

Scott's shoulders relaxed, and he nodded to the sticky note

near the glove compartment. "There is a list of movies and times. I thought you might like to pick. I'm fine with anything." It did not surprise me he was thoroughly prepared. I looked through the list.

"Oh, this one is a romcom, and I saw the trailer last week. It looks fun."

Scott grinned and nodded. "Sounds great."

It sounded great. Dinner and a movie with Scott sounded really great. Is that bad? How serious are things? Do I need to tell him about the no-babies thing? That seemed a little premature. Right? Or I could go with "Hey, I know we kissed one time, and this may or may not be our first date, so you're obviously thinking about what it would be like to marry me."

I looked out the window and watched the sagebrush hills. A tightness in my stomach tried to grow, but I reminded myself to take a slow breath. I didn't need to rush anything. We kissed, sure, but we haven't talked anything long-term. Dates with Scott before we both went our separate ways sounded fun. Fun wasn't serious.

"Is a romcom with dinner too much of a date?" I glanced in his direction.

Scott glanced my way. "Would it bother you if it was?"

My stomach erupted in a volcano of butterflies. I pulled on my undershirt. I wanted this.

Scott glanced over at me as he passed a tractor with flashing lights making its way to another field to harvest. "I know you have rules . . . but I would—"

"I may reconsider those rules." At the moment, I was reconsidering everything. From thoughts of returning to Hillsdale and running the B&B, to the no-date rules . . . everything felt new. Exciting and scary.

Scott grinned. "Perfect. Let me know if there is anything I can do to help you restructure the rules because I would love this to be a date."

My hand started shaking. Whew. Okay. Date. I mean, I already kissed the man. Why does a date seem scary? "What about the London trip?"

I couldn't stop myself from asking. Would it ruin the moment?

"I won't stop you if that is what you want, and I'll still help you plan it. I have no intention of getting between you and your happiness." He was serious. This wasn't just about me. He had a future that didn't include me either.

"What about your plan? Penthouse suite and all that. I didn't see this on that dream board," I gestured to me.

Scott chuckled and shifted his arm closer to me. "We could take everything one day at a time. No need to 'ruin it all with logic', as you like to say." He winked at me.

I loved his smile. Oh my, I was not prepared for this version of Scott. It shouldn't surprise me. He was fully committed to everything he did. *How would it feel if that was all pointed at me?*

I slid my arm to the center console until it brushed against Scott's.

"Let's call it a date then," I grinned.

"Perfect." Scott reached over and laced his hand in mine. "Let's go to the movie first, then dinner, because we can make the earlier showing." Scott looked at me. "Is that okay with you?" His eyes locked with mine and I had to remind myself to breathe. I could only grin and nod.

Throughout the rest of the drive, each time Scott rubbed his thumb along the length of the back of my hand, tingles rushed through my veins like miniature energy shots. We walked into the theater hand-in-hand, and he let me pick the seats. Scott asked if I wanted any popcorn, but my stomach wasn't ready for food.

The lights went out in the theater, and I was drawn to Scott like a magnet. It was a good thing this theater had arm rests between us because it was the only thing keeping me from retrying that kiss. I couldn't concentrate on the movie. Several times the audience would laugh, and I had to refocus. The only thing that caught and kept my attention was Scott. Scott brought my hand to his lips, and I felt his warm mouth press into the back of my hand. Scott must have been thinking about our kiss too. I was attracted to him the moment I met him in the corn maze, but it was much stronger now. The bands around my heart were loosening.

Was this okay? It was safer because it was short-term, but that didn't mean it would break my heart any less when it ended. I reminded myself that this was for fun, and I shouldn't get attached.

At the end, the lights turned on and Scott leaned in closer. "Did you like it?"

I grinned. "What? The movie?"

He laughed and nodded. Shoot, what was I supposed to say? Did he like it? I shrugged and was honest. "I don't know what happened. I kept getting distracted."

He chuckled and raised my hand to his lips and brushed a kiss along the back, causing my arm to erupt in goosebumps. "Me too."

Whew, I was playing with fire. Hot, hot fire. He grinned. We stood to leave the theater, but I didn't drop his hand. It was awkward to walk out of the row with my arm twisted behind me. I relaxed my grip to drop his hand, but my hand stayed in his. I glanced over my shoulder as I shuffled through chairs. Scott was watching me, his eyes still stormy. My foot caught on the chair in front of me, and I pitched forward. In an instant, Scott's arms were around my waist, pulling me back into his chest.

"You okay?" Concern etched on his face, and he leaned down and kissed my forehead. I shivered as his nose brushed against my neck. I cleared my throat.

"Yep, should just watch where I'm going."

He chuckled, and I made it to the end of the aisle without further embarrassment.

"Dinner?"

"Sounds great."

We went into a little cafe and ordered burgers, fries, and hot cocoa with whipped cream and cinnamon. I felt the heat rush to my cheeks.

"I did this way before I found out you smelled like cinnamon. It's the best." I blanched. *Why did I say that out loud? Ugh!* I closed my eyes and tried to erase the moment.

He chuckled, and the server left with our orders.

"Cinnamon, huh?" The left side of his mouth turned up in a grin.

"Maybe." I felt my cheeks turn bright red.

"I think you smell like green apples."

That was my shampoo. I liked that he'd noticed.

"Tell me more about you." I wanted to remember every piece of him so I could remember him when I left, or when he moved on. We wouldn't last, but the memories could.

"What do you want to know?" Scott reached across the table and took my hand.

"Anything, everything?" I shrugged. With the trunk-or-treat over Halloween was on my mind. "How about a fun Halloween costume?"

Scott looked up at the ceiling in thought. "Once, when I was in second grade, I wanted to be a vampire for Halloween at school. Well, we didn't have Halloween makeup, but mom promised her makeup was even better. She went and grabbed her makeup and put it all over my face. She was so happy and loved doing it, but I was wearing my mom's makeup . . . to school . . ." Scott smiled and shook his head. "I was so embarrassed, I knew that the kids were going to tell. I hid most of recess so my class wouldn't know I was wearing women's makeup. Later that day, I got a big prize for being the most mysterious vampire. I guess they all thought I was in character, hiding in the corner with my cape."

I could picture him huddled in the corner with his cape drawn around him. We both laughed so much we cried. The rest of the night we shared stories of growing up, mostly silly ones, but some of the hard things too. I brought up London, and what I wanted to see. The drive home went by too fast, and I realized I had spent five hours with Scott, but it felt like only minutes.

I was falling for him. He was charming. He was strong, but soft in all the right ways. My heart beat like I was on the edge of something scary and I didn't know if I wanted to run toward it or far, far away.

Scott walked me to the front door after the date. We'd held hands the whole night, and I wasn't in any hurry to drop his. I wondered if I could ever let go. The thought sent chills through me. At the front door, his stormy eyes searched mine before they stared at my lips. He was going to kiss me once more.

Was I ready for this? Did I want to be more than friends? This kiss would differ from before, not a quick moment of joy, but the start of something.

Scott bent to me, searching my eyes for permission. I knew what way I wanted to fall. I wanted to fall into Scott. Into his safe arms. Into his serious side and his goofy one too.

It wouldn't work. We were both leaving. My thoughts screamed in protest.

Ugh. No planning. Just falling. I reminded myself I didn't like plans anyway.

I grinned and leaned towards him. His lips parted as he breathed me in. We finished the perfect night with the perfect kiss. It was sweet and earnest at the same time and left me wanting more. I reached my arms around his neck and pulled him into a hug. He pressed his lips onto my forehead. "Thank you for tonight," Scott whispered against my hair.

I looked into his eyes and grinned. "It was amazing. I'm glad I changed my rules." I bit my bottom lip and his eyes dropped to my lips once more. He grinned, but then stepped back.

"You better go in or I won't let you go for a while." I felt the fire in his gaze.

I chuckled. "Thanks for the date." I turned the doorknob.

"Anytime . . . like any time."

I sighed and leaned into the door as I opened it behind me and stepped through.

"I told you it was a date," Nan hollered as I shut the door.

Chapter Twenty-Three

MARISSA

"Look Marissa, honey." Nan sat on my bed, waking me up with a show of her hand, which now held a ring with a square diamond on it. "I'm getting married!" She clapped beside me as I sat up.

It had been a week since my date with Scott and it felt like yesterday and forever at the same time. Bert got home a few days ago after visiting his grown children, but I had been so focused on things with Scott that I had hardly noticed his return. Nan pushed her hand closer to me.

"What? Wait. When did this happen?" I rubbed the sleep from my eyes. I had stayed up too late texting Scott.

Nan giggled and pulled me into a hug. "Bert proposed last night. He had white roses and everything." She looked down at her hand with swollen knuckles and sunspots, staring at the ring that now glittered on her finger.

"Wow. You're engaged!" I shook my head, trying to make sense of it all. I'd always imagined that if I had to live my life one day without Nan, it would be because she died, not because she got married. "Does it seem fast? You have only been dating a few months . . ."

"Oh honey, at my age, I could die in a month." She reached down and squeezed my hand.

My chest tightened at the thought of Nan leaving. Then I would be alone. And what would happen to Nan if Bert died? He was pushing early eighties. This was all happening faster than I had imagined. Would he take care of her? I had watched him fawn over her, and then laughed as she tried to learn to text so she could message him. I had to admit, she seemed happier than ever.

"Are you sure this is what you want?" I looked down at her soft hand on top of mine.

"Oh my sweet Mar." She reached up and cupped my cheek. "I know you've been scared of love and people leaving you behind ever since your parents died." I closed my eyes and leaned into her touch. She waited for me to look at her again. "Trust me, my dear, you get far more from love than what it takes when it's gone."

Gone. My chest hollowed. I was better off having loved Nan and my parents. I could see that. But it was still.

"The love I shared with your grandpa was fleeting, but it gave me your mom, and your parents love gave me you." Nan pulled me into a hug, and she rested her frail head on my shoulder.

"Yes, but what about when it leaves?" I whispered, voicing my fear. I was going to end up alone.

"Love doesn't leave." She patted my back. "It grows, and it changes. It's always there, a whisper of happy memories and shared kisses. I've never regretted loving. It has blessed me to love and to be loved by many." She pulled out of our hug and looked at me. "And it has blessed you too."

I thought of my scars inside and out. "But it can hurt."

"It only hurts because you care, which is far better than the alternative. Which is to not love, or care for anyone. Living life in a shell of existence is no way to live."

I thought about how I had opened up to Scott, and about

facing my fear of running the B&B. I even met Carol there for breakfast yesterday and we had talked about her memories of my mom growing up. It had been scary but good. Maybe Nan was right. Maybe love was worth the risk.

But this wedding wasn't my choice or about me. It was Nan's. "Does he make you happy?"

A wide smile split her face. "He does. I'm thrilled. He makes me laugh, and it feels like I'm a teenager again instead of a decrepit old lady." She chuckled.

She knew the risks as much as I did. If she was happy, I would be happy for her. Even if it pulled her away from me. I leaned my head against hers. Her white wispy hair tickled my cheek, and I let out a deep breath. "I'm happy for you, Nan." She looked at her ring, rubbing it with her thumb.

"I've lived a full life, Mar, but even now I can still find such happiness. Life is a gift." Nan patted my leg and leaned her rounded back away from me. "Now, I know you're planning on running off on a trip to Europe, but you have to be back for my wedding."

"Wouldn't miss it for the world." I kissed the top of her head. Wow . . . Nan was getting married.

"Any more thoughts about taking over the B&B when you get home?" Nan leaned into my shoulder.

The thought of returning to Hillsdale and setting down roots used to terrify me. But the trunk-or-treat was over, and I realized I was missing my connection to the property. I loved the idea of helping people in the community. How or where would I even start?

"Who told you?" There were no secrets in Hillsdale.

Nan waved off my question. "Oh, Carol mentioned she was hopeful you were at least considering it this time around."

"I can say for the first time, I'm considering it. As well as other options. I don't know . . . it seems like a lot to take on."

"Right, it's like you need a hot, tall, strong business owner to partner with." Nan grinned. "I wonder where you could find one of those . . ."

I rolled my eyes. "Nan, it's not that serious with Scott. We're both planning on leaving Hillsdale. This is all about temporary fun."

"Mmm . . ." Nan wiggled her eyebrows. "Well, you better get ready for work, and I'm meeting Arlene for brunch to tell her the news." Nan hopped off the bed with more energy than she had shown for a while. Either the new hip was working wonders or Bert had put a spring in her step. She was willing to give love a chance again. I smiled as I lay back on my bed.

I grabbed my phone and texted the group chat.

Marissa: Guess we are planning a spring wedding!!

Rose: . . .

Faith: Wow! Marissa, I'm happy for you, but I don't know if you know Scott that well . . .

Did they think I meant me? I laughed.

Marissa: NO

Marissa: Not me!

Faith: . . .

Rose: HAHA it's Nan!!

Marissa: Yep!

Faith: Aww, that is sweet! I'm so happy for her.

Rose: She's crazy, but I love her.

Rose: Wait—is the trip still a go?

Marissa: That's the plan.

London was the plan, right? I thought about Nan and her opening herself up to love and life. Was I running to London like Carol suggested, or was it something else?

Faith: I LOVE WEDDINGS!

Faith posted a set of happy clapping and party GIFs.

Rose: You would. When do you leave for London?

Marissa: I don't know, I'm still figuring some things out.
Rose: . . .
Faith: Like Scott? Or about running the B&B when you get back!!

She sent kissing and dancing emojis.

Marissa: Whoa Faith, slow down!
Rose: No longer playing the friend delusion card?
Rose: Have you told him about the kids situation?

Had I told him I couldn't have kids . . . no. Was that really his business yet?

Marissa: Ugh, just let me live in this moment.
Rose: We are coming over for lunch on Sunday. Let Nan know, looks like we have a lot to talk about.
Marissa: Alright, gonna be late for work. Talk later.

I was not looking forward to all their questions, but they could all wait until this weekend.

My phone continued to go off like a machine gun. I refused to open it. If I did, I wouldn't be able to keep myself from spilling all my feelings for Scott and I wasn't ready to say them out loud yet.

I hurried through the motions of getting ready. Scott had been picking me up on the way to work this week, saying something about not trusting my car to not dent his.

Rose was wrong. Looking too far ahead would ruin everything. Better to just enjoy the moment. Because in this moment, I was happy.

I heard Scott pull up. I gave Nan a quick kiss, congratulated her again, and rushed out the door.

Scott was halfway up the sidewalk by the time I made it outside. His cheeks were red from the cold, and he was blowing on his hands. It was official. All the leaves had dropped and so had the temperatures. I rushed the distance between us and threw my arms around him.

I felt his warm breath on my cheek as he let out a little chuckle. "I should've known you would be a morning person." I felt him smile. His hands traced down my back and along my arms. Grabbing my left hand, we turned toward his car. "It's freezing. You have more than that jean jacket, right?"

"Yeah, I wear this one as long as possible." Based on my shivering, it was time to swap it out for winter.

He looked at me from the side, waiting for why it mattered.

"It was my dad's."

He nodded and gave my hand a little squeeze, then held the car door open for me. Once in the car, he adjusted the heat. "I should've guessed. At least he left you a cool jacket. I would be forced to wear bright Hawaiian shirts if I wanted to wear things that belonged to my dad."

I snorted as I took in his button-up and khakis. He had eased up on the suits, but Hawaiian shirts were a bit much. "I can't picture it."

He shivered. "Me either. I used to think my dad and I were opposites. But now I'm not sure."

What did he mean by that?

Scott reached over and picked up my hand, kissing the back of it. "You can tell me soon enough. He's coming into work today."

"Wait . . . seriously?" I wasn't sure that I liked the idea of meeting his dad. What did that mean about us?

"Yep, he is coming to check in on the office and help for the day."

Oh right, he was coming for work . . . not me. What was I thinking? I sunk deeper into the warm leather heated seats. Luxury sure had its perks. Scott chuckled and turned the heat higher.

As we pulled into the parking lot, I was surprised at the beat-up old truck waiting in the parking lot.

"Not a shiny fancy car?" I tipped my head at the truck.

"Nope. I think my dad would have no problem fitting into a place like Hillsdale. He could live here forever without a problem."

"What about you?" I was still trying to make out Scott's character. Part of him seemed like he couldn't wait to move on with his big fancy plans, then another side seemed content here in Hillsdale. I held my breath, unsure what I wanted him to say. He looked down at our combined hands.

"Is it bad if I don't know?"

I had no idea what I wanted, and that he was questioning his future filled me with hope. I didn't need all the answers right now. I could enjoy this for now. "Nope. I hate plans, remember?"

He laughed. "Oh, I know." He opened his door and came around to meet me. Holding my hand, he walked us to his dad's truck.

Should I drop Scott's hand? What would his dad think? I decided I would let Scott lead with the whole dad thing. The door to the truck groaned in protest at opening.

"Scott, my boy." His dad stepped out in a green and yellow Hawaiian shirt and cargo pants. He hugged his son. There was something about his dad's face that was cheery, like he knew a joke and was excited to tell it.

Scott hugged his dad without dropping my hand. Scott held up our hands. "This is Marissa."

"Oh yes." Scott's dad pulled me into an enormous hug and his warm bear arms drew me in. He stepped back. "Thanks for helping my son. Heard he was quite lost here without you."

I shrugged. "I'm just glad he didn't fire me after the black eye."

His dad threw his head back and laughed loudly. "That was you," he chuckled. "Small world."

"Yeah, well I'm freezing. Let's go inside and go over the books." Scott headed to the door.

"There's my Scotty boy, always so serious." He grinned. "Just a second." His dad turned to his truck and grabbed a box of cookies off the seat. "Here are the cookies you asked for from Bella's Bakery. I even got extra of the sprinkle kind you asked for." He looked at me. "Have you developed a sweet tooth, Scotty?" He grinned and shut the truck door and started walking to the front door.

"Something like that." Scott smiled at me and jitters took over my stomach. Although maybe it was just about the cookies.

We all went through the office door. Scott was different from his dad. He was less colorful and not as loud, but there was something deeper that was the same. I couldn't quite put my finger on what it was.

Chapter Twenty-Four

SCOTT

It was pie and pumpkin judging day at the fairgrounds. *Apparently, that was a thing.* As I walked toward the long white building on the Hillsdale fairgrounds, I realized I must have missed a memo. Everyone was dressed in boots, jeans, and a flannel button-up. At least I got the jeans part right. I had made myself change out of the dress slacks, even though I was a judge. There was a small petting zoo with the animals protesting the cold, food vendors, and a stage blasting country music.

Somewhere along the way, I'd begun to feel differently in Hillsdale, less of an outsider. I now planned an extra thirty minutes every time I went to the grocery store, for when people waved me over to chat. I saw Mrs. Bates at the Mercantile the other day. She was buying a rake and milk. I apologized for our first encounter and told her I would make it up to her by raking her leaves that night. The woman may have had an army of yard gnomes, but she made the best homemade jam I had ever tasted.

It was certainly a unique place, quirky but loyal to their own.

"Hey. You ready for this?" Marissa snuck beside me and

wrapped her arms around my waist. I smiled down at her. I loved that as soon as she was near me, we were holding hands or touching. And kissing. Lots of kissing.

"Should I be worried?"

"Yep. Come on, pie contest this way." Marissa pulled me to the large white building. "A word to the wise. Be careful, these ladies seem sweet on the outside, but if you don't give their pie a good review, it's likely to turn lethal."

My eyebrows shot up, and I looked at Marissa. Was she teasing me again? She looked serious.

I followed Marissa up the wooden ramp into the building. It had warped floors, plastic folding tables, chairs, and space heaters sprinkled throughout.

"Oh, thank goodness." Ashley was wearing a dress that made me feel cold. She sighed and rushed to my side. "I was worried you might not make it."

Marissa stiffened beside me.

Ashley eyed Marissa. "Did you learn to bake and enter a pie?" Ashley's words sounded sweet but were full of venom. "I would've looked after Mr. Elliot for you if you were busy." She reached up and touched my arm. "By the way there sugar, I'm not sure if Marissa has told you about her past, but—"

Marissa flinched and pulled away. I leaned down and kissed the top of her head. "I'm always happier when Marissa is with me, and if there is anything Marissa wants to tell me about her past, I'll hear it from her." My voice was bold and sure. I refused to let this harpy hurt her. At that moment, I realized how true my statement was. I was relaxed and happy when Marissa was at my side.

Ashley stepped back. "Yes, of course. How silly of me." Ashley's lips pouted, and she turned to join the others.

Marissa relaxed and leaned back into me. I looked down at her. She was smiling up at me, then reached up and kissed my cheek. I had been proud of a lot of my accomplishments in school and life, but somehow it all paled next to making Marissa happy.

Marissa led me to the front room and showed me to my seat. Two other men with deep scowls and gray hair sat beside me. I smiled at them. "Lucky for us to get to eat all these pies. I'm Scott."

They both nodded gruffly and stuck out their hands. "Name's George, this is Doug, and trust me, no luck here boy, you'll see."

The man on his left turned to a stern woman wearing an apron at his side. "Now Martha, I already told you, I have no desire to be a judge this year. You were mad at me for three months last time."

She put her hands on her hips and glared. "You'll judge, and maybe choose the right pie as the winner this time, or you'll have no pie for the rest of the year." She scowled and left to join the rows of folded chairs.

"Blasted woman, this is a trap if there ever was one." Doug pulled his hat over his eyes.

Hmm, this might be tricky.

A few teenagers with 4H leadership shirts began bringing out plate after plate of pie and sat them on a table. Cream pies, fruit pies, ones piled with meringue, and others covered with intricate dough . . . art? The room was packed with about thirty pie bakers. Each sat on the edge of their seats and stared at me and the fellow judges. Poised, ready for an attack.

Ashley stood up from her chair in the front and cleared her throat. "I think it would be easiest if we start with the same varieties of pie, then narrow it from there." She chirped. "Let's do pumpkin first."

A gray haired woman from the back jumped to her feet. "You are trying to cheat again. Hoping the judges will get bored before they make it to the cream pies!"

Ashley smirked. "Now, Marie, no one can know who made what pie. That's confidential."

Marie scoffed. "Ashley, with you, nothing is confidential."

"What does that mean?" She raised her hand over her heart.

There were cheers as some women stood and shuffled around

each other, forming groups. They all began yelling, and I was sure I saw dentures hit the ground.

This was escalating into a full-on pie brawl. I stood and held both hands in front of me. "Excuse me." I waved my arms and looked at my fellow judges. They offered no help, only pulled their hats lower over their eyes. I put my fingers into my mouth and whistled.

Everyone stopped and looked at me. I gazed over the stunned faces and met Marissa's kind eyes. She gave me a wink and a nod of encouragement.

I exhaled. I had seen some disorderly courtrooms, but this might take the prize.

"Excuse me, ladies," I nodded at them. "If you'll all please take your seats." I knew how to use my voice to make a suggestion feel like a command. They all glared but accommodated. "Now there seems to be a debate on where to start."

The uproar began again, but I raised my hand, silencing it before it got out of control. "I believe I have a solution." I moved over to Doug on my right and reached for his hat. "May I?" The man shrugged and handed me his hat. I took it and asked one teenager if they could find me some paper and a pencil. After I had all the needed supplies, I wrote the different pies on paper and put them in the hat.

"Ok, we'll draw out the order for pie tasting. It will be impartial." I walked back to Doug. "Would you mind pulling a name out of the hat?" He looked up at me in fear, his eyes glancing toward the women. It was obvious he had no wish to be part of the choosing. "Very well, both of you judges mix up the names and hold them up high above my head and I'll reach up and draw the order." I turned to the room of women. "Any objections to this plan?"

"I still think we should start with pumpkin," Ashley grumbled.

"Draw the order," shouted someone from the back. I nodded and pulled out a slip of paper, unfolding it. "The first type of pie

judged will be . . ." I unfolded the paper. "Cream. Followed by . . ."
I reached back into the hat. "Fruit." I heard a cheer from the back.
I continued the process. "Next meringues." I reached up for the
last. "Which leaves," I unfolded the paper, "pumpkin."

"That's not fair," Ashley whined.

"I assure you, it's as fair as I could make it on the spot." I
gestured at the teens caught in the cross hairs. "Now, if you'll
please bring out the pies in that order."

"Which one is first in each category?" The teen whispered,
afraid to start another riot.

"This year, we will have each category brought out in alphabet-
ical order. I believe first will be," I searched the table of pies,
"banana cream. I suggest next year you set up a rotation on which
you all vote and agree."

I sat back down in my chair. It felt good to solve a problem
with words instead of fists. Words could do damage, but they
could also heal and diffuse.

For the next forty-five minutes, I tried pie after pie, making
notes in my phone notepad, being meticulous and fair. I praised
something specific about each bite, which was difficult with the
mustard banana cream pie. I noted textures, colors, and overall
taste.

We needed to come up with a winner, runner-up, best crust,
and filling. The other two judges were happy to let me take the
lead. If I had a guess, it was because both of their wives were somewhere in that crowd. We needed to collaborate without witnesses.

"Ladies. Thank you so much for your pies and the time you
spent making these masterpieces. I cannot speak to other years, but
these are some of the best pies I've tasted, other than my mother's."
I smiled, and they all chuckled. "Now, please excuse us. We'll be
back with the results in fifteen minutes." I nodded to the other
two judges. "Gentlemen, let's go for a drive."

I stepped over to Marissa, giving her a quick kiss. "Be right
back."

"Good luck," she whispered. I grinned back at her, fighting the urge to kiss her again.

Both judges followed me out of the room, doing their best to dodge their wives' glares. Once we sat in my car, the two men livened up a bit. After being sworn to secrecy, they had great insights to offer with the pies.

A few loops around the town, and we'd reached our decisions. Returning to the building, a crowd had gathered. I stood in front of the room with the ribbons and a rolling pin trophy.

"Again, I would like to reiterate that the pies were all wonderful, and I was grateful to be a part of the judging process." I took the paper out of my pocket. "The winners and runner ups are as follows. Best overall pie this year went to pie C in the cream pie section. Runner-up was pie D in fruit. The best crust went to pie A in meringues and the best filling to fruit pie A."

The 4H teen leadership held up the pies that won, followed by hoots and jeers. Although the biggest smile of all belonged to my fellow judge Doug, whose wife Martha was crying happy tears and running up to take her trophy.

I knew I was walking on thin ice trying not to offend anyone, but everyone seemed to accept the results without a fight. Ashley was not pleased, but I was glad for it . . . which may have been childish of me.

As we left the building, Marissa squeezed my hand and leaned her head on my shoulder. "Now that was impressive. You know, if you weren't already one, I'd say you should become a lawyer."

I chuckled. "Glad to know I made the right choice to diffuse the baking club. Haven't had many opportunities to practice actual law here." We wandered to a little wooden picnic table to the left.

"Hey Mar." A woman with long brown hair and acrylic nails came up to the table, followed by a blonde. These were her friends from the corn maze. I had heard a lot about them, but had never been introduced. I stood and held out my hand.

"Hey, nice to meet you. I'm Scott."

The one with the extra-long lashes tipped her chin. "Umm, yeah, everyone knows who you are."

I nodded. High heels, long dark hair, painted nails, and sass for days. "You must be Rose." I pointed to the shy, smiling blonde. "And Faith, I presume?" She gave a shy smile and nodded.

"It's almost time for the pumpkin weigh-ins," Faith spoke softly. "I figured you wouldn't want to miss it."

Marissa stood and nodded at me. "You coming?"

"Is this *the* pumpkin weigh-in?" I leaned away so I could see her eyes.

"The one and only." She giggled and pulled me off the bench. "Let's go see if Frank keeps his title." She kept my hand in hers as we walked across the open grass field toward a dirt parking lot. "In fact, I bet you'll have some new cases on Monday all about pumpkin drama."

"Lucky me," I said.

Actually, I did feel lucky. With Marissa's hand placed in mine and the bonus of not having to take any older ladies to the hospital, today had been awesome.

"Good to see Mar finally got you out of wearing suits." Rose looked over her shoulder. "I also think we need to get you some cowboy boots."

Faith clapped. "Oh, and a big hat!"

"No, no hat," I stated. "That's where I would draw the line." Marissa giggled and reached up and pressed a kiss on my cheek.

Chapter Twenty-Five

MARISSA

I sat on the worn navy-blue couch flipping through wedding magazines that Faith had brought over. Weddings used to be an avoided topic, but I didn't mind it as much as I thought I would. I flipped the page. Wow! A cookie bar. If I got married, that would be a must. *Wait. Focus on Nan.* More and more, I had wondered what it would look like if it was my wedding we were planning.

Faith squealed in excitement. "Oh, Nan look. What about a Cinderella cake?"

Nan chuckled and looked at the page. "Faith, I don't think "fairy tale" is quite my style. At my age, I'm more the fairy godmother than a princess."

Faith tipped her head and looked at the cake. "Nan, everyone is a princess at their wedding."

Rose turned the page to show Nan what she was looking at. "What about this cake?"

"Oh geez, Rose." Nan leaned forward to get a better look. "Does that one have skulls on it?"

Rose shrugged and kept turning pages. "I guess that's a no. Where are you thinking of having it?"

Nan sat back in her chair. "I'm thinking something simple."

Faith scooted closer to me. "So . . . just planning Nan's wedding, right?" Her bright blues shined with hope. "You've been with Scott an awful lot."

"Whoa, Faith. Slow down. That's temporary." But nothing about the way I felt was temporary.

Faith tilted up a shoulder. "What if you didn't leave?"

Rose sat up straight. "Oh please, she has been wanting to leave forever. Besides, Scott is hot and all, but I bet London guys with accents are like Scott dipped in chocolate and served with ice cream."

It was hard to picture someone I would rather see Europe with than Scott. Between working together and spending each night texting, I couldn't imagine anything without Scott.

Would he want to go see it with me?

What if he was just playing some game? Stuck in this town and only with me for as long as that lasted. His dream board had no woman on it, and I would never fit in with his penthouse vision. Had his dreams changed? Or been put on hold? What about my dreams?

"Earth to Marissa." Rose was waving her magazine in front of my face.

"Oh, sorry." I blushed.

Nan giggled. "Someone was dreaming of Scott again?"

"No stop. It's not like that."

Nan looked at me. "Oh, please! My eyesight isn't that bad."

"Ok fine, it isn't like that for him. Maybe?"

"What do you mean? That man has been here every night drooling over you." Nan gestured to the place on the couch that had become Scott's spot.

"I admit I like him, but it can't go anywhere."

"Why?" Nan shifted in her chair.

"He's leaving. He doesn't know about the whole kid thing."

"Oh Marissa, you are more than your reproductive parts." Nan waved her hands in the air. "I'm not getting married to pop out babies."

"I know, but he might expect something else." I leaned further into the couch.

"Then ask him." Nan rolled her eyes.

"Is London off now?" Rose slapped down her magazine and scowled.

I rubbed my forehead, feeling a headache forming.

"No, Ugh . . . it doesn't feel as pressing right this second?" I leaned back on the couch.

"Ugh. It is, I knew it," Rose said.

"Rose, relax. Give her time to figure it out," Faith pleaded.

I sat forward. "Can't you just let me enjoy this?"

Faith bumped her shoulder. "What if he is the guy?"

"Then tell him." Rose's eyebrows lifted in challenge.

I held her stare. "Weren't you saying it doesn't matter? It doesn't change my worth."

Rose leaned forward, not backing down. "Oh, telling him isn't to test your worth, it's testing his."

Faith reached down and squeezed my hand. "Telling him is not a terrible idea. It isn't about your worth, or Scott's worth." She glared at Rose. "But it's something you should have a conversation about, before it hurts more if . . ."

"If he is a complete dirtbag," Rose threw in.

This felt scary. If I said something, it could change everything. "Guys, look, yes, I like him, but I'm questioning everything right now. I don't know . . ."

There was a big part of me that thought my reproductive organs shouldn't make a difference, but the smaller part of me whispered, *but what if it does?*

Faith nodded. "Marissa, why have you wanted to go to London?"

"Because it's where my dad took my mom, and we talked about going when I graduated."

"Why else?" Faith prodded. Leave it to Faith to not take my simple answer.

"It's away from the expectations of Hillsdale." I closed my eyes, surprised by my confession.

"What expectations?" Faith asked.

I tried to form the right words, but they jumbled and spilled over each other as I spoke. "I don't know. Everyone here has the same routine. They go to school, get married, then have babies. The end." I sat back on the couch, my fingers urging to fiddle with my shirt. "It's what everyone talks about. How are the kids? How are the grandkids? How is motherhood treating you? I change those plans." A piece inside of me fell in on itself. "They couldn't have that with me. Everyone here knows that." I wiped the tears from my cheeks, unsure when they appeared or how I had started this conversation. "Everyone here looks at me like I have no future worth having. Like I'm broken." I don't think I had ever said that out loud before, but every word rang true.

Faith leaned against my side. "Are you?"

"Am I what?"

"Broken? Do you have a future still worth having?" I felt Rose move on the couch to sit on my other side.

"Yes . . . No . . . I don't know." All my nerves rose to the top of my skin, burning with heat.

Faith squeezed my hand. "Maybe that's where you should start? I still have the contact information for my friend who's a counselor, if you want it."

Faith had pressed counseling the last few years. Maybe she was onto something.

"I don't want to talk about it anymore tonight. I'll think about it, but maybe I should figure out if he wants something serious before I talk about babies." I wiped away all the evidence of tears.

My phone vibrated. Several texts from Scott were waiting on the screen. I couldn't help but smile.

"Bye." Rose bumped my shoulder and grinned.

I scoffed. "What? No, I'm staying and helping plan this thing."

Nan yawned dramatically. "I might need a nap."

Faith grinned and nodded for me to answer my phone. "I have lesson plans calling my name."

Scott: I miss you.

Scott: What are you up to? Want to go to lunch?

"Are you sure you are ready for a break, Nan?"

She rubbed her eyes and forced a yawn.

Marissa: Sure.

I heard a knock at the front door and jumped. Was that Scott already? Did it look like I was crying? I dried my eyes one more time and took a deep breath.

Reaching the front door, I opened it, surprised to see him. I stepped back. How long had he been there? Had he been listening?

Scott's mouth lifted in a shy grin.

"Hey Marissa, sorry to just stop by, you didn't answer your phone and well . . . I was going to come knock, but then I tried to text one more time." He blushed. "This is awkward that I'm already here. Should I go home and come back later?" He flinched.

Nan hollered from inside. "Who is it?"

"It's Scott." I could hear the giggles. We couldn't stay here. "Let me grab my phone and jacket." I closed the door, leaving him on the porch. There was no way I was having him inside the house right now. Who knew what they would ask?

"Did you leave him on the porch?" Faith sounded disappointed.

"That was rude, Marissa." Nan stood to let him in.

"We are heading to lunch, and I know if he came in, you guys would bombard him with questions. It would've been ruder to let him in." I rushed over and grabbed my jacket. "Bye."

"Don't forget . . ." Rose hollered.

I opened the door to find Scott standing a few feet away. I could see the confusion in his eyes at being left on the porch.

"Sorry, there is a lot of wedding planning going on in there. I didn't want you to get roped into it."

Scott's eyes widened, and he looked at my hand. Was he wondering if he accidentally proposed? I held up my hands. "It's for Nan." I chuckled.

"Oh, right." He sounded relieved.

What does that mean? He doesn't want to marry me. Or he's just surprised?

"Does Nan need your help? I hate to take you away if you're needed here." Scott walked beside me as I headed toward his car.

"Nope. I'm good. Besides, I'm starving." I wasn't hungry. I had been snacking all day. But I needed to get away from the questions I wasn't ready to face.

Scott reached over and grabbed my hand in his. Electricity shot up my arm. I reminded myself to breathe. This relationship was temporary. He swung his car door open and held it for me.

"Where to?" he asked as he climbed into the driver's seat.

He began rubbing little circles on the back of my hand. My body kept forgetting the idea that *Scott and I together* was temporary. Was this desire to always be with him going to destroy me? I couldn't allow this to grow into something more than it was. But what was it? Just fun? Or something else? I told my heart to get back in its cage, and I locked the door to keep it from trying to burst. Scott put his car into drive, and we started down the street.

"Hey," Scott's voice was low and laced with concern. "You okay?"

I shook my head and replaced my concern with a smile. "Yep. I'm good. Let's go to Merritt's."

Scott shook his head. "No, don't do that with me." He pulled over and put the car in park. He turned to face me.

"Don't do what with you?"

What was he talking about?

"What you do with everyone else." He dipped his head to look at my eyes. "You feel something other than happiness and you push it down, smile, and change the subject."

I looked down at my hands. I hadn't realized that he had recognized that about me.

"You don't have to be happy all the time, Marissa." He reached over and moved my hair out of my face. "I would rather you be real." He reached over and tipped my head to look at him. "You don't have to pretend with me." His eyes were earnest.

I glanced at his face. His eyes were soft, and he brushed his thumb across my cheek. "Don't pretend. Be real with me," he repeated in a whisper.

"I'm not used to talking about actual emotions. I might not be good at it. What if you don't like the real me?" What if I don't know if I like the real me? Do I even know the real me?

One corner of his mouth lifted. "You know what they say about practice." Scott tipped his head to the side. "I think we will both love the real you if you give us a chance."

Had he meant the L word . . . he didn't take it back or fluster over it. The pause stretched, full of pressure. Fall or run? It was time to choose.

"Let's try again." He picked up my hand and brought it to his lips. "What were you thinking about before?"

"Are you sure?" I could barely push out the words.

"Yes." He matched my volume. The air felt heavy around me.

Closing my eyes, I pulled in a deep breath and nodded. Nan was right. I was better off for knowing and loving my parents, loving and knowing her. He gave my hand a light squeeze. It allowed me time to think, but now he was still here. I would not run. This time I would choose love.

Okay. Here we go.

"I'm wondering what this is." I pulled up our joined hands and opened my eyes.

"Oh, I'm sorry. Am I pressuring you?" Scott went to let go of my hand, but I held on tight.

"No, that's not what I meant." I shook my head. "I enjoy holding your hand." I smiled and looked at him. "A lot." I saw hope reflected in his eyes. "But I'm curious . . ." I closed my eyes, trying to form the words, pushing down the urge to run. "Are you with me because you are bored and know I'm leaving or for something else? Where is this relationship even going?" The last part was barely audible. Scott leaned in, trying to hear me, and I looked anywhere but his eyes.

His hand brushed back my hair. "I was hoping to talk about this today, but was worried I would chicken out." Scott raised one side of his mouth in a soft grin. "Marissa, I don't know what the future will bring. Everything is too new to say." He tightened his grip on my hand. "But I know I read your texts looking for hidden meanings in everything. I know when I go to bed, I'm thinking about you, and when I wake up, you are the first thing I think about. You are comfortable and kind, but you drive me crazy at the same time." He reached up and felt a strand of my hair, rubbing it back and forth between his fingers. "You're unexpected in the most refreshing way."

I couldn't breathe. Was this really happening? To feel loved and accepted was what I wanted but could never have. A tear fell. What would happen when I told him everything? Would the fairy-tale end?

Scott caught my tear on his thumb. "Us together is not easy. Our futures are unsure, and that scares me. I've thought of nothing else than trying to get you to postpone your trip this last week. That or trying to see if I could somehow come too." His cheeks turned red, and he glanced away.

I squeezed his hand. Aww! "You would come with me?"

Scott nodded. "The thought of you in another country, being so far away scares me. Partly because I want to keep you safe, and partly because of all those males with British accents."

I giggled, then stilled. "You're not with me because it's easy and you know I'm leaving?"

Scott laughed. "There is nothing about us that is easy."

I liked that he'd said *us*.

"But it's worth every hard thing to be near you."

I traced his knuckle with my thumb. "What about all your dreams and ambitions for a big career? Nothing about us has ever felt long-term. Maybe that's why it works?" There I said it. It couldn't work. It wouldn't last.

"No. I refuse to believe that." He shook his head. "Nothing about my feelings are short-term."

I looked up into his eyes. He looked adamant.

"But what about your plan?"

"Plan schman." Scott smiled.

I shot him an incredulous look.

"Let's take it one day at a time. We can figure it out, but I don't want to rush everything to the point we end it because we don't have the answers." Scott grabbed both of my hands in his. "I guess what I'm trying to say is, Marissa, would you be my girlfriend and see if we can make this work? We can plan or not plan. Whatever you want. Just don't run or push me away. Give us a chance?"

I sighed. He said we could go slow and figure it out. "I can do 'figure things out as we go'."

Scott grinned. "Really?"

I chuckled. "Yeah. Let's try it."

Scott looked at me with wonder. His eyes flicked to my lips. I bit them, this time on purpose. His eyes burned as he looked up at me. "If we are officially dating, I'm no longer okay with kisses goodbye. I want kisses hello, and middle, and all day long." He reached over and pulled me closer.

I grinned. "That seems like a lot . . ."

Scott tipped his head to the side. "Sounds like the perfect amount." He put both of his hands along my jaw and leaned forward and whispered in my ear. "I've been dying to kiss you since you walked by smelling like apples." Chills erupted over my arms, and I shivered. He showed a cocky grin, liking the effect he had on me.

Fine, I could play that game too. I unbuckled my seat belt and kneeled in the seat of his car, so I was taller than him. Leaning down, I kissed his neck just under his ear and my lips barely grazed his skin, then I nibbled his ear. I heard his breath catch. I was supposed to be teasing him, but found I enjoyed it just as much.

Looking into his eyes, I felt safe and excited about the future for the first time in what seemed like forever. His eyes were focused on my mouth. I leaned forward and brushed my lips against his. The kiss was soft and tentative. He reached for me and pulled me onto his lap as he deepened the kiss. I let myself fall on him, to fall into the future and into something sweet and new. I wanted to make plans, I wanted to chase dreams. I wanted to be with him.

I also felt myself fall off balance as my knee slipped and my backside bumped into the steering wheel, causing the horn to blast. I jumped and tried to hop off Scott, but he laughed and pulled me further onto his lap. His laugh was full and cheerful, and he put his forehead to mine. I couldn't believe that it was me who made him happy.

"Do you think everyone heard that horn?" I grimaced.

Scott nuzzled into my neck. "Thank you for talking with me Marissa. Thanks for giving us a chance." He kissed me again and again. I melted into him, buzzing with happiness.

Scott reached up and rubbed his thumb down my cheek, and I leaned into his touch.

"Let's go eat. I think we gave her enough of a show." Scott nodded to the sidewalk where Ashley stood with her mouth open. Her phone was prepped for a picture. "Or should we give her something to really take a picture of?" Scott whispered wickedly in my ear.

I laughed and shoved his shoulder. I slid off his lap, laughing, and waved at Ashley. Rolling down the window, I called out. "Hey, would you send me a copy of that one?"

Scott laughed as he pulled back out onto the road.

"Guess what?" I pulled his hands to my lips. "I'm considering plans too. Aren't you proud?"

He kept driving. "Wow. That is big."

"Yep. I've been thinking of maybe trying to do the whole Carol B&B thing." I sucked in a tight breath. It was scary to say out loud.

"Wow. Um, Marissa, that's—wow."

"Huge, I know! I've never thought of my life beyond London and leaving Hillsdale." I shrugged. "I'm not sure or anything, but even thinking about a future plan at all, I thought would make you proud."

Chapter Twenty-Six

SCOTT

Work had never been so unproductive, and I had never been happier. I handled anything that was pressing, pumpkin complaints and coach disputes included, but everything else could wait.

I especially ignored Clyde Johnson's calls and emails. Every time I saw something pop up on my phone or email, I felt sick. A few days ago, when Marissa mentioned she was thinking about a future in the B&B, I almost vomited. It took all I had to not spill about the Raymond & Johnson Law Firm. She was only *thinking* about it. I could picture it though, her running the community events, and me, coaching a recreation basketball team. Getting old in Hillsdale, living the small-town life. Kids running all over the place. It was the opposite vision of everything I had planned for so long, I couldn't tell which was right for me. The law firm was getting persistent, and I was expecting them to retract the offer any day. I needed to find where my future was headed.

Scott: You home yet?

Marissa: I just got home. Are you watching me? I can't decide if that is cute or creepy . . .

Scott: Let's go with cute. Is it too late to come over?

Marissa: Lol. Umm you can, but I told Nan I would spend the evening with her and Bert talking about wedding plans and beating them at Wheel of Fortune and Jeopardy. If that's not a party for you, that's fine.

Scott: I'm game. Maybe if we team up, we stand a chance.

She sent back a smiling face.

Scott: Be there in five.

Marissa: Are you sure? It's going to be boring, and I'll see you in the morning.

Scott: Nope. Too long.

She sent a rolling eye emoji.

Marissa: Fine, but if I'm tired tomorrow from staying up too late, you have to tell my boss it's all your fault.

Scott: Deal, I'm pretty sure I can take him if needed. I chuckled at my joke.

Marissa: I'm in my PJs. If you show up in something fancy, I will throw you out.

I wondered what she wore for PJs. I changed into shorts and a t-shirt, to put it out there to the universe. The thought of cuddling her in shorts and a tank top, her soft skin against mine, made me rush for my keys.

Knocking at their door, I couldn't help my stupid grin. I was excited to be near her. It had only been a few hours, but I couldn't wait to see her. She was in a tank top and joggers. I pulled her into a hug and kissed the top of her wet hair. We went to the couch, settled into our designated spots, and pulled the gray blanket from underneath the coffee table we always used.

"What couldn't wait till the morning?" Marissa asked as I placed my arm around her shoulder as she leaned into my side.

I shrugged. "I just wanted to see you."

She chuckled. "No huge pressing secrets on your conscience."

That made my back stiffen. Had she found out about the B&B? What would happen if she knew? That place held so many memories of her parents and was the first place she saw herself having a future. I knew I couldn't sell it. I couldn't do that to her. I should resolve all those threads and let her know.

Would this ruin the progress we had made? Was honesty worth the risk? What if she says no?

"For tonight, I just wanted to see you." I shrugged. "Any secrets from you?"

I could sense there was something she wanted to say, but then she sighed. "No secrets for tonight."

But not no secrets for either of us . . . my stomach felt tight. What did that mean?

Marissa put her head on my chest, and I used my right hand to play with her hair. We agreed to take it a day at a time. It would take a while to learn everything about each other. It didn't mean I needed to worry.

Bert nodded at me. He had put two lazy boys close enough that he could hold hands with Nan while they sat in their chairs.

Nan grinned. "Alright you two, you can be as lovey as you want, within reason. But whoever loses tonight has to wash the dishes."

Marissa chuckled and yawned. "It's on, Nan."

"How are the wedding plans going?" I asked Bert and Nan.

"I've no idea. I'm happy with whatever she chooses. My only stipulation is it be as soon as possible." Bert grinned.

"Can't stand to be without me?" Nan wiggled her eyebrows.

"No. I can't." Bert kissed the back of Nan's hand.

With that, the music for Wheel of Fortune started.

"Who's being all lovey now?" Marissa rolled her eyes. "I'm super tired and I don't want to end up doing dishes by default when I fall asleep."

A FEW HOURS LATER, WE HAD WON AT JEOPARDY, BUT lost at Wheel of Fortune. Bert had gone home, and I rested on the couch, Marissa sleeping in my arms.

I dozed off and woke up there with Marissa still in my arms in the early morning. My left arm was screaming in protest from loss of blood flow, but at this point I was happy to lose it, rather than move. It was dark in the house, other than a faint glow coming from near the TV. I could lay here forever, feeling Marissa in my arms.

My phone went off again and again with notifications. The world was yelling for attention, but I didn't care. There was nothing that mattered more than right here, right now. I rubbed Marissa's hair in my fingers and pressed a kiss to her forehead. She was gorgeous.

Marissa murmured something in her sleep and stirred. She sat up, tipped her neck to the side, and lifted her arms up in a stretch, nearly hitting my face. Her nose wrinkled, and she flopped down on the couch in the other direction. She had exposed her stomach, and I stared at the vicious lines that ran across it. The car wreck must have been terrible to heal like that. I leaned over and pulled her shirt down, knowing she would be more comfortable with the scars covered.

I turned and grabbed an extra blanket to cover her up, then stretched and stood. I should head home.

"She almost died, you know."

I jumped but refused to let the yell escape my lips and wake Marissa. I put my hand to my heart and turned to see Nan standing nearby watching Marissa.

I looked at Marissa and thought of what the world would be like without her in it. My world would be gray. Nan shuffled closer.

"Did she get the scars from the car accident with her parents?" I whispered. Marissa had opened up about a lot of things, but with the accident, she could only seem to share a tiny piece at a time.

"Yep." Nan sighed. "The poor thing was out cold for forty-eight hours. She woke up to a world forever changed. Left her home and moved in here with me." The pain in Nan's voice was clear as she relived that moment.

"That must have been a very hard time for you both. The grief of losing people you loved and navigating new life together."

Nan leaned against her chair. "She never talks about it. The crash, her scars, any of it. I didn't handle it right at first, too much in my own grief. And by the time I was in a space I could try to help her, she had walled off that part of her. I've tried to discuss it with her for years, but she wouldn't even talk with me." Nan turned and looked at me. "That's when I knew you were important to her. She told you when she didn't have to. She has even started opening up to other people since too. I've seen so much change in her."

"She didn't tell me much," I whispered. Marissa was such a walking contradiction of strength and softness. Laughter and pain. I wanted to take part of her burden. I wanted to be with her.

The only life I wanted was one with her in it. Marissa, with her long dark hair and dusting of freckles. The things in life I was pushing for, the fancy car, big job, penthouse, were all empty now when I pictured them. They didn't glow the way thoughts of a life with Marissa did.

This was what I wanted.

This was my new plan. The thought startled me, but I didn't let it scare me away. I knew this was right.

My center had become Marissa. A magnet, a new life plan. With more life and love than I could imagine.

Her quirks, her laugh, her curves, her lips, I wanted it all. I turned to Nan. "I better get home." I pointed to Marissa. "Should I leave her there?"

"Yes, she is fine there. And Scott," Nan's eyes held mine. "Do not break her trust. It's rarely given."

I felt my breath catch. I needed to come clean. In fact, I was going to talk to Carol today. I knew she guessed, but I needed to tell her about how I was working with the Raymond & Johnson Law and hoping to get a job. I didn't need her to sell anymore because I no longer needed to leave, but I also wanted no more secrets. I would let the firm know I wasn't interested in their deal.

When I got to the B&B, it was five-thirty in the morning. No use in going to bed now. I decided to make Carol some breakfast. Everything was better with food.

The only thing I knew how to make was scrambled eggs and toast, or cereal. I was certain cereal wouldn't set the tone for the conversation we needed to have. I rummaged throughout the cupboards and found an old toaster and grabbed some eggs from the fridge. I left the toast to do its thing as I grabbed the milk and stirred the eggs. I added it to the hot pan, mixing frequently.

The smell of smoke permeated the air. *What the?* I turned and saw a small fire coming out of the toaster and dark gray smoke clouding the room.

Crap!

I grabbed a nearby kitchen towel and smothered the fire and went to open all the windows. The smoke was making me cough, and then the smoke alarm started blaring.

"Did someone set fire to my kitchen?" Carol rushed in, hollering in panic. She spotted me in an apron, standing on the stool and fanning the smoke alarm.

"I may have burnt the toast." I shrunk. "Sorry . . ."

She rushed over and removed the now burnt eggs from the stove. "Oh honey, I think you about burnt down the house." Carol waved her hand in front of her, clearing smoke. She gestured at me to get off the stool and motioned to the table. The beeping stopped. "How about we start with coffee?"

"Coffee sounds great." I grabbed some cups and sat in the chair. The previous evening's emotion caught up to me and I was exhausted. Carol sat across from me and stared me down. "I need to tell you something."

"Ready to come clean, eh? It took you long enough." She placed her arms on the table and blew on her coffee.

I spluttered and wiped the coffee from my chin. "How did you know?"

Carol rolled her eyes. "You may be a talented lawyer, but I would not suggest going into acting."

I rubbed my tired eyes. "You should be a private investigator or something." I thought I could read people, but I had nothing on Carol.

"Alright, how about we start at the top, where you used Marissa to convince me to let you stay, so you could trick me into selling to that nasty firm?"

I went through it all, sparing no detail. The contract, why I took it, the life I thought I had wanted, and falling for Marissa and a change of plans.

Carol nodded through it all, as if it was all old news. "Are you still wanting a job with the that big city firm? Do you think it's a good idea and you can protect the town?"

I turned the cup in my hand. "Yes and no." I shook my head back and forth. "It was all I wanted before I met Marissa. Part of me still wants that prestigious career. Selling would also give you the life you deserve, one with far less work." I took a sip of coffee. "It would bring jobs to the town that could help, but there are also risks that this place would never be the same when the client takes it over, and that would be unfortunate." I looked around the kitchen. I loved these bright, chipped cabinets and mismatched glass dishes. Not only that, I loved this town.

"I don't know what Marissa wants, and every time I bring up a long-term future together, she changes the subject." I pinched the bridge of my nose and sighed. "I know there is something she's not telling me, but it isn't fair for me to ask for her secrets when I've got some of my own." I ran my hand through my hair. "I need to come clean about everything, but now I'm worried if I tell her I used our friendship to get a place here, she won't even let me explain before she rushes off to London."

Carol nodded and took a long sip of her cup and looked me in the eye, waiting for something. "Well, I'm sure something will work out, whether with the firm or someone local." She set down her cup. "I trust you. You're one of us now." She rose from the table and set her cup in the sink. "I'm heading back to bed. Please don't make me breakfast ever again." She smirked and walked off.

I sat there spinning my cup. I had the choice. I could help Carol sell this place and get the job I had always wanted or live a life different from my original expectations. What was best for the town? Would the boys still have a place to practice? Could the town still have a trunk-or-treat here?

I also needed to figure out if Marissa was interested in a life with me. I checked my phone. My mom had texted several times last night asking if I was coming home for Thanksgiving in a week, and if I had a plus one.

Scott: Yes, hopefully on both accounts.

I then texted Marissa, hoping it wouldn't wake her up, but I also didn't want to chicken out.

Scott: Would you come to Thanksgiving with me and meet my family this Thursday? If not, can I come wherever you'll be?

Chapter Twenty-Seven

MARISSA

The couch and I were fighting. I stretched my neck, trying to release the kink. Apparently, I was too old to sleep on it without consequences. My brain was fuzzy as I tried to piece together memories from the night before. I remembered Scott cuddling on the couch. I remembered falling asleep. And I was pretty sure I woke to him rubbing my hair between his fingers and feeling his lips on the back of my neck. I assumed the extra blanket was also Scott's doing. I grinned as I pictured doing this exact thing with him for years to come. Years. That wiped off my smile in a hurry.

Not days, or even months, but years. I wanted years. I searched for my urge to run, but found it overpowered with my desire to stay. To try.

If I ran, I could lose years of cuddles on the couch and watching Scott bantering with Nan. I would miss the small circles he always rubbed on my back and hand. I would miss the smell of cinnamon and the hope he gave me for a future I wanted to plan for. I stood and stretched and wandered to the kitchen for a drink of water. I noticed the dishes dried and stacked to the side. I think I was supposed to wash those. Whoops. I heard Nan come into the kitchen behind me.

"Sorry about the dishes."

"Oh, I didn't do them. I beat you guys fair and square. Although he may have been distracted watching you sleep."

"Scott did them?"

"Yep. Then rushed right back to the couch and held you. All night, I might add."

I felt my cheeks turn red.

"He only left a few hours ago." Nan leaned against the counter.

I checked my watch. It was almost eight.

"What are you going to do?"

"What do you mean?" I set my cup near the sink.

"I mean, you love that boy."

"What? I don't know . . . I mean, maybe?" My heart rejected the words. Yes. I loved him. I knew it with every piece of me.

"Oh honey, you do." Nan came closer. "What are you going to do about it? Are you going to let your fear push him away? If you are going to pursue it, it's time to tell him everything."

"I don't want to run." I faced Nan, searching my heart. "Honestly, I want nothing more than to see where this goes."

Nan grinned and nodded. "It does my heart good to see you happy."

I gave Nan a side hug. "That's dramatic. I've always been happy."

"Nah baby, you have always pretended to be happy." She hugged me back. "This is different."

I met Nan's sad eyes. "That's not true. I've been happy here with you."

"You have had happy moments, but you have been holding tight to a whole lot of sad. Running away from anyone or anything that reminded you of your parents."

I flinched. I hadn't meant to hurt Nan. I was scared. Nan nodded towards the living room couch.

"Let's have a seat." I followed her to the couch. She sat with a humph, and I sat next to her and picked up her hand.

"Nan, I've always loved you and been grateful you took me in. I didn't mean to make you think I was unhappy."

Nan patted the back of my hand. "I know that, but you have also refused to let anyone else in this close. This town, and other boys—especially after what happened with Tyler's mother. Even your friends . . . you have a hard time letting anyone in." Nan sighed and looked her age. How hard had it been for her to raise a teenager so late in life?

I leaned my head on her shoulder, and she put her arm around me.

"For the longest time, we were both stuck in our grief, both drowning. I surfaced, but I never knew how to help you. Any time I tried to help, you would run off."

It was true. I had carried my past around with me, refusing to set it down. "I think I was worried at first about facing it. Now I'm worried that setting it down will betray them somehow. What if it means I forget them?"

Nan patted my head with her hand, smoothing my hair. "You can keep the good, and sometimes you can be sad. But honey, you can't live in the hole of grief forever. You have to climb out." Nan leaned her head on mine. "And it's a climb. I've been praying for someone to come and show you how amazing you are. To help you let go of the past and be truly happy. Just as you are."

I rubbed my hands on my PJ pants. "It felt good to talk to Scott about it, even though I haven't told him everything. He has been patient and happy with what I share."

"What are your thoughts of London and finding your worth?" Nan asked.

"I'm not sure. I've found that I might not mind this town as much as I thought. I think it was so hard as I was grieving, and everyone wanted to talk about things I wasn't ready for. It was easiest to push them all away and be angry at them for not letting me forget it."

"Anger, grief, and running. Marissa, that's heavy to take with you everywhere. You need to stop thinking about everyone else and think about yourself. What do you want your future to look like?"

I pulled my knees into my chest and thought. "I don't know yet. Anytime I tried before, all I could see was a bunch of cats or something?" I rested my chin on my knees. "I knew you would eventually die and leave me. It was safer to plan on being alone."

Nan sighed. "Mar, you have so much to offer this world, you just need to see it. What are three things you love about yourself?"

I fought the urge to be self-deprecating and looked a little deeper. "I love living with you." I bumped into her with my shoulder. "I loved bringing the community together with the trunk-or-treat. I love how Scott makes me feel."

"Those are all wonderful things, but Mar, those are things you do. What if you did nothing? What about on the days where you just exist? You need to love that girl too. The girl that isn't based on a to-do list."

Wow. That felt like a big ask. I closed my eyes.

"I'll try."

"That works for me. Alright dear." She patted my hand. "I'm going back to bed. I'm too old to keep the hours of young love." She kissed me on the cheek and heaved herself out of the couch and waddled towards her bedroom.

"Nan."

She stopped and turned.

I looked up at her kind eyes and wrinkled beautiful face. "Thank you. Thank you for raising me, and loving me, just how I am."

"That, my dear, has been one of my life's greatest pleasures." She winked and went to her room.

Maybe Nan was right, maybe it was time to drop some of the

weight I had been carrying. Counseling wouldn't be a bad idea. I should text Faith. I wanted to face my past so I could love my future.

I checked my phone. I had a message from Scott. I wrapped myself up in a blanket as I opened it. It was time. Time to be honest with myself and him. It would be worth the work of facing my past if I had Scott as my prize at the end. Regardless. It was time to let some of the pain go.

I opened my text.

Scott: Would you come to Thanksgiving with me and meet my family this Thursday? If not, can I come wherever you'll be?

Yikes. Meet the family. What if his family didn't like me? I pushed back my doubt. It would take time to learn to trust and love, but I was ready for the chance to try.

Marissa: I would love to come to Thanksgiving with you.

It was time to tell him and stop running.

Marissa: Scott, I need to tell you something . . .

I hit send the same time a text came through.

Scott: Marissa, I love you.

Wow! I leaned back on the couch smiling so wide my face hurt.

Marissa: I love you too.

I couldn't wait to see him, to kiss him.

Marissa: I've never felt like this. You make me happy and feel safe.

Scott: I'm amazed and honored you feel that way.

Scott: What was it you wanted to talk about?

Ugh. I couldn't bring it up now. It would ruin the magical moment. And I wanted to bask in it.

Marissa: I'll tell you later. I just want to enjoy this feeling, but I think we need to talk . . . about future expectations. But later.

Scott: Since you're awake, can I come see you?

Marissa: See or kiss?

Scott: Both.

It was magic. It had to be. I didn't want to ruin my chance at this. I texted Faith.

Marissa: Who was that counselor friend you recommended to me? I think I'm ready to face my past a bit.

Faith: Marissa, that's amazing. I'm proud of you. I'll send over her contact card and let her know to take the best care of you!

She sent several heart emojis.

My future was looking bright.

Chapter Twenty-Eight

MARISSA

I FLUNG OPEN THE DOOR AND SAW THE MOST GORGEOUS man holding flowers and smiling at me. I flung my arms around Scott, almost knocking him over. He chuckled and handed Nan the flowers and wrapped his arms around me. He took me to the couch and pulled me onto his lap.

"I missed you." I nestled my face into his neck. "And I love you."

"I missed you too." He kissed my lips. "I love you too. I'm excited for you to meet my family today."

It had been several days since I heard Scott say he loved me for the first time, but it still felt like a fairy tale. Me. This gorgeous, amazing man loved me! Faith's counselor friend Sarah had already reached out, and we met over the phone. It was a little intimidating, but I knew Faith loved me and trusted her, so that helped.

"Alright, you two lovebirds. Are you gonna help me load these pies, or are you going to make me do it by myself?" Nan hollered from the kitchen.

I laughed and hopped off Scott's lap, grabbing a pumpkin pie. I was floating. I was done running. I was ready to live.

"Are you sure you don't want to come, Nan?" Scott asked Nan.

"Nah. I'm going to spend the day with Bert." She shooed us away.

The drive was full of songs and discussions of our best Thanksgiving meals and memories. I was nervous to meet his family, but he kept reassuring me I had nothing to worry about.

We pulled up to a beautiful brick house full of history and charm. The white picket fence, bright potted flowers, and the swing on the large porch made me feel like I was looking at a painting. This house had the feeling of a home.

Scott held the pan of pies, and I looped my arm through his. Taking long breaths, I tried to still my racing heart.

Scott reached the front door and pulled it open. "Hey everyone," he smiled, "I know you're dying to meet my girlfriend . . ." Scott set the pies on an entry table.

I giggled at his huge grin. Following his announcement, I heard steps rushing towards us.

"Uncle Scott!" A little girl with blonde hair in pigtails rushed at his legs and grabbed on tight. Scott chuckled and scooped her up. "Jelly Bean!"

She placed her hands on his cheeks and looked him in the eye. "Why can't the turkey go to church?"

Scott chuckled. "I don't know why?"

The girl started to giggle. "Because he uses fowl language." She leaned closer. "Mama said that means he says naughty words."

Scott threw his head back and laughed. I had the sudden vision of him as a father.

Whew. Okay. Don't run.

I needed to have the no kids talk, but it never felt like the right time, and now watching him with his niece felt like a knife in the gut. *This is it. This is what I always wanted.*

What I couldn't have . . . but he could . . . with someone else.

I took a step backward but felt the sweet reassurance of Nan telling me not to run.

Look to the future; don't focus on what ifs and the past.

I took a shaky breath. Scott looked at me and must have seen the fear in my eyes. He set down the little girl and came over and wrapped his arms around me.

"Hey don't worry, they'll love you." Scott whispered into my ear.

"There you are." I looked up to see what must have been the girl's mother. She was very pregnant and looked exhausted. She was holding hands with her husband as she came over.

"Mama, Scott thought my joke was funny!"

The mother smiled and stepped to me and Scott. I was pulled into a hug. Her bulging stomach turned to the side.

"Hey, I'm Jessica. Sorry if she overwhelmed you at all." She motioned to her husband. "This is my husband, Blake." He shook my hand and gave me a quiet smile.

"Nice to meet you," Blake added.

Jessica smiled at her daughter. "She can be a lot, and Uncle Scott is her favorite."

"Hey, I heard that."

I saw a man who had to be Scott's twin standing in the doorway. He looked a lot like Scott. Tall, with light hair. Michael's presence exuded confidence as he strolled over. I knew Scott had mentioned several girls choosing Michael over him when they were younger, but as I stood there holding Scott's arm, there was no comparison. My twin was beautiful inside and out.

Jessica smiled but did not take it back.

"Huh, I guess your girlfriend wasn't imaginary after all." His brother gave Scott a light slug on the shoulder. After that, his parents walked in, his dad's arm draped around the mother's shoulders. I could see the love radiating between them. Love for each other and the beautiful life they had created.

"Good to see you again." Ron pulled me into a side hug and Emily embraced me in her arms.

"Thank you for taking care of my boy," she whispered. "I'm Emily."

I didn't know what to say to that, so I blurted, "I brought pie . . ."

"Thats great." Emily grinned and looked towards Scott. "Your father burned the last pan of mine."

"It isn't my fault. You distracted me." The parents chuckled, and the siblings rolled their eyes as we walked towards the dinner table.

"LET'S GO AROUND THE TABLE AND ALL SAY THINGS WE are grateful for." Emily's eyes shined. "I'll start. I'm grateful that my family could all come and celebrate Thanksgiving. For my wonderful children," she grinned and looked at her granddaughter, "and grandkids. And to my wonderful husband and the life he has blessed me with." She leaned to him, and they kissed.

"I'll go next, if only to keep you two from embarrassing us all," Scott piped up. "I'm grateful I have a wise father who told me that sometimes life works out better than you could ever plan." He grabbed my hand and brought it to his lips, kissing the back of it. "I never expected to be so happy living the life I didn't plan on, or expect. It's so much better with you." He kissed the back of my hand again, and I blushed.

"Looks like you might be grateful for more grandkids before too long," Michael said, turning to his parents.

I felt my spine go rigid, waking me from a dream.

"Oh, you hush." Emily chided Michael. "Looks like it's your turn now, and if you tell me you are grateful for your lines of never-ending dates again this year, I will throw this roll at your face."

Everyone giggled, and I was glad they were no longer looking at me. My skin flushed with heat.

"Hey, you okay?" Scott whispered into my ear, and I realized I was squeezing his hand tight. "I'm sorry about Michael. He always feels the need to be the center of attention."

I shook my head. "It's fine." But my voice shook and betrayed my calm exterior.

"Hey, no it's not. Remember no pretending with me." He brushed my cheek.

"Okay, you're right. I have something to tell you about the whole kids thing. But can we enjoy Thanksgiving first?" Scott's eyes searched mine in worry. "On the way home, okay?"

"Of course, if that's what you want."

"It is." I had started the conversation. The knots in my stomach untangled a little.

Scott nodded and dropped the subject. I loved that he trusted me enough to know I would talk about it when I was ready.

"Marissa, don't feel pressure to join—but if you would like, it's your turn."

I looked around the table and all eyes were on me. I had missed the rest of the thankful messages in my haze. "I'm grateful for Scott, and that he is patient. And I'm grateful you have let me come to Thanksgiving."

Michael scoffed. "Scott's not patient."

Out of nowhere, a roll soared across the table and hit Michael right in the face.

"Ouch!" He bent over and held his eye. "Really, Mom? In the eye!"

"Yes, well, that part was an accident, but maybe it's karma catching up to you and that mouth."

The table erupted in laughter.

After eating way more than I should, we went to the backyard, and I sat on a porch bench and watched as the family tossed the football back and forth. The little girl always got to score a touchdown.

Scott was free here, and so happy. This was the life he deserved. Would it be better for him to not be with me? I sighed and rubbed my forehead. I needed to tell him and let him decide what he wanted. I felt sick to my stomach. Nan was right. I wouldn't regret loving Scott either way. He'd changed me for the better and helped me face my past.

"Do you mind if I sit?" I looked up to see Scott's mother, Emily.

I scooted over. "Not at all."

Emily looked at her playing family, smiling. "I'm glad to finally meet you," she said without looking away from her family. "I could tell a while ago that you must be special to create the change in Scott I was hearing about."

"I don't know about that." I felt myself blush.

"I do."

"Wait, what change?"

His mother shrugged. "Scott is a wonderful person. But he always seemed to chase something he couldn't grasp. Top of the class, best this or that. It would consume him at all costs." She frowned. "Never feeling content or like he was good enough." She raised her shoulder. "It was like he couldn't believe in the good in himself and his worth until you showed him."

"What do you mean?"

"It's hard to explain. He seems content."

I wasn't sure I liked the idea that I made him settle.

Emily laughed, reading my expression. "No, not like that. It's like he has been trying his whole life to be someone else, be enough for someone or something. Fiercely trying to prove that he's the best. And now he just seems . . . more whole."

I felt myself blush. "He's pretty great."

"I won't argue with you there." She chuckled and picked up my hand, giving it a squeeze. "Thank you for joining us for

Thanksgiving. It was lovely to meet you, and I hope to see much more of you." She smiled.

"I better go check the pies. I wanted to warm them up a bit." She gave me a brief hug and walked away.

I made my way down the steps and walked around the trees in the large yard, trying to clear my head and find the words to face my fears for the drive home.

Emily hollered that dessert was ready, and I headed back towards the house. Scott was walking with his brother. I jogged to catch up.

"I missed you." Scott kissed my cheek and wrapped his arm around me.

"What do you mean, you haven't signed the contract?" Michael asked from Scott's side. "I thought everything had to be completed this next week to sell the B&B?"

"I haven't missed the window. Let's talk about this later, okay?" Scott sounded angry and went rigid at my side.

What contract? Was he hiding something?

"You're gonna sign the contract, right? You aren't gonna keep the firm in Hillsdale, right? What about moving to Haven Falls with me?" Michael scoffed. "Last time we talked, the plan was to trick your secretary into getting the B&B lady to sell and then you'd ride off into the sunset."

I stopped walking. Scott's eyes held panic when he looked at me.

"Wait, what?" I felt as though someone had punched me in the gut.

Scott swore under his breath. "Michael, drop it!" He pushed his brother away.

But he didn't say it wasn't true. Was Scott using me this whole time, just to trick Carol into selling? Was everything a lie?

My breath was coming in gasps. I had to know. I stepped around Scott and went straight to Michael. "What do you mean, Scott was using some girl to get what he wanted?"

Michael waved his hands. "Oh, you don't need to be jealous." He winked. "Just tricking a receptionist and an old lady to sell some B&B. I'm sure he'll still want to see you. You should come check out Haven Falls, the night scene—"

Scott pushed his brother hard enough he fell to the ground.

"Hey! What the heck!" Michael hopped up.

"Michael. Shut up. You don't know what you're talking about!" Scott turned, his eyes were guarded. "It's not like that, Marissa."

I took a step back, shaking all over. Shards of ice ran down my spine at Michael's words. Scott had used me. It all made sense now. How I fit into his plans. He hadn't changed his at all. He never wanted me. Why would he?

"You were using me all along . . ." My eyes burned hot, but I pushed the tears down. I had been stupid to think I could have this life. That I could have him. I buried the feelings of hurt and loneliness. *His plan at all costs, I was part of those costs.* No longer able to hold back tears, I turned and ran to the side gate.

"No, Marissa, wait . . . let me explain . . ." Scott reached for my hand and grabbed my arm.

I pulled it free and turned, full of anger. "Explain which part? That you are using me to get some job? That you would let those investors bulldoze the B&B? I was just a part of your plan . . . I can't believe I trusted you." Tears seared down my cheeks, but I refused to acknowledge them.

"It's not like that."

"Which part is wrong?"

Scott shrank. "Well, it was like that, but it isn't anymore. Please, just let me explain." He reached for me again, but I stepped out of his reach. He had used me, pretended to like me.

"No. Your mother was right. You'll sacrifice anyone and anything to win." I begged my tears to dry, but now that they were flowing, there was no stopping them. "Even me."

"What are you talking about?" Scott shook his head. I stepped farther away.

No. I wouldn't let him hurt me further. I built a wall back around my heart. "Thank your family for their hospitality today. Tell your mother it was delicious." I turned and went through the side gate, closing it behind me.

"Marissa, let me at least give you a ride home." Scott's voice was full of pain and he begged me to let him back in. And I wanted to let him in. I wanted to hold him. I was a fool. I couldn't trust myself near him.

"No, thank you."

Scott came through the gate and grabbed my hand, tears in his eyes. "Please don't push me away. Please. Let me explain."

I ripped my hand away from his. "I believed you. I thought you loved me. I thought you liked our little town. But you were using all of us. You didn't care at all. Does Carol even know you are using her, too?"

"Carol knows."

I felt the air sucked out of me. "Wow, just me then." Did Carol know he was using me? What about her wanting me to take over? I looked at the house and the future I was planning only hours before. I set the last brick in place around my heart. I turned and walked a few steps down the street. I would have the Uber pick me up at the gas station on the corner.

"Marissa, I was going to sell and leave. But I changed my mind. My dream was wrong . . . I was wrong." I looked back at him, his mouth pulled down, his hands in fists. His eyes were worried and pleading. "I made a mistake, but that mistake allowed me to get to know you, to love you." He whispered and reached for me. I shook my head.

"No," I stepped further away. "I made the mistake. I trusted you. I thought the future could be worth planning for, hoping for. I was wrong." There was no way I could see him after this. Ever. I wasn't strong enough. "Scott, I quit."

"Please, wait." He crumpled in defeat. "I haven't signed the contract with the Raymond & Johnson Law Firm, and I wasn't going to." He ran his hand through his blond curls. "I was thinking, what if instead we run the B&B together? We could fill it up with all the babies you want, wear matching costumes, and live happily ever after. I had the wrong plan."

I started walking backwards; the sucker punch turned into a knife. I couldn't be what he wanted . . . ever. I couldn't have the fairytale ending. I was broken. "It's okay Scott. This is for the best." I took a deep breath, shoving down the pain. "I haven't told you everything about me either. That vision you saw of us with kids and the perfect life. That's not real."

"It's real. I know it can be." Scott stepped towards me with his hands extended.

"No. It can't." I straightened my shoulders. "Scott, I can't have kids. After the accident, things were . . . too damaged to repair." I watched as the hurt and confusion registered on his face.

"Why didn't you tell me?"

"I guess we both had secrets." I caved in on myself. "I was foolish to believe we could have worked. Sell the B&B or whatever, get the dream job, have the life you want. Don't worry, I won't hold you back."

"Marissa, please, wait. At least let me give you a ride." I could tell it took every bit of willpower for him to not run after me.

I closed my eyes. If I looked at him, I would break. "That's okay. I will call an Uber." *I needed to get away. Needed to run.*

When I peeked at him, his head was down. He looked defeated. "Please Marissa, don't do this. Let's talk it through. We can figure it out." Even now, he was beautiful. Even now, I wanted to soothe his pain and tell him it was all okay and let him in. I couldn't risk it. He couldn't be trusted. What we had wasn't real. I bricked my pain back behind a wall and turned and ran towards the gas station.

"Don't call me!" I yelled over my shoulder.

<h1 style="text-align:center">Chapter Twenty-Nine</h1>

SCOTT

UGH!

I had the wrong plan, but if she would just let me explain . . . I watched Marissa until I could no longer see her. I didn't want her paying for an Uber home, but there was no way she would take a ride from me. Watching Marissa run away caused my pain to turn into anger. Anger at Michael for his big mouth. Anger at the world for showing me something good and then ripping it away. Anger at me and my stupid plans.

She couldn't have kids. The plan I envisioned was wrong again. Why hadn't she told me before?

I rushed inside. Michael was blocking my way into the living room. "Dude, I'm so sorry. I had no idea she was the same woman."

I shoved him out of my way. "Of course you didn't. You're always looking for the next joke. Always needing to be the center of attention," I growled. I headed for the kitchen. *Mom or Dad would give her a ride. There was no way I would ask Michael for help.*

"Yeah, well, you and your ridiculous plans are easy to make a joke of." Michael glared at me. "Did you really start dating the woman you were using to further your career? And I thought I was bad with women." He shoved me back. I turned, ready to lash into him with every ounce of pain and anger that radiated through my body.

"Boys! That's enough!" We both looked to the kitchen doorway, where Mom untied her apron and threw it across a nearby chair. "You're old enough to control your tempers. Stop acting like toddlers. Now, what's going on?" She put her hands on her hips.

I turned to my mom. "I need your help."

She stepped toward me.

"Please."

She looked around. "Where is Marissa?"

"How was I supposed to know his girlfriend is the one he was tricking to get out of Hillsdale?" Michael folded his arms, leaned against the wall, his eyes shooting daggers at me.

"Oh Scott, what did you do?" Mom looked at me, her scowl heavy with disappointment.

"Me!" I pointed to Michael. "What about him?"

Mom placed her hands on her hips. "I told you at the start, I didn't like the idea. I didn't know it was Marissa. Scott, how could you do this?"

I felt my anger crumble. She was right. This wasn't Michael's fault, this was mine. *Why didn't I tell her sooner?* I collapsed against the wall, sinking to a sitting position on the floor. "I was going to tell her. I changed my mind about working with Raymond & Johnson Law Firm. I hadn't figured out how to tell Marissa yet. I was going to. Now she won't let me explain."

Mom flinched. "Where is she now?"

"Walking to the gas station and getting an Uber." My head fell into my hands. "She won't let me get close enough to her to even explain."

Mom nodded and hollered towards the kitchen. "Ron, I'm going for a drive. Keep things running here."

I looked past my mom to see my father standing in the doorway. He nodded and grabbed her keys, handing them to her.

She pointed her finger at me and Michael. "I've raised you both better than this. If you don't learn to stop using people to get what you want," she looked at me, "or to feel more important," she glared at Michael, "you'll both end up alone." Her words stung my wounded heart. "Now apologize to one another and play nice. I'll be back later." She kissed Dad. "Try to talk some sense into these two," she said, then stormed out the front door, slamming it behind her.

I felt my phone vibrate. Maybe it was Marissa? I pulled it out as fast as I could and opened it.

Please be her.

Nope. It was from Raymond & Johnson Law.

Great. Just what I needed.

Scott, I'm getting worried that you don't understand our offer. How about you come to the Christmas party next week and we can talk?

-Clyde Johnson

I closed my phone and chucked it across the room to the couch and covered my face with my hands. "This is all my fault."

"You're not wrong." Dad walked over and patted my shoulder as he eased onto the floor next to me. "The question is, what's next?"

Michael sat on my other side. "Scott, I'm sorry." He sighed and dropped his head. "I was trying to ask about your work because I want you in the city with me. I miss us being close." He bumped me with his leg. "I would never hurt you on purpose."

I thought back to high school and how all his friends used to make fun of me all the time. He had never been on my side. "Maybe you didn't, but everyone you hung out with did."

He leaned his head back against the wall. "Do you have any

idea how many fights I got in over that? I punched Alex in the face twice after he made fun of you in the cafeteria when you tripped."

"What do you mean?" My mind went blank. I couldn't remember a single time when Michael had gotten after his friends for mocking me.

Dad nodded. "True. Went to the principal's office several times over it." He chuckled. "She was never thrilled when I didn't punish you, but I told her if he was sticking up for you, Scott, then I was proud of him."

"What?" My head felt cloudy. "I always thought you got detention for not caring about your grades and the pranks you pulled on the teachers."

Michael chuckled. "Well, there may have been some of that too. But Scotty, I'll always have your back. I'm sorry you didn't know that. We are brothers, more than that we are twins. If we don't have each other's backs, who will?"

I leaned my head against the wall and closed my eyes. I didn't know who I was anymore or what was real. All the pieces that had fit in my life no longer made any sense.

"So," Michael bumped my shoulder. "Like Dad said, What now?"

I sighed. "What do you mean, what now? I blew it."

Dad chuckled. "Aw, Scott, that's our curse as men. We blow it. But we can usually find a way to fix it too."

Michael popped his knuckles. "Maybe you just need a new plan. What do you want for your future? Do you know?"

"She can't have kids." Michael and Dad were quiet for a minute.

"Well, do you want kids?"

I remembered my vision board from a month ago, the prestigious job and lifestyle. Then I thought of the vision my heart had created with Marissa, a future with kids and the picket fence. I thought about it. Did I want to have kids, like my own kids?

Yes?

I don't know.

Ugh. We had *both* kept secrets. But did her secrets change how I felt? Or what I wanted?

"I thought I knew what I wanted a few months ago, then I had a new future planned out until only a few minutes ago, and now. . . I have no idea what my plan is." I rubbed my forehead and tapped the back of my head against the wall.

"Hmm," Dad said. "That's hard. My only advice is to go with the choice you can't live without."

I dropped my head into my hands. I had a fierce headache coming on. "What if it isn't up to me? What if she won't give me a chance?"

"Well, I figure you'll cross that bridge once you're on it. One step at a time. First, you need to decide what you want in your life." Dad reached over and gave me a side hug. "Alright, let's have some pie."

Dad and Michael stood and headed to the kitchen. I think they could tell I needed space to think. What did I want? I thought about the two different lives that stood in front of me. One bridge led to the plan I'd always wanted before; the other bridge had Marissa standing at the end of it. I knew what I wanted. I didn't want pie. I wanted Marissa. I hated the thought of her hurting, knowing I was the cause. I stood and walked to the couch, picked up my phone, and dialed Marissa's number.

Voicemail.

Listening to her cheery voice was a knife in my gut.

I texted her. I needed to tell her everything. No more secrets.

Scott: Marissa, please let me explain. Yes. My original plan was to use you to allow Carol to let me stay, then convince Carol to sell to the Raymond & Johnson Law Firm. If she agreed to sell by December, they offered to hire me and give me a big enough bonus to save my parents house and have the job I always wanted. Someone else would take over at Hillsdale.

Yep, I sounded like a complete jerk. Maybe I was one.

Marissa: Looks like it worked—congrats.

I was relieved that she answered me at all.

Scott: No, that's the thing. It did work, but along the way, I realized the life I'd planned for wasn't what I wanted. I picked the wrong plan. You showed me that there is more to life than prestige and external importance. You've taught me so much, Marissa. Please, give me another chance.

Marissa: Your plans changed once. I'm sure they can again. You can't have the life you want with me, either. Please don't text me again, don't make this harder.

Ugh! I set my phone down on the ground next to me. I needed to listen to her, but she wasn't listening to me. Doesn't it matter that I changed my mind?

I felt numb and empty. What was I supposed to do?

I would wait until Mom got home and ask her how Marissa was doing. Maybe Mom would know how to save this? If I could come up with a good plan, Michael and Dad would help in any way they could. So would Jessica. I had a great family that would always have my back. How had I refused to see it before? I was so focused on the wrong things for too long, I could only see the reality I'd created for myself.

I paced back and forth, waiting. I heard a car pull into the driveway and rushed out the front door, meeting Mom at her car and opening the door. "Mom, is Marissa okay? She isn't answering me. She won't talk to me. What do I do?"

Mom sighed and stepped out of the car.

"Honestly, Scott, we hardly spoke. I offered her a ride, and she sat pulling at her shirt, wiping her tears, and looking out the window. She was crushed, Scott." She jabbed me in the shoulder, hard. "You'd better fix this. That girl deserves better than someone like you right now. You need to be better. I hope she gives you another chance."

"How do I convince her to let me try?"

"I don't know if you can." She walked around the car heading towards the house. "You'd better think of something big. Put her happiness in front of your own for a change."

I walked to my car, which I always took so much pride in. I sat and stared at the now empty seat beside me. The tears that had threatened to fall all evening now fell without reserve as I thought of Marissa sitting there beside me, her feet up on the dash and a sprinkled cookie in her hand. I was stupid.

It wasn't the car I wanted. Not anymore. I cared nothing about this car.

If I needed some big gesture, I knew who I needed.

I opened my phone and texted James.

Scott: Hey James, I need some help with a woman, and I need something big and fast.

Chapter Thirty

MARISSA

Monday, I sent Rose and Faith to pick up my stuff at the office. I forgot to tell them to leave the fake lilac. Stupid purple flower, reminding me of Scott learning about my mom, making me think he cared.

Did he care? Was I just a piece of his plan? Why had I let my stupid heart believe in the possibility of a happy future?

I grabbed another tissue. I rubbed my nose raw, and my eyes were puffy. I needed to shower but lacked the energy. I sat up in my bed. Tissues fell around me like confetti. I should've never let him in. I shouldn't have wanted the B&B. I knew better.

My phone was going off. I picked it up, sending Scott to voice-mail again. I couldn't listen to the messages. It would be a mistake to open my heart up again.

I stepped over to my closet and shoved my phone into my sock drawer before plopping back down on my bed. *Stupid Jeopardy. It made me wish he was still on my team, stupid B&B for making me hope, and stupid Ben & Jerry's for not fixing my pain.*

I tried to cancel my appointment with Sarah this coming week, but Faith said she would buy me more ice cream if I promised to keep it. I was running low. I could go buy my own, but in a town this size, I might see Scott, or Carol, or Ashley, or anyone. I still needed to talk to Carol. What was I supposed to say? "Hey, turns out I let a snake into your B&B . . . Turns out you knew and let me fall in love with him . . . Turns out he is going to demo the place."

I buried my head in the pillow, suffocating any thoughts of my parents wedding, trunk-or-treat, or Scott.

I wanted ice cream, but I had my limits.

"I turned on the shower," Nan hollered from the other room. "If you aren't in there in fifteen minutes, I'm going to throw away every bit of ice cream or cookies that come into this house for a week." She threw open my bedroom door and waddled inside. "Plus, you don't have a job and neither of us can afford a higher water bill. Time's ticking, princess."

"Ugh, Nan. Leave me alone." I grabbed another pillow, pulling it over my head to erase her voice.

"I did. For a week. Now you stink and you need to do the dishes." Nan left the room, and I closed my eyes, begging for sleep to swallow me.

"Oh, look, the last carton of Ben & Jerry's . . . It would be a shame if I . . . Whoops." I heard it hit the trash can. "The last of the cookies that Faith brought . . . What if I . . . Oops?"

"Nan! Stop!" I jumped out of bed in a panic. I stepped out of my room. "Ugh, alright, I'm up."

"And showering?" Nan glared from the kitchen, a cookie held hostage in her hand.

"And showering." I came into the living room. Each of my muscles cramped at the movement and my eyes ached. My soul felt heavy as I shuffled my feet toward the bathroom.

"You can't avoid him forever." Nan leaned against the door frame to the kitchen. "He's called nonstop, and he sat on the porch for two hours yesterday yelling all my Jeopardy answers through the window. Maybe it's time you talk to him."

"Nope. I learned my lesson. Besides, he'll just lie or pity me now and I can't hear it. Any life he has pictured doesn't include me. We're both better off this way. Leaving Hillsdale."

"How do you know?" Nan folded her arms across her chest. "Sounds like he has no reason to lie to you. Not that he lied at all." She huffed and turned to the kitchen.

"What do you mean? Of course, he did." He lied, and he used me.

Nan faced me. "I mean what I said. He may have misled you some, sure, but it's not like you have told him every little thing about you before." Her eyebrows raised in question.

"He had plans, none of them included me." My body was exhausted trying to keep myself from collapsing.

Nan threw her hands in the air. "You both had lives before. You can't blame him for that. Besides, you didn't tell him about your injuries in a way that gave him a chance to process. You threw it at him and ran."

I grabbed a towel from the cupboard in the hall. "I don't want to talk about it."

Nan's shoulders dropped. "I know you don't, but honey, I ain't going anywhere and I don't think Scott is either. This town is mighty small to stay inside forever. So, what's your plan now?" Nan took a huge bite out of one of my last cookies.

What was my plan now?

It couldn't be to stay. "I guess it's time for my trip to London and finding my happiness."

Nan huffed. "Don't be ridiculous. Your happiness won't be found anywhere when you are running from who you are. London won't solve your problems, just like a lifetime supply of ice cream won't."

I stomped to the bathroom and shut the door harder than necessary. "I might as well try."

"You are as stubborn as your mother." I heard Nan huff and walk away.

My mother . . . my parents. The old pain rushed up my throat like it'd never left. Searing and red hot. I leaned my head against the door and closed my eyes. The emotions and pain rolled through me like a storm. I usually had my walls up when I got one of these pangs. The pangs that reminded me I was alone, and my parents were dead. This time, I was too raw from Scott. I wasn't ready. My emotions dragged me under, choking me from the inside.

I cried.

I cried for the life I thought I would have.

I cried for the memories I didn't get to share with my parents. Prom, high school graduation, everything.

If I got married, if I graduated from college, if I changed the world for the better, they wouldn't be there for any of it. And Nan was getting married and was old enough that she would be gone one day too. And I really would be all alone. With my scars and my pain.

Tears ran down my face. It was too heavy. I gasped for air as my throat burned with pain, and I crumpled to the ground. A weight sat on my chest, pressing me into the floor, pressing every breath from my lungs. Drowning. Shaking. My chest burned from the lack of oxygen, and my throat felt like it was bleeding.

I need help and I needed to let myself heal.

I crawled towards the sink and stood. I looked at myself in the mirror, at my drooped shoulders, puffy face, and red eyes. I lifted my shirt and examined the wounds of my past. Ones that had not healed quite right. Just like me.

My fear wasn't about not having children. I was afraid to be left behind. To be alone. That's why it hurt when I thought I had something real with Scott. That's why I hated planning my future.

And now that he was gone, I was left in the cage I had built for myself. The one that I chose to be alone in—that way, it wouldn't hurt as much when it came true. It turned out that I had believed a lie—drowning alone was far worse.

I looked in the mirror and remembered that younger girl who

was still a part of me. The one who had woken up with tubes and wires everywhere, in a white sterile room that smelled of antiseptic. Nan was on a chair, but where were my parents?

A doctor's stilted apology and explanation of why he couldn't save my parents lived inside my head. The pain came on me full force and swallowed me whole. I couldn't even say the word dead, it felt too permanent. People giving me hugs and apologizing before I could accept their deaths were even real. The tears had fallen then until I was hollow and had nothing left to cry. Until my throat had been scratched raw. My legs were broken, but I was wheeled around at the funeral. Hugs and sad looks. Questions and apologies. Where would I go now, they asked. What would I do? It was too much. I was suffocating.

Fifteen-year-old me did what she needed to survive. She pushed it down. If she had tried to face it, she would've drowned. But maybe now it was time to let it go. To breathe. I told the younger version of myself that I loved her, and it wasn't her fault. She fell asleep during the drive. It wasn't her fault she lived when they didn't. I told her that one day it would hurt less. She didn't need to carry it anymore.

By the time I got in the shower, the water was ice cold, which wasn't ideal. The water dripped over my face and down my back. I imagined it taking little pieces of those pains and worries with it. I needed to continue therapy. I needed to face my past and still plan a future I was excited about.

When I emerged from the shower, I was beyond exhausted. I wrapped my purple towel around me and put on a clean pair of pajamas. I picked up the tissue confetti in my room and brushed and braided my hair. Nan had left some hot cocoa by my bed. It brought new tears to my eyes. Not sad or angry tears. Tears for Nan and how amazing she was. She had never left me alone.

Maybe Nan was right. I couldn't find happiness elsewhere until I faced my past and learned to love the person inside. I wondered if a change of scenery might give me permission to do it in my own way without so many witnesses.

Maybe London was what I needed. But not because I was running—because I needed space to find something. Plus, I couldn't stay, waiting for Scott to leave and the future I envisioned at the B&B to be demolished would be torture. That would be way too much to handle.

Chapter Thirty-One

SCOTT

I LEANED MY HEAD AGAINST THE SOFT LEATHER SEATS OF my Mustang and looked up at the building that used to hold all my dreams. I had reluctantly agreed to come to the Christmas party at the Raymond & Johnson Law Firm. Plus, Carol was still considering selling if they would honor her wishes. I still thought Marissa would be a perfect fit, but I would look at all Carol's options in case Marissa didn't want it. Carol was ready to relax, and this was the least I could do for her.

I stepped out of the car and straightened my tie. Somehow, the clothes that I used to wear every day felt more restrictive now. Walking into the office entry, I met the same scowling receptionist and cold industrial building I'd encountered on my first visit. I rode the elevator up with other lawyers with straight suits, pinched frowns, and "I'm too important to talk to you" vibes.

I followed the crowd to the conference room, listening to them talk about cases and prestige, vying for the upper hand. New cars, new apartments, who worked the most hours.

I stepped to the full-length windows. Across the street was a park. There was a Christmas tree, and people holding hands skating on an ice rink, groups of families admiring the lights.

"Looks miserable, right?" The guy on my left in a navy Italian suit and gray hair nodded to the activity outside the window. He looked to be in his mid-forties.

The other guy next to him pointed to the parking lot. "Look at all those minivans. You can bet every one of those men has a nagging wife and a brood of kids with sticky hands and used clothes." He held up his cup of wine in a sad salute to the proverbial man. They both laughed.

These men were jaded in the worst way. I saw the old me in them and was ashamed. I had been on the fast track to being a capital jerk. "Are none of you married?"

"No way," the man in the Italian suit held up his hands. "Almost did once, but then she was always complaining about my work schedule. Said I would have to choose her or the paycheck." The guy scoffed and added, "I went out and bought new golf clubs that day with the money I saved."

More laughter.

I shook my head in disgust.

"Aww, you must have someone. Get a prenup, right Jack?" He nodded to the man on his side. "He's on his fifth wife and knows all the best loopholes. Saved several of us thousands." He gestured around the room.

Wow. I needed to change the subject. "Have you started your Christmas shopping?" It was a sorry attempt at conversation, but I no longer wanted to talk about failed marriages and fake lives.

"I don't have time for that. A secretary will send a box of fruit to any address you give her. My parents like the pears."

"You send your parents fruit for Christmas?" I couldn't keep the disdain from my voice.

"Yep. I never see them anyway. They send me a card with money. We all live busy lives and wouldn't have it any other way."

I looked around the room and saw my vision board come to life. Fancy food, successful careers, and prestige. This was who I would've become without Marissa. I realized now, standing in the middle of my dreams, how empty and exhausting this life was. After thirty minutes of small talk and free food, I was sick to my stomach. *I needed to get Marissa to talk to me. To get her to see I was here to stay.*

I walked out of the party into the hall, where pictures of the "top lawyer of the year" hung on the walls. I walked down the length of space, studying each face. They looked proud but also exhausted. What were their lives really like?

When I reached the end of the photos, I froze, recognizing the man staring back at me. He was younger and not wearing a Hawaiian shirt, but it was my dad. I double-checked the name. Ron Elliott. What? I felt like someone had ripped the ground out from under me. How could this be?

A rustle of fabric sounded from behind me. I turned to see Clyde Johnson looking at the pictures too.

"He was one hell of a lawyer." He sighed.

I shook my head, trying to clear the fog. "My dad worked here?"

"More than worked here. We were partners. Ran this firm together before he dropped it all. No one could compete with his work ethic or cutthroat court room persona. Even me, and that's saying something." Clyde raised an eyebrow, glancing at me. "That is, until your mom convinced him to help her save some old houses from becoming a parking lot."

I looked at the picture. It was still Dad, but his cheery smile was hollow, and his eyes were dull. It wasn't the man I knew and loved now.

"Huh."

"Enough about the past. Now tell me where things stand with the bed-and-breakfast."

I straightened my jacket. I was not here to beg for a job. This place held nothing for me now. I was here for Carol.

"I've talked with Carol and she is interested in selling—"

"You did it!" Clyde slapped me across the back.

I stepped out of his reach. "But there are a few stipulations she would like to keep."

Clyde scowled. "Like what?"

"She wants to ensure the community can still use the facility. A clause that they would have access to the property and amenities at a steep discount. Also, she wants a rec center built on the land for the town to use."

Clyde laughed, "She really is mad."

I didn't laugh.

"The investor plans to bulldoze every piece of property and turn it into a resort, not turn it into a community handout. The town will be lucky to have the source of income as jobs."

I figured that would be his response. "She won't sell without those stipulations in place."

"Your job offer is on the line, you know that. You don't have what it takes if you can't persuade a little old lady to—"

"I'm no longer interested in working here."

Clyde took a step back. "You can't be serious. You're going to throw it all away for some old lady? Just like your dad. The apple doesn't fall far from the tree. Your dad and his dead-end investments, barely scraping by." He gestured to the prestigious building. "Now, I might overlook that last comment if you talk to Carol again. You can have so much more. I'm sure you dreamed bigger than the life your dad has, or you wouldn't have applied here. Don't throw it all away like he did."

I thought about the two lives that sat in front of me and I knew which one I wanted.

I thought about family dinners, the community trunk-or-treat, and helping the boys with basketball. And hopefully I could do all of it with a fiery wife who loved sprinkled cookies and had a B&B to run. I wanted to be with Marissa and share the special little moments of everyday life.

"My dad has a better life than I ever will working here." I nodded, resolute. "Sorry, it didn't work out." I turned and began down the hall.

"This is my last offer," he yelled.

"I understand." I walked to the elevator and loosened my tie before I even made it to the front door. In the foyer, I saw the intern, Becky. I stopped her.

"I need to tell you, you can do better than this. You can be happier than this. These people are cruel and don't deserve you. If you ever find yourself in need of a change, email the Elliot Law Firm in Clifton. Tell them Scott sent you. It's less money, but it turns out money cannot buy happiness." I left her speechless and nodding.

I left the Raymond & Johnson Law building happier than I went in. I understood my dad more at this moment. One day, he made the choice to put people first and found true happiness and worth. I was just like my dad, and proud to be so.

I knew my future was in Hillsdale, and now that I chose that path, I needed to fix things with Marissa. James said if Marissa's happiness was in London, I should change my name to London, then I would make her happy. He was crazy, but he was right about something. *I could give her London.* I sang along to the Christmas songs on the radio as I drove up to the used car lot. I only prayed that she'd still want me after meeting all those British accents.

Nan might not answer, but I knew I could wait her out. Marissa's car was gone. It was the perfect time to talk about my plan.

I had already purchased a three-week vacation package for Europe with no return ticket. Marissa needed to decide when and if she wanted to come back. I couldn't cover the three months she was hoping for, but this was a start. Plus, after trading in my car and settling a deal with Carol, I only had fifteen thousand dollars left.

I bundled myself in the blanket on the porch and sat by Nan's front door. I wouldn't force my way in, but I also would not give up. After listening to Jeopardy through the door and hollering the answers as loudly as I could, Nan must have conceded, because the door flew open, and I fell flat on my back.

"Alright, you can come in, but only because I want to beat you good and proper." She placed her hands on her hips. "No speaking to me about Marissa. That's between the two of you to work out."

I couldn't agree with that. "How about I get one question about Marissa for every answer I get right?"

Nan sat in her chair with a sigh, looking exhausted. "Why did you do it, Scott?"

My stomach dropped to my feet. So much for not talking about Marissa. "I made that stupid deal before I even knew Marissa. I didn't sign the contract. And not because of her, but because of the life I now want. I was focused on the wrong plan, but Nan, I've changed." I ran my hand through my hair. "I can't sleep, I can't focus, and I can't live like this. Life is gray. I know there is a chance she won't forgive me, but I'll never forgive myself if I don't at least try. Please, hear me out."

Nan raised an eyebrow. "You hurt her again and I will poison your food."

I chuckled. "Agreed."

"You're aware she's not able to have kids. Are you fine with that?"

"No . . . I mean yes." I rubbed my jaw with my hand. "What I mean is . . . it's not what I thought our future might look like." The vision of kids in the yard had faded, but Marissa was still there. "But it changes nothing. The life I want is with her. Adoption, or whatever we do, it doesn't matter if she's with me."

"Good. Now, how are you going to fix this?"

I stepped out onto the porch and pulled in the purple luggage.

"I'm going to give her London." I held out the tickets.

Chapter Thirty-Two

MARISSA

I WAS MAKING PROGRESS, AND THAT HAD TO COUNT FOR something. The therapist Faith had suggested, Sarah, had been another one of those angels Nan had told me to watch for. She listened and was patient. She didn't pity, but instead validated my pain. Healing would take time, but I could see how much therapy had already helped me shift my mindset. I wanted to be okay in my own skin and love myself. I closed my journal that held the exercises Sarah suggested doing every day. I was ready for the next step. No more sulking about Scott, and how things didn't work out as I planned. I was still better off knowing Scott, and I would be better for loving him too, eventually.

The Christmas movie marathon with Faith and Rose was a great distraction last night, but it was time to come up with a plan. I tossed back the covers and Nan knocked and threw open my bedroom door. Faith and Rose were right behind her. It was early for Rose to be up, and shouldn't Faith be at work?

Was it a weekend? Since I had no job, my days all fused together into one long, fuzzy stretch of time.

Faith rushed to my bed, followed by Nan. Rose leaned against the door frame with a smirk on her face.

"What's going on?" I would've assumed someone died, except their faces were all lit with grins.

"We have a surprise for you." Nan scooted closer on the bed and handed me a purple envelope. I grabbed it from her and held it in my lap as the smell of lavender enveloped me. I looked at the fake lilac, still in the trash.

"What's this?"

"Just open it." Faith squealed as she bounced on my bed.

I didn't even know they made purple envelopes, but from here on out, everything I sent would be in a purple envelope.

Marissa was written on the outside, and for a second, I hoped it was from Scott. Then I remembered we were better off separate. Besides, he was probably signing his contract and leaving by now. Inside the envelope was a ticket of some sort. I pulled it out. It was a plane ticket.

To London.

With my name on it. "Wait, what's this?" It came out a whisper. Was I dreaming?

"A ticket to London," Faith squealed and pulled me into a hug.

"Yeah, but how . . . I didn't buy it, I can't afford it. Especially without a job." I glanced back at the envelope. I pulled out the folded papers. It was a reservation confirmation for a hotel for three weeks.

"It's already all paid for." Nan smiled. "And Scott brought your last check by, and a slight bonus, which should cover your return ticket." Nan handed me the printed paycheck.

No return ticket? I could choose if I came back. *How weird.*

Scott. My last check in Hillsdale. I had always wanted to leave, now I guess I could. I looked at the check with Hillsdale Law printed in the top corner. It had been such a big part of my life for so long. Everything in this town had been. What did it all mean now? I chewed on my bottom lip. This was all a dream come true, yet my stomach felt sick. It could be the steady diet of ice cream and cookies though. "Who paid for this?"

"I didn't," Nan squeezed my hand in hers.

"Faith . . . Rose . . . was it you guys?"

"Not us." Rose smirked.

I leaned my head against my headboard and closed my eyes. Was *it a pity trip from Carol or Scott?*

I sat up straight, my stomach dropping. "I don't want it if it's from Scott selling the B&B. I can't even go there." Carol had stopped by a few days ago, but I did what I do best. Pretended that I had never cared. I'd smiled, said I didn't want to talk about Scott and that I was sorry, but I hoped her future was everything she hoped it would be.

I wanted her to be happy, but since I had pictured my future tied to the B&B, now it was all murky again. I could never offer her what she deserved for it.

She was better off this way.

"It's not from Carol. It's also not from Scott selling the B&B." Nan rolled her eyes.

"Then who?"

Rose plopped on my bed next to me. "What does it matter, Mar? It's your dream vacation, and it's *paid!* Maybe not a whole three months worth, but three weeks is a great start."

"I don't like handouts, or being pitied."

Nan laughed. "If anyone hears of a free pity vacation for me, sign me up!" She picked up my hand in hers. "Trust us, sweetheart. None of us paid for it. And none of us are going to tell you who did. Just enjoy it, it's a gift. Unless you don't want it?" Nan reached for the purple envelope. "I'm sure I could send it back and let them know you weren't interested."

"No!" I grabbed the envelope, held it to my heart, and I couldn't hold back my grin. "I'm going to London!"

"It's Fate! I knew it was going to happen." Faith sighed.

"I don't know why I doubted you, Faith." I grinned.

Rose nodded to the envelope. "What's in it?"

I opened the purple envelope and smelled lavender. I pulled out a dried lavender flower and a paper.

Your trip includes the following:

Big Ben and the Houses of Parliament, Buckingham Palace, Westminster Abbey, the London Eye, Trafalgar Square, Kensington Gardens, Hyde Park, the British Museum, Piccadilly Circus and more!

I was going to go, and it no longer felt like running from my past, but excitement to find myself and take some time to think about what I wanted my future to look like.

I glanced through the papers again and felt my eyes prick with tears. I was going. On the trip I had always planned, the one I dreamed about with my parents.

Faith bumped my shoulder. "It's a Christmas miracle."

I chuckled. "I guess it must be."

I continued to scan the papers. The next page was about my flight. I scanned for the date, wondering if it was all too much to be true.

Your flight leaves—

"Wait . . . *tomorrow?*"

Rose smirked. "Well, it's not like you have to take off work."

"This is perfect." Faith grinned.

Nan stood and went out of my bedroom and rolled in a brand-new hard shell lavender suitcase. "Well, don't just sit there. Looks like you need to get packing."

"Good thing my passport isn't expired." I stood and rushed over to the beautiful purple case, running my hand down the handle. Whoever set this up must know about my mom and purple. Was it Carol?

Nan grinned and gave me a hug. "You deserve this, Mar. This and much more. I hope you go explore and love all you see." She put my face in her hands and leaned closer. "Especially learn to love yourself." She patted my cheek. "Alright ladies, I pass the torch to you. Get this girl ready for her vacation."

Faith squealed.

Rose walked out of the room and came in with a metal tote. "Let's start with those nails." She grinned and came over to the bed.

"Mani/pedis!" Faith cheered.

Could this be happening? I was going to London! But at whose cost? I would've wondered about Scott since we talked about it, and he knows about the purple, but Nan had said it wasn't from him. Who else could it be though?

Was this Fate giving me permission to be happy and find myself? I wanted to know who it was from, but not enough to give away this chance to go to London. Whoever it was, Fate, an angel, or a Christmas miracle, I knew I would be forever grateful.

I set the suitcase on the bed and opened it. Inside was a box of charging adapters, and a note.

I hope your trip is all you have dreamed it to be and more. Please be happy.

Scott flashed in my mind. No. I shook my head. I was moving on, and so was he.

Whoever put this together sure did their homework.

"You guys swear you and Nan had nothing to do with this, right?" I asked.

"Promise. We're only in charge of getting you ready to go," Faith said.

I thumbed through my flight details for the next day at five a.m., there was a little handwritten note at the bottom.

I picked up the note and turned it over, hoping for a clue of who might be the sender.

P.S. You'll receive emails from me about trip details and receipts should you need them. Feel free to ask if you have questions. Also, please let me know when you arrive safely.

Happinessinlondon@gmail.com

Hmm, this had Scott written all over it. A more romantic side of Scott, but still him. I could not take this trip if it was earned from him using me. *It was my pride maybe, but it is what it is.*

"Guys, you promise it isn't from Scott selling the B&B?"

"Promise." Faith shook her head.

"I swear it," Rose nodded as she pulled out the nail polish remover.

"Well, it looks like happiness in London is waiting." I wrapped my arms around each of my friends.

I was taking a vacation, but part of this vacation was about rediscovering who I was and what I wanted. About accepting who I was, and that I was enough. It would take time, but I knew where I wanted to start. I walked over to my closet and opened the drawer that held all my undershirts. They were in terrible shape. Sweat stained and filled with holes. I had worn one of these every day since I was fifteen.

"Be right back," I said.

I made my way to the box of garbage bags under the sink, pulled out a white bag with a red drawstring, and walked back to my room. I looked at the drawer. It was time to let go, to love all of me and stop hiding my scars. I picked up a handful of shirts and tossed them into the trash bag. "It's time to let these go. No more covering up."

Faith gasped from the bed and ran over and pulled me into a hug. "This is huge, Marissa! I'm so proud of you."

I smiled. I was proud of myself too.

"Can I buy you a bikini for London now?" Rose smirked.

"Um, I think it's too cold for that." I did not want to even imagine what tiny fabric swimwear Rose had in mind. I wasn't ready for that, but maybe by summer a tasteful two-piece or a crop top would be in my future. One step at a time. I finished bagging the undershirts, and then the three of us went to the dumpster to throw them in.

Chapter Thirty-Three

MARISSA

I was in London! I would've asked someone to pinch me to see if I was dreaming, but my aching back and stiff legs told me it was real.

What was it about sitting all day that was tiring? After getting through customs, I found an Uber driver to take me to my hotel in Central London. Even though it was well past midnight, London was still wide awake. Stores were open and not just bars. People walked down the streets in suit coats and dressy clothes. Scott would fit right in. I pictured him when he first came to Hillsdale with his starched shirts and bruised eye. The only thing I regretted about Scott was the way things ended. I didn't regret loving him, or how he helped me learn to love myself, and hope for a future I loved.

I looked toward the crowd and saw street performers and billboards for theaters.

"First time in London?" The Uber driver had an aged face but kind eyes as he looked at me through his rearview mirror.

"Yep! I've always wanted to come."

He smiled showing a wide smile with a chipped front tooth. "Why's that?"

I placed my hand on the purple envelope in my lap. I had read through the contents several times, but somehow it was still comforting to hold.

"My parents were going to go with me after I graduated high school, but then they passed away. It seemed important to go anyway." I shrugged. That I was talking to a stranger about my parents was a testament to how far I had come.

"Oye, sorry miss. I hope London is all you hoped."

"Any recommendations for me?"

He nodded. "A lifetime worth. The theater up on West End. The plays and the buildings are both a must see. Little Venice in West London has these house boats and river cafes. You have to try Marty's Fish and Chips." He looked at me through the mirror. "Oh, and there is the flower market in East End on Sundays, and the Bermondsey beer mile." He chuckled. "You might have to stay awhile or visit again."

"Sounds like I might."

I thanked him for all the tips and checked into my hotel room. I plopped down on the white poofy bed. My room was gorgeous, decorated with warm earth tones, gold accents, and oil paintings everywhere. The whole hotel screamed luxury.

This trip had to have cost a fortune.

I plugged in my phone with the plug adapters and checked my email and saw three emails from Happiness in London.

The first was a reminder of the time I would need to meet the group in the lobby for tomorrow's tour. We would see Westminster Abbey, the Houses of Parliament, get to ride the London Eye, and see Big Ben.

This was for sure the way to travel. I smiled as I opened the next email. They sent it at one a.m. London time, which was ten minutes after I landed.

Marissa,

I hope this trip is amazing and you enjoy every minute. Please let me know when you land.

-Happiness in London

I checked the time on my phone. It was almost three a.m., and the last email was sent ten minutes ago.

Marissa

Did everything go okay? Are you safe? Did you make it? If I killed you somehow, I would never forgive myself!

Please let me know ASAP.

-Hoping you are actually in London

I rubbed the sleep from my eyes. I better respond or search and rescue would be out any minute looking for my remains.

Happiness in London,

That is way too long a name. I'm going to call you Lony for short.

I'm in London, just checked into the hotel. Everything went great. I feel like I'm going to be indebted to you for the rest of my life. This couldn't have been cheap.

-Marissa

I walked to the floor-to-ceiling white tiled bathroom to change into PJs and pull on the complimentary robe. Who would spend this kind of money on a trip for me and why? The only person I could think of was Scott, trying to ease a guilty conscience. I didn't want him to feel bad. We both had secrets and lives. I didn't want him to change his dreams for me. I wanted us to both move on and find futures we wanted.

Who else could it be? Carol? Nan also said it wasn't Carol.

Something wasn't adding up, not that I was complaining. This was all amazing. I wanted to know who I would owe for the rest of my life.

I brushed my teeth. I hated how I left things with Carol. She had always been so kind to me. She loved my mother, and she loved me. Even if this trip wasn't from her, I should call her and thank her for always watching out for me.

I checked my phone was set with tomorrow's alarm.

There was a reply email from Lony.

Marissa—

I had already looked up the London police, it's called metropolitan police and I'll attach their info in case you end up needing it. Thanks for your response.

As for the money, don't worry. You can repay me by being happy and enjoying every minute. I know it's late, and you have had a long day. I hope you sleep well and please be safe.

Lony is a boring name. Let's choose something else. How about the most amazing person in the world that is the bringer of all my happiness?

Mapitwtitboamh for short.

Sincerely yours,

—-Mapitwtitboamh

I snorted and rolled over in my bed, propping myself up on the plethora of pillows.

Mapitwtitboamh . . . Seriously . . .

Umm, I think the name needs work.

The reply was quick.

I'm open to suggestions.

I tried to come up with something witty, but my brain was empty.

I will think about it, but I'm too tired right now.

Wait, after all that bringer of happiness stuff, I think I need a cooler name than Marissa.

-Marissa

The reply came before I could close my email.

Marissa is a perfect name. I wouldn't change it or you for anything. Good night, Marissa. Be safe.

-Hoping you're happy.

Whoa. Okay . . . that was romantic in all the best ways. Everything in me hoped it was Scott, but that was a bad idea. I was too tired to trust myself, so I did the sensible thing and went to sleep.

Best to face these questions when I was rested. I set my phone on the nightstand and lay back on the cool pillow, pulling the comforter to my chin. I was in London. I needed to stop thinking about Hillsdale and enjoy being here.

DAY ONE, I WAS OFF AND RUNNING. I MET WITH THE tour guide in the lobby way earlier than I was ready to be awake, and kept hustling all day. We visited Westminster Abbey, the Houses of Parliament, and Big Ben. I followed along with a group of tourists in puffy coats and cameras. Over lunch, our group chatted around the table. There were people from all walks of life: grandmas, teens, honeymooners. There was talk of loved ones, death and life, different religions, failed relationships, and work goals. Some had kids, some never wanted kids. Some were successful, some were barely scraping by. Everyone had a different story and goals. Each life was unique. Each path was different. But everyone there was focused on living their lives to the fullest. I joined in the conversation versus always turning it back to others. I talked about Scott, my scars, and how this was the trip I'd planned to take with my parents. I was scared and overwhelmed and knew no one, not even myself. But I was determined to be open and not live in fear. I would hope and dream for the future and honor the pain of my past.

After lunch, we headed to Buckingham Palace. This was it. The same place my parents had taken a picture on their honeymoon. I reached into my backpack and pulled out the small 5X7 framed picture. The picture I always looked at when I thought about going to Europe. Dad with his big goofy grin and Mom making faces at the palace guards to make them laugh. I ran my finger along the glass and wished with every part of me they could be here with me. I used my shoulder to wipe a tear from my cheek.

"Are those your parents?" A teenager from the group looked down at the photo.

"Yep." I smiled and held it closer to her.

"You look like your mom, but I think you have your dad's smile." She studied the picture. "I'm sure they are happy to be taking this trip with you." She nodded to the picture.

I felt the surety of her words. They were here with me, like Nan said. The ones who leave us are never truly gone. We carry them with us, a part of who we are.

"Want a photo?" The teenager motioned to the area to our left, the same background as my picture.

"I would love that." I handed her my phone and held the 5X7 in front of me as she took the picture of the three of us in London.

She handed my phone back to me and I stared down at the image. "Thanks," I whispered.

Carol would love this picture too. Maybe Carol would get to travel now. I thought of Carol's life. She didn't have children, but she had a thousand kids. Everyone who walked through her door for cookies, played basketball on her property, or had parties at the B&B became one of her kids. Including me.

I sent the image to Carol.

Marissa: Thanks for all you did to help raise me and so many other kids in Hillsdale. I hope you take the money from selling the B&B and get to go on that cruise you've always wanted. The town is better because of you. I'm better because of you. Thanks for being a second mom to me. I love you.

I sent the text with the picture.

Marissa: I can't express how much this trip means to me and this moment. I have a feeling you had something to do with it all. If so, thank you.

We were dropped off at the hotel.

I ran to my room to freshen up, then hit the streets. I passed by a pub with a rooster above the door and a crowd singing from inside. I stepped inside for dinner. I wanted to have the full

London experience, which included fish and chips. Unfortunately, I was allergic to fish, so sandwich and chips it was. The woman who brought my basket set it down on the table. "Can I get you anything else, love?"

"No." I thought about the rooster. "Well, can you tell me why the pubs have rooster signs above them?"

The woman put her hands on her hips and laughed. "It's been this way forever. That way people who couldn't read could still find a pint." She pointed at me. "We sure got our priorities right." She winked and walked to the next table.

THERE WERE LITTLE SHOPS EVERYWHERE, AND I FOUND the cutest ceramic gnome holding a flower. I knew the moment I saw it, I had to get it for Mrs. Bates. The shopkeeper talked to me about gnomes and how they can bring good luck. That was one thing London seemed to have in common with Hillsdale. The people were happy and wanting to chat, or at least help. I got lost twice and had no problem finding help.

Christmas came and went; I missed Nan and my friends. I people-watched from a shop as couples kissed, a little girl in pigtails chased pigeons the size of chickens, and a bus passed with people drinking and singing "Sweet Caroline."

The more I saw of London, the more I realized that while I loved every second, I wanted to share it with the people I loved. The people of Hillsdale, although challenging at times, were my home.

Even without Carol's B&B available to me, maybe I could run a community center of my own.

I couldn't have kids, and I had some past issues I was working through, but I could still have a wonderful life. And share it with someone I could dream and plan with. Maybe someone like Scott.

A text message came through on my phone. It was Carol. It

had been several days, which was not like her. Maybe she lost her phone as she was packing up the B&B.

Carol: My sweet Mar, that picture means the world to me. I'm sorry it took so long to reply. Betty Ann lost her cat, and in the process of looking for it, we broke my phone. Please tell me everything!

I wondered if Carol would like to travel more. If she had the time, maybe we could take a trip together.

Marissa: London has been fabulous. Was good to have some time to think about life, I want to come back again too. Maybe bring you with me. Thanks for always being a second mom to me.

Carol: I'm glad to have the honor of being in your life, and although I could never replace your mother, I'm happy to help you in any way I can. As for the trip, I admit, I knew about it, but that is it. It's all Scott's doing. Maybe this next summer when things slow down at the B&B we can go to London again. Safe travels.

Wait, *What!* It was from Scott . . . and Carol was still at the B&B. Didn't that mean she didn't sell? None of this made sense.

Nan promised it wasn't Scott, right? I thought back to the conversation. She said it wasn't from him selling Carol's B&B. He wouldn't have the money otherwise.

I texted Nan.

Marissa: Nan, Carol said this trip was from Scott and she isn't selling B&B . . . I don't understand.

That night, I still had no reply. There was a seven-hour time difference and I knew it was going to be a long night.

Chapter Thirty-Four

MARISSA

The next morning, I still had no reply from Nan as I took the train to Windsor. I was excited to see the castle and go on a boat ride on the Thames. Once again, I met a group of travelers wrapped up in coats and scarves as we made our way to the castle.

Had Scott done all this for me? If so, why? Guilt? And if not from selling the B&B, how?

I should've answered one of Scott's many calls before I left, but I hadn't because I was scared. It was my perfect out. I could blame him, say we wouldn't work, and run.

That way, it wouldn't hurt even more later. Later, when I loved him more and he realized we wanted different things in life. It wasn't fair of me. I had run away before facing Scott because I had convinced myself being apart was better, safer for both of us.

I texted Nan for the tenth time in twenty-four hours.

Marissa: You said this isn't Scott, right?

Nan: dydjnj't say thakt exactly

She still struggled with texting, but I knew what she meant.

Marissa: Nan! What do you mean?

Nan: I'm noit going to tecft this ca;; me latr.

Nope. No way. I called her right then.

I heard Nan pick up and sigh. "Marissa, surely this can wait. It's four in the morning. Aren't you in the middle of something?"

"Yes, I'm in line to go through the Henry VIII Gate and security check for Windsor Castle. I will send pictures." I looked over and saw a woman in dark sunglasses giving me a smile. "I need to know, Nan. Is this trip from Scott?" I didn't wait for her reply. "Carol said it was, plus I thought through it all. The purple envelope and bag, the notes, and details—there are subtle hints of him everywhere." I couldn't make sense of it all. "Nan, you promised it wasn't from him, right? Was this all out of guilt? I don't get it."

"I didn't say that . . . I promised it wasn't from him selling the property."

"He had to sell the property for it. How else would he come up with the money for a trip like this?" I was too tired to play this game. "Was it Scott? And how did he pay for this trip if he didn't sell Carol's place?" The woman nearby *tsked* in my direction and started talking in French to her friend. I was holding up the line. I moved forward.

"Mar, hun, he sold his car. Used the money, plus all his savings to send you to London."

My mind emptied. "Wha . . . Wait . . . What?"

She spoke louder into the phone, "He sold his fancy car to pay for your trip."

"You don't need to yell Nan, I heard you."

I heard her huff. "Then why did you say 'what'?"

I was next in line but felt like the ground was ripped out from underneath me and I was falling. "Why?"

"Scott is still here in Hillsdale. Helping Carol with the B&B and running Hillsdale Law. I think he's waiting for you."

His car? It was his most-prized possession. "He sold his car to send me to London?" My breath caught in my throat. "Why? He loved that car . . ."

"Yep, guess he loved something else more."

The woman nodded at me to keep moving. I gestured for her to go in front of me as I tried to put the pieces together of what Scott had given up to send me here.

"Did he just feel guilty?"

"This isn't guilt, Mar. Guilt would be 'I'm sorry' and then leave. He is still here."

She was right. Scott loved me. Even after I told him about not having kids, even after I pushed him away. He loved me and he was waiting for me.

A heavy weight lifted from my heart. I loved him too. "Wow . . ."

A little piece of me shouted, *what if it doesn't work?* I told that side of my brain to shove it and focused on leaning into joy. Leaning toward something good.

"So," Nan continued. "How are you going to show him you love him back? After he has done all this, seems like you need to do something back."

I chuckled and stepped back in line.

"You're right."

"Go see that castle hun, I'm going to go back to bed. Call me later."

"I will. Love you, Nan."

Now it was my turn to show him I loved him back. I didn't know how, but I was excited to figure it out. I went through security and got my audio for the tour.

It was time to stop running . . . again. Time to love myself and let others in too.

I would start with Lony. I didn't want to give away that I knew it was him, but I needed to talk to him. I opened my email.

Lony,

This trip has been amazing. I owe you for the rest of my life.

I had to tease him, just a little.

Hyde Park has a shockingly-low number of dukes. Here I thought my happiness might include a horse and carriage.

-Marissa

The audio informed me I was now walking in the Quadrangle, and I sat in the Moat Garden. It was cold outside, but I felt myself warming from the inside out. I was so lucky. Lucky in life, family, and love. I refreshed my email again. I knew it was early and likely he hadn't read it yet. But I had to check.

I had a reply.

Mar,

Do you even like horses?

-Lony is still boring.

I chuckled and hit reply.

Boring Lony,

I'm not sure if I like horses, but I feel like a duke romance should always be on one's itinerary. I'm sitting in some castle grounds, maybe today will be my lucky day for my duke to find me.

-Marissa

I smiled, hoping he would take the bait.

Marissa,

Well, I will now have nightmares. Maybe that will bring you happiness. If not, you should know all my cookie preferences now have sprinkles. Because sprinkles remind me of happiness, sunshine, and you.

-Dreaming of dukes.

I couldn't stop my laugh. Nearby tourists looked down at their audio device, clearly waiting for the joke that had me laughing. My cheeks were stinging, but not from the cold. I couldn't erase my grin.

That also meant Carol hadn't sold. Would she still want to? I had little saved up, but I could work out a payment plan or something. Maybe I could ask Scott if he wanted to partner with me? He was great with the boring business side of things.

Lony,

I'm not sure I deserve this trip that you have given me. I probably should've turned it down, but my only excuse, pathetic as it sounds, is I have a long history of running, and where better to run than London?

I think the only thing that would make it better would be someone to share it with. Someone to plan with.

Side note: I might need a business partner. Are you interested?

-Marissa

I could picture a wonderful, happy future. It held so many possibilities. Hopefully Scott would see it that way too. I made my way to the round tower to climb the stairs. I wanted to see everything I could in this moment and save it to my memory.

Marissa,

Still a no for Lony . . . we could shorten it to bringer of your happiness (BoyH). Maybe your next trip will be for two?

I'm intrigued. What's your business idea? Does it involve dukes?

-BoyH

I chuckled. A woman in her twenties bumped my shoulder. "I don't know what you are listening to, but it seems far more exciting than what I have."

I smiled. "I paused the tour and am talking to a man."

"Rightfully so, anything that screams happiness like your smile takes precedence."

I was happy. Very, very, happy. I couldn't keep from smiling. It looked like I might have found my happiness in London after all, although it wasn't at all what I had expected. Scott was always making me happy. London wasn't where I found my happiness. Loving myself and allowing myself to love Scott was where I would find my happiness.

What was a business idea I could share? I couldn't tell him I was hoping to run the B&B and community center, and hopefully with him. Not yet.

BoyH isn't working for me. Makes me wonder about Boy A-G.

Two might be good, if I could find the right person. Still no to the whole duke situation. Or at least a good, starched shirt. My business idea . . . How about Everything Pumpkin! Growing, baking, chucking . . .

-Marissa

I admit it. I laughed out loud at my own joke.

Mar-

I have a personal aversion to pumpkins flying through the air. Any other ideas? I'm ecstatic there seems to be a low number of dukes available.

It was the middle of the night for him, and I should let him sleep.

I will let you sleep. Let's message tomorrow when you are up. I need to explore this castle. But I needed to apologize first. You may know I have a tendency to push relationships away. I think it's because I'm scared of getting hurt. Plus, I'm still figuring out how to love myself. I think it's important to start that journey too.

Is it worth the risk of pain to love?

-Marissa

I took a deep breath. I hoped this would end better than last time. Although the reason it went bad last time was largely due to me running.

The reply was quick.

Marissa,

I'm putting all I have into hoping it is.

I closed my email and opened my contacts and clicked on Scott's number.

Marissa: Goodnight Scott. Thanks for London.

Scott: Good night, Mar, I miss you.

Oh, my goodness, I loved this man, and I was going to make sure he knew it in front of everyone. Thinking of our first night together and the auction gave me an idea. This time, I would bet on Scott with all I had. I knew my little town would help me win him back. I needed to get back to Hillsdale.

I started a group text with Rose, Nan, Carol, and Faith.

Marissa: Alright girls, looks like I have a man to win, and I need your help. I was thinking of an auction to raise funds for a youth program at the B&B. Maybe Carol could add a certain lawyer contestant to the auction so I can bid on him.

Marissa: Also, a side question for Carol. Are you open to a business partner? I don't have money, but I have energy and passion for days. Also, if I'm lucky, I'm hoping a certain lawyer might join me.

<h1 style="text-align:center">Chapter Thirty-Five</h1>

SCOTT

I FINISHED THE LAST COAT OF PAINT IN THE UPSTAIRS third bedroom. Nothing like an anxious mind to keep a guy on task. The three weeks were up, and Marissa still wasn't back in Hillsdale. She sounded like she wanted to give us another try, but was I reading way too much into it? When would she be coming back?

"Scott, you need to take a break." Carol picked up my paint pan and started to the sink.

"Staying still drives me crazy. I spend the whole time worrying about Marissa and what she's doing and if she was safe. And more importantly, if she will give me a chance once she gets home."

Carol sighed. "Yes, well, let's not die of exhaustion while we are waiting for her."

I chuckled and rinsed out my roller and set it on a rack to dry.

"No use borrowing tomorrow's worries." Carol set the paintbrush on the rag and made sure the lid on the paint was sealed tight.

At least I knew Marissa would come home for Nan's wedding, if not before. That was in five months. I knew I couldn't wait that long. I wouldn't let her go without a fight, that much I was sure of, even to a duke. I looked out at the snow-shoveled path to the barn. Faith and Rose were walking towards it, their arms full of boxes.

"Is something going on?"

Carol nodded her head to the stairs. "Yeah, it's a fundraiser for the community event center. I could use your help on it. Let's go chat."

We went downstairs and settled in the kitchen in our usual two chairs. Carol's shoulders drooped and she let out a long sigh. She was so tired. I hoped I didn't do the wrong thing for her by not going through with the Raymond & Johnson Law deal.

"I was thinking we might try to raise enough to add an after-school program. But all of that comes with extra costs."

I had lots of ideas about how to make the B&B more profitable, but those things took time.

"So," Carol continued, "we're going to have a fundraising auction here in three days. I invited the whole town to auction different things and all the money will go to a fund for building a community center on the property. I was hoping you could help me set up over the next few days. I already signed you up as an auction prize."

My eyes opened wide. "What do you mean? Like legal services or something?"

Carol shrugged. "Something like that. You're also a great handyman, you could auction that service for a few hours. It could help get the auction going, you know. You don't mind, right? I figured you would be happy to help get the kids in town a more permanent place to be after school."

"Oh, okay. Yeah, that's fine."

When I had told Carol about not selling to Raymond & Johnson Law, she told me she hoped that Marissa and I would take it over all along. That woman's scheming levels were above my mother's. Carol would like to stay on as an investor but spend more time in Florida. I couldn't speak for Marissa, but I loved the idea.

As for the auction, it wouldn't be the first time; I had done it before. So much had changed since then. I checked my watch for the date again. Marissa could have been home four days ago, and still wasn't. This auction would be good to help me stay busy.

"What do you need help with?"

Carol waved me off. "Oh, not much. Faith and Rose have spread the word. Will you go out to the barn and see what else they need? Maybe there is something your parents would auction as well?"

Dad and Michael had been down a few times to help patch the leak we found in the roof of the B&B. "I'm sure they would be happy to contribute. This is just the thing my mom would go crazy over." Speaking of Mom, I had a crazy idea pop into my head. "Have you ever looked to see if the B&B would qualify as a historical building?"

Carol raised an eyebrow. "It was old when we bought the place and now I'm ancient. If it doesn't qualify, I don't know what would. It's the oldest building in Hillsdale."

I clapped with excitement. "I have an idea of how we can restore the B&B and keep investors away for good. I can't believe I didn't think of it before!"

Carol sighed. "That sounds wonderful, Scott." She reached over and patted my hand. "You're a good kid . . . for a lawyer." She chuckled.

I grabbed a coat and gloves and headed out the front door down the icy path to the barn. Helping Faith and Rose with the auction was the perfect excuse for me to talk to them about Marissa; hopefully they'd be more inclined to help me than to tell me to get lost. I walked into the barn and saw a mess of tables, signs, and papers. Faith and Rose were bickering in the corner about something.

"Excuse me, ladies." They didn't hear me. "Excuse me," I said, a little louder.

They both turned and looked at me. Their eyes were wide with surprise.

"What are you doing here?" Rose scowled.

Maybe not on Team Scott then? Maybe I would ask Faith when Rose wasn't nearby.

"Carol sent me over to help with the setup for the auction."

Faith's eyes sparkled. "Perfect. I know just what to do with you." She pointed to the ladder in the corner. "Will you help me hang these signs up high?"

THE DAY OF THE EVENT I PLOWED THE FRESH SNOW from the parking lot with the four-wheeler and set up extra space heaters and blankets in the barn. We'd had a nasty storm all day, but it looked like it was blowing over just in time.

I dressed in a button-up shirt and khakis and went to the barn. I helped people find their seats and pointed them to the various tables with donations.

I walked over to the folded tables that held silent auction. There were baked goods to sell, a free manicure from Rose, and a handmade patchwork quilt. There were music lessons, a free eye exam, and paintings by Josh. It was a painting of Big Ben. I was brought back to the trunk-or-treat with Marissa and our first kiss. Yep, I would bid on that one for sure. I started the bid at thirty dollars. The way this town pulled together to help each other was amazing.

The research I had done this week said many people didn't want to be the first one on the silent auction papers. I made several other offers, hoping to be outbid since my cash flow was tight right now. Everyone mingled around, talking about crops, weather, sports, grandkids, and how Coach Peters had missed an opportunity for the win at state by not playing their kid.

I checked my watch. The live auction was supposed to start forty minutes ago, but each time I reminded Carol, she insisted we wait longer before we started. I looked around. The place was packed. Why did it feel like she was stalling?

I kept checking my watch and watching the reaction of those in attendance. No one seemed too bothered that they were running late. I didn't want it to affect their willingness to support the cause.

Carol stood up on the platform and grabbed the mic. I sighed and sat next to my mom.

"Alright, everyone, find a seat. We are going to get this party started." People wandered to chairs. The lateness made me antsy.

Carol nodded to the left, and one of the boys brought out a cheesecake. "Let's start with Dorris's famous pumpkin cheesecake. Can I get five dollars?"

A hand shot up.

"Great, how about ten?"

Another hand. It continued and ended up selling for thirty dollars. I thought that was a great start. The auction continued through different desserts and Randy auctioned one of his new car inventions.

Ashley auctioned off her designer handbag. Nan was selling some of her rolls, and Steve sold fifteen dollars off at the Merc. Frank offered a bag of his fertilizer, and Mrs. Bates a set of garden gnomes. Merritt sold her pumpkin pie recipe. Gasps sounded through the crowd as Carol called it out. I recognized several women from the pie contest standing, raising their hands in the air.

"One hundred dollars," one yelled.

"Two hundred!" came a shout from the other side.

I looked beside them where their husbands were trying to pull them back to their chairs as they swatted them away. I chuckled. This town was something else, in the best way.

I noticed Faith near the entrance, checking her phone, wringing her hands, and tapping her foot. She was worried about something.

Should I go see if she needed anything? I stood and headed that way, but a man with a baseball cap and jacket that said Hillsdale Coach got to her first. I waited and watched to see if she wanted me to help. Faith looked at the coach, but then she smiled. Looked like she wouldn't need saving after all. I headed back to my seat. Mom tilted her head toward me. "Great idea about turning this into a historical building. It will take some paperwork, but I really think it might work."

My shoulders sagged in relief.

"Scott Elliot, will you come up here please?" Carol said through the mic. "He is our last item of the night. Don't hold back."

I sighed. The other things that had been on that stage were items. I felt strange being the only human auctioned off. But I owed Carol, and I would do as she asked.

I walked up to the platform. I noticed so many familiar faces in the crowd, grinning up at me with wide smiles. I would be happy to help any of them with house repairs or legal matters.

"Alright, Scott has kindly offered two hours of his services for auction. He is great as a handyman and as we all know, graduated top of his class at Harvard Law." Carol chuckled, and I rolled my eyes at the reminder of the man I had been when I first showed up in this town. I chuckled too.

"What should we start the bidding at?"

"Twenty-five dollars!" Mrs. Bates shouted from the back.

"Thirty," came from the left.

"Scott is single. Let's auction him for a date!" Betty Ann yelled. Several other women cheered, and the bidding skyrocketed.

Whoa. This was not what I had in mind.

"Wait." I held my hands up to stop the momentum, but the price kept rising. Ashley was fighting to win. I glanced at Carol, begging for help.

"Scott, come on, it's just a date. It's for the kids," she whispered back at me.

I groaned. *Not again!*

Chapter Thirty-Six

MARISSA

My flight was an hour late because of a storm, and then I was at the back of the plane. I watched everyone stand and slowly grab their bags. I tried to keep my fidgeting down. I glanced at my watch. At this rate, I would miss the whole auction and Scott would end up on a date with someone else! Probably Ashley.

I leaned to the man in front of me. "Excuse me, but could I maybe sneak through? I'm late for something important."

He scowled. "The plane was late. I'm sure everyone on here is late for something."

I flinched. It was true. I was sure I wasn't the only one in a rush. "I know. And I apologize, but this is very time sensitive," I begged.

The man shrugged in confusion but let me through.

I made it halfway to the front before the doors opened and people began shuffling off the plane.

"Come on . . ." I checked my phone. Now that airplane mode was off, seven texts from Faith came through.

Faith: Where are you?

I had never meant to cut it this close. All I could do at this point was speed and hope I didn't get caught. I rented a car at the airport and drove like mad.

Faith: Mar!!!! Stalling!!

Faith: Can't stall any longer

Faith: Mar . . . we have to start the auction soon . . .

I sped as safely as possible. I should've planned better.

I got caught.

It was just outside of Hillsdale by Sheriff Max. "Mar, aren't you supposed to be winning that lawyer of yours tonight?" His scruffy eyebrows pulled down.

I sighed in relief. "Yes! My plane was late and now I'm worried it will be over before I get there."

He nodded. "This is serious," he gasped. "I got you. Follow me."

I never expected a police escort to help me get a date. Only in my town of Hillsdale! I smiled as I followed the lights to the B&B and parked in a lot full of cars. I had gotten a text from Faith that Scott was going up to the stage.

I jumped out of my car and started running for the barn, careful of the ice.

"Thanks Max!" I waved over my shoulder.

I made it through the doors in time to hear Betty Ann yell about auctioning Scott for a date. I watched Scott's face turn from smiling to worry. This was perfect. I stared up at the man who had given up so much for me. I also loved this town. I spent so long trying to run away that I missed the goodness I had right in front of me. I reached Faith's side and gave her a quick hug.

"Thanks for stalling." I tried to catch my breath.

"You just about gave me a heart attack." She hugged me back.

They were really bidding Scott up, although to be honest, I wasn't sure if Ashley was here to help me, or if she wanted Scott for herself.

"Two hundred dollars going once," Carol called. She winked at me. "Going twice . . ."

"Wait!" I hollered. All heads turned in my direction. "I have three hundred dollars, some animal shelter coupons, and a chance on forever."

At the sound of my voice, Scott went rigid and frantically began scanning the crowd. I walked up the center aisle toward the stage and when his eyes found mine, I was home. A smile erupted from his face.

"SOLD!" he yelled as he jumped off the stage and rushed to me. I couldn't contain my laughter as he picked me up and spun me in a circle in front of the whole town.

"I can't believe you are here! I was worried you might not come back. Marissa, I'm so, so sorry. I—"

I reached my arms around his neck and silenced his lips with mine. He kissed me back. I saw my future in that kiss. Whatever my future brought, I wanted Scott to be a part of it.

When he set me back down, we stood there, our foreheads touching as we held each other.

"Scott, I know I already told you I can't have kids." It was time. Time to trust and hope and love. Time to embrace every piece of me without guilt or shame. "And although this isn't the life I expected, it's still going to be a great one. And if you'll give us a try, I still want to plan my future with you."

Scott rubbed a stray tear from my cheek that I didn't know was even there.

"Mar," he whispered and pulled me into a tighter hug. "I'm sorry for your pain."

I leaned into him for support. "Are you disappointed?" I couldn't keep the tremble from my voice.

"Never." I looked up at his eyes, searching for the truth. "Sure, I thought one day I might have kids." He shrugged, and I deflated. He tipped my chin up to see his eyes. "But Marissa, I know what I can and can't live without." He kissed the top of my forehead, my salty cheeks, and my lips. "I choose you, over and over again. I choose you and whatever life that comes with it. Adoption, travel, pets, chaos, flying pumpkins . . . anything. Marissa, you are my happiness."

"And you're mine." I reached up on my toes and kissed him. Kissed him as my hurt and fear melted away. I had found a way to love myself and let others love me. I had so much life I wanted to live and experience.

I wanted to plan and dream, to take on the world, and I wanted to do that with Scott at my side. "Maybe we could use those coupons and get a dog, for starters."

He chuckled and held me tight. "I've missed you." I felt him reach up and touch my hair.

"Alright, you two lovebirds," Carol said over the mic. "Some other people here want to say hello."

I laughed and let go of Scott. He shook his head no and grabbed my hand, pulling me close again. "Take me with you," he whispered as he rubbed his thumb against my hand. I nearly exploded with happiness.

"Always."

We walked around the room so I could say thank you to everyone who helped me pull this off. This was the life I wanted. One surrounded by love and the people I cared about. Scott's mother, Emily, was one of the first in line. She hugged us as she wiped her tears.

I searched the crowd for Carol. She had always had my back and helped shape me into who I was. "Carol, I think we have some paperwork we need to work through. Do you know a lawyer that can help our business arrangement become official?"

Scott's eyebrows pulled down. "Now, what are you doing?" The corner of his lips pulled up in a grin.

"Oh, you know, just getting a new business partner on a whim, wanna join?"

Scott threw his head back and laughed. "That's my girl," and he pulled me in and kissed me again.

Epilogue

FIVE MONTHS LATER

MARISSA

Nan glowed with happiness. She had so much love to give and a life to live. Nan never stopped fighting for her happiness.

She was my hero.

I finished putting the last little flower into her hair and leaned over her shoulder, giving her a hug.

"Nan, I'm so happy for you."

"And I for you, Mar." She glanced towards my ring finger. "Still no rock, eh? It's coming soon, I'm sure of it."

I laughed. "There is no rush." Although I hoped it was someday soon. For now, we were moving Hillsdale Law into the B&B and going over business and marketing techniques. And kissing, lots of kissing.

Nan decided on a light purple dress for us both in honor of my mom. I could almost feel her there in the room. Talking boys and causing trouble.

"Alright, well, we better not keep that man of mine waiting. Don't want him to die before I say I do." Nan chuckled at her joke as I helped her stand and grabbed her small bouquet of roses.

"Don't let me trip," Nan pleaded.

"I would never." I wove her soft arm in mine and kissed her.

She reached up and patted my cheek. "I'm proud of how far you have come these last few months. You've come into your own and you're finally seeing that you're the amazing girl I've known all along. I love you."

My eyes watered. Where would I be without this fierce, wonderful woman? "I love you. Thanks for all you have done for me."

"No ma'am, no tears. If my mascara runs, it will get caught in one of my face craters and I'll never get it cleaned out in time." We walked out the front door of the B&B to a lawn full of tulips and lavender. "I love spring. Nothing like celebrating new beginnings."

We rounded the corner, and I watched as Bert waited for Nan. His back was hunched, and his hands shook, but his eyes were filled with love and wonder. I handed Nan over to him, then went and sat next to Scott.

"That's what I want," he whispered in my ear.

"What?"

"I want to look at you like that forever."

I leaned in and gave him a quick kiss and watched as Nan and Bert started a new adventure together.

"I WAS THINKING. IT WOULD BE A SHAME FOR YOU TO stay at Nan's house all by yourself now that she is moving in with Bert." Scott bumped my shoulder as I walked to my car after the wedding. It had been a beautiful day, but a very long one.

"Hmm, that's true." I grinned up at him. "I still have those coupons for the animal shelter. Maybe I should go pick up a puppy."

Scott frowned. "Hold on." He picked up his phone and started dialing a number.

"What are you doing?"

"I'm seeing if the animal shelter will do me a favor and turn you down. I'm hoping you'll take me home instead."

I laughed at his joke as he put away his phone. Then he stopped by the tree where we shared our first kiss. He knelt and grabbed my hand.

"Marissa, you are my sunshine, like sprinkles on cookies. You are unexpected and have turned my life upside down since those flying pumpkins."

I gasped and put my hand over my mouth as he reached into his pocket and pulled out a little blue velvet box. Oh my gosh, he was proposing!

"You're as necessary for me as air. I feel like I'm directionless without you. The only plan I want for the rest of my life is one with you in it." He squeezed my hand. "I beg you, make me the luckiest man alive and be my wife."

My eyes filled with tears. I loved this man with every part of my heart. I couldn't wait to see where life would take us. It didn't even matter where, as long as we were together.

"Marissa, will you marry me?"

"Yes! A thousand times yes!"

Scott rose to his feet and slid the white gold, square-cut diamond ring onto my finger and grabbed my face and kissed me. The crowd cheered. I had no idea everyone was waiting for this to happen. Faith waved as she continued to record.

"I told you it was coming!" Nan hollered as she got into Bert's car.

I couldn't stop the tears streaming down my face, and my cheeks hurt from smiling. I was so lucky. Lucky in life, and in love.

Lucky that Scott saved me that day from flying pumpkins and started me on my path to finding my happiness. I pulled him closer and kissed him again.

"Here's to happiness and planning our happily ever after!" I cheered.

THE END

For a free sneak peek into Scott and Marissa's wedding join my newsletter at www.kiripatterson.com

Author Note

The topic of infertility can be a tricky and painful subject. I hope I caused no additional pain to anyone through this story.

Although I have children of my own, for which I'm grateful, this story came to me when I was in a mental slump. I love being a wife and mother, but it had consumed all I was. My wonderful genetics and a hormone imbalance didn't help.

Medicine, counseling, and supportive family members all helped me find my footing again.

My counselor asked me once who I was without being a wife and mother.

I couldn't think of a single answer. Nothing. I was empty.

This led me to lots of thoughts of worthiness and where our worth as individuals lies. Brené Brown's wonderful talks about our hustle for worthiness were essential.

If I had no children, would my worth be different? No.

If I had a prestigious career, would my worth be different? No.

On the days I get through the never-ending to-do list, is my worth different? No.

On the days I do nothing, is my worth different? No.

Is my worth different based on relationship status? No.

That is where this story found its way into my life. The story of people hustling for their worthiness, when they were worthy of love and belonging all along.

And so are you.

Acknowledgments

Wow! I had no idea how hard it is to write a book and how many people it would take to get me this far!

First off, thanks to my family and their love and support with limited complaints for bad dinners and unwashed clothes when I'm focused on a project. To my husband, who doesn't read, but read my romance book more than once, you are simply amazing.

Thanks to Jentry Flint and Camille Smithson who taught me about writing. Thank you for allowing me to tag along a bit and learn so much from you both.

To Melody J Williams and Casi Holman, thanks for keeping me going. For the *many* pep talks, plot chats, helping me rewrite over and over, and the all the times you read parts of my story. You are both amazing. Melody as you know, grammar is my nemesis. Thanks for your patience.

Thanks to all the author friends, editors, mentors, and social media rockstars who have been so willing to share information and help along the way. What a beautiful community.

Biggest of all, thanks to you!

Thanks for taking time out of your busy lives and choosing this story out of all the wonderful books out there. I hope it brought you a few smiles and moments of happiness.

About the Author

I grew up in small-town Idaho and communicate through movie quotes and song lyrics.

I taught myself to read before kindergarten and have loved reading ever since. Especially books with lots of kisses, strong characters, and lots of witty banter—ingredients I hope to have in all my stories.

I try to survive on chai tea, Dr. Pepper, and dark chocolate. Other guilty pleasures include marathons of BBC period dramas, Harry Potter anything, documentaries, and french fries.

I live in Star, Idaho, with my hot husband, four rapidly growing children, a strong belief in happily ever afters, and pink laptop—a nod to my belief that everything is just a little better in pink.

Sign up for my newsletter for sneak peek chapters and upcoming releases.

https://www.kiripatterson.com

www.ingramcontent.com/pod-product-compliance
Lightning Source LLC
Chambersburg PA
CBHW021413010826
48972CB00014B/1861